HOW TO MURDER
YOUR
MOTHER-IN-LAW

Other Books by Dorothy Cannell

THE THIN WOMAN
DOWN THE GARDEN PATH
THE WIDOWS CLUB
MUM'S THE WORD
FEMMES FATAL

HOW TO MURDER
YOUR
MOTHER-IN-LAW

Dorothy Cannell

BANTAM BOOKS
NEW YORK   TORONTO   LONDON   SYDNEY   AUCKLAND

Mother-in-law dear,
Pray do come to dine,
We'll have roasted pheasant,
And a fine hemlock wine.

To DIANE DAMARIN

a friend for all seasons.

Book design by Donna Sinisgalli

ISBN 0-553-07493-8

Published simultaneously in the United States and Canada

Bantam Books are published by Bantam Books, a division of Bantam Doubleday Dell Publishing Group, Inc. Its trademark, consist-
ing of the words "Bantam Books" and the portrayal of a rooster, is
Registered in U.S. Patent and Trademark Office and in other coun-
tries. Marca Registrada. Bantam Books, 1540 Broadway, New York,
New York 10036.

PRINTED IN THE UNITED STATES OF AMERICA

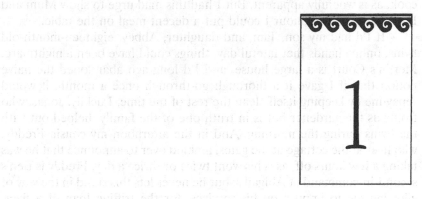

Some women are born to meddle. They lurk in bathrooms, sticking their noses into medicine cabinets and rehanging the toilet paper. They lecture other people's children and put their neighbours' houseplants on diets. They would tell God what was wrong with heaven if they got half a chance. Enough is enough! I say they should be shot at dawn, every last one of them, including Mrs. Bentley T. Haskell, of Merlin's Court, Chitterton Fells; for if anyone should have the words *I will mind my own business* monogrammed on her forehead, it is I.

In a flush of family feeling I decided to host a wedding anniversary dinner party for my parents-in-law—Magdalene and Elijah Haskell. Nothing elaborate, you understand. Just a beef stew with a slight French accent, a salad jardin, and perhaps a chocolate blancmange masquerading as a mousse. "Ellie, you're the salt of the earth," Dad would say. And Mum would pipe in with "I don't know why it's taken me so long to appreciate your wonderful qualities." Being the occasional wet blanket, my husband wasn't keen on the idea. How I wish I had listened to Ben! And how sad it is to say that all I ever seem to learn from my mistakes is how to make new ones. When the big day arrived, I was still feeling on top of my game. Ben had offered to come home early from Abigail's, his restaurant in the village, but I stuck to my guns. I know I'm not as eclectic in my choice of lettuce as is my beloved. And I once wore out a pair of shoes looking for clarified butter in every supermarket in town. I eat a lot better than I cook, as is woefully apparent. But I had this mad urge to show Mum and Dad that in their honour I could put a decent meal on the table.

If I'd had my son, Tam, and daughter, Abbey, eighteen-month-old twins, on my hands that fateful day, things could have been a nightmare. Merlin's Court is a large house, and I'd long ago abandoned the naive notion that if I gave it a thorough go-through once a month, it would repay me by keeping itself clean the rest of the time. Luckily, Jonas, who fronts as the gardener but is in truth one of the family, helped out with the twins during the morning. And in the afternoon my cousin Freddy, who lives at the cottage at the gates, ambled over to announce that he was taking a few hours off, as is his wont twice or thrice a day. Freddy is Ben's second-in-command at Abigail's; but he never lets this stand in the way of allowing me to impose on his services, for the trifling loan of a fiver. Abbey and Tam, who adore Freddy, with his ponytail and dangling earring, greeted him with gurgling cheers and toys tossed in the air.

Everything was going swimmingly, for—not to sound like a pampered puss, I was additionally blessed in having the assistance of Mrs. Roxie Malloy. Mrs. Malloy always "does for us" of a Monday. She had graciously consented to come in a little earlier than usual and stay on through the evening to help with the clearing-away and washing-up.

After flying about the house like Batman, zapping windows and mirrors with ammonia, buffing the furniture with Johnson's Lavender Wax, hosing down the bathrooms, making up beds, and feverishly wiping away fingerprints as if we were expecting a visit from the constabulary instead of my in-laws, I met up with Mrs. Malloy at four o'clock in the wainscotted dining room.

"What a team!" Smiling smugly, I faced her across the great divide of linen-clad table, set out with the Indian-tree china and crystal that had belonged to Abigail, the former mistress of Merlin's Court. "My in-laws aren't due for several hours and here we are, almost ready."

"Not so cocky, Mrs. H." Mrs. Malloy thrives on gloom and doom. "Them candlesticks could do with a trimming." She eyed the pair as if they were a couple of naughty schoolboys. Hands on her stalwart hips, she looked the room up and down for all the world as if she were Lady Kitty Pomeroy, the terror of our little community, checking out the stalls at St. Anselm's Summer Fête.

Mrs. M. would lend character to any room. Her jet-black hair always shows two inches of white roots as part of her fashion statement, not because she is between dye jobs. Her rouge would appear to be applied with a trowel, her lipstick is a violent purple, and her eyes are done up like stained glass windows. Since that memorable day when she took me on as a client (strictly on six months' approval), we have had our run-ins.

"The candles are fine." I adjusted the dripless beeswax in their pewter holders. "And dinner is all set. The beef ragout is in the fridge, waiting to be heated up. The salad dressing is made, the endive rinsed, and the rolls rising for the second time."

"What about the chocolate goop?" Mrs. M.'s damson smile assured me of her complete faith in my ability to flub dessert.

"The mousse is chilling in little glass dishes. What took the time was finding the baking chocolate. Some nameless person had stuck it on the top shelf of that cupboard, where I keep the aspirin and cough syrup."

"Think the silver could do with a buff-up?"

"The secret of successful entertaining is to know when enough is enough, Mrs. Malloy." My voice was as crisp as the folds in the damask serviettes. I leaned against the sideboard, already groaning under the weight of enough silver chafing dishes to keep an industrious fence in business for a year. "The mantelpiece clock does not need winding, the pictures do not need straightening, and Jonas does not need to be reminded to take a bath."

Arms folded beneath bosoms, as always in danger of popping like a pair of overblown balloons, Mrs. Malloy pursed her butterfly lips and looked sad. "Pride goes before a fall, Mrs. H."

"For heaven's sake!" I laughed blithely. "What are you trying to do, put a curse on me?"

"Don't have the knack." Mrs. M. gave her organdy apron a twitch and assumed a modest mien. "I leave that sort of thing to me former friend, Edna Pickle. Edna's great-great-grandma was a witch, and they do say that sort of thing crops up, like twins, every so many generations."

"What do you mean"—I fastened on the juicy part of her statement —"former friend? You and Mrs. Pickle have been pals forever. You're always going in to see her at the vicarage on your way home from here."

"We've had words," she replied meaningfully. "No, don't ask me any more, Mrs. H., me lips is sealed."

"All right," I said.

"Go on!" She let loose a bone-weary sigh. "Force it out of me. Yesterday Edna was telling me she has high hopes of winning the Martha —that's the trophy given at the summer fête, in honour of the woman who was always scrubbing the kitchen sink in the Bible. It goes to the person who comes in tops among the winners in the homemaking events —jam-making, marrow-growing, and all that nonsense. But you know that, Mrs. H. And when I answered, nice as you please, that I couldn't sit listening to that sort of talk, what with you being this year's chairwoman, Edna turned right nasty."

"What—Mrs. Pickle?" I couldn't believe it. The woman never seemed to me to have enough energy to get worked up about anything. Whenever I went round to the vicarage, it invariably took her two hours to answer the door and another fifteen minutes to troop down the hall to the study to announce my arrival to her employer. I wasn't greatly surprised that Eudora Spike kept her on, because our deacon is an immeasurably warm-hearted woman. The wonder was that Mrs. Pickle also worked as a daily for several other people, including the exceedingly formidable Lady Kitty Pomeroy.

"Edna's got an 'orrible temper when roused," said Mrs. Malloy, who never forgot her haitches unless the situation called for major emphasis. "The old story of still waters running deep, if you get my drift. And along them lines, Mrs. H., you haven't said one word about how the mister is taking this dinner party of yours."

"It's for his parents."

"And he's jumping for joy, is that what you're telling me?"

"Oh, you know how men are," I hedged.

"After four husbands, I should say I do, duck." Mrs. Malloy could be incredibly sympathetic when her nose got the better of her.

"Ben wasn't immediately in favour of the idea." I busied my hands straightening knives and forks that didn't need straightening. "But it's not as though I were talking about entertaining the postman and his wife. He's known his parents for years."

"So what was his problem?"

"He went on about the journey, as if Mum and Dad would have to take the dogsled from Siberia instead of the train from Tottenham. If it had been dead of winter instead of June, he might have had a point. But what it came down to was his belief that Mum and Dad had never made any fuss over their anniversary and he thought they'd be happier with a nice card. You know the sort, with the satin heart that you can use for a pincushion later, and a verse on the inside such as 'Still singing love's song, while the world hums along.' "

"Spit it out." Mrs. Malloy blew on a serving spoon before giving it a buff with her apron. "How did you bring him round?"

"The babies. I reminded Ben that the last time his parents saw the twins, they weren't putting words together, let alone staggering all over the house. And the moment he started to waffle, I picked up the phone and issued the invitation."

"And I suppose your in-laws was over the moon?"

"Well, I wouldn't go that far," I admitted. "Dad hemmed and hawed a bit about having to bring the dog, and I could hear Mum in the background saying she didn't want to be a burden. But I knew they really wanted to accept. Why wouldn't they? And in the end it was all arranged that they would come down today for the dinner and stay the week."

"So when did you come up with the bright idea of including Mrs. Haskell's long-lost friend in the invite?"

"Just a few days ago," I said, looking around as if the walls not only had ears but their own telegraph system. For this was to be the *big* surprise. "Last time she was here, Mum mentioned she had learned through the grapevine that her girlhood pal, Beatrix, lives a few miles from here. And that her married name is Taffer. But when I suggested ringing up and inviting her over for lunch or tea, Mum went on as she does about not wanting to make work for me. Such a shame, because I knew she had to be dying to see her friend and chat over old times. So when I got down to organizing the dinner party, I rang up and spoke to Mrs. Taffer's daughter-in-law. The old lady couldn't come to the phone herself because she was upstairs doing her exercises—arthritis I suppose, poor dear. But Frizzy Taffer couldn't have been nicer or more excited about Beatrix having a night out."

"Very nice." Mrs. Malloy gave a lordly sniff. "But if you ask me, you've got your work cut out for you."

"I keep telling you, everything is under control."

"Says you, Mrs. H., and what I says is you're forgetting your mother-in-law can be a real pain up the rear."

"That's unkind."

"What was unkind"—Mrs. M. drew herself up on her stilt heels—"was her calling me the Harlot of Jerusalem when her hubby gave me a peck under the mistletoe last Christmas. Then again, perhaps I took offence where none was meant. My third—or was it me fourth?—husband always said I was too sensitive for me own good. But we can't none of us change our natures."

I was wondering what Eudora Spike would have to say about that. Uncannily, Mrs. Malloy proved to be a mind reader.

"Take a lesson, Mrs. H., from our poor vicar."

When Mrs. Spike had arrived at St. Anselm's Vicarage as a temporary replacement for the Reverend Rowland Foxworth, there had been quite a few chauvinistic grumbles, but, after a few months, most parishioners seemed to forget she was a mere deacon; and Mrs. Malloy wasn't unusual in addressing her as "vicar."

"What sort of lesson?" I asked.

"Where've you been living, in an igloo? Her mother-in-law came for a fortnight the beginning of May and is still buggering up the place."

"Really?" Not only had I not seen the elder Mrs. Spike in church, but Eudora hadn't brought her to visit me, or invited me over to the vicarage to meet her.

"I expect they've been busy cutting each other's throats," Mrs. Malloy said kindly. "I've been getting the lowdown from me ex-chum, Edna Pickle. Edna's not like me, Mrs. H., for as I told you the first day I walked through your door, I don't do drains, I don't do cellars, and I don't gossip about me clients. As I said, I'm too meek and mild for this world, and I worry about you and your good intentions, Mrs. H.; I tell you straight and no mistake, you'll end up looking like Lady Kitty Pomeroy's daughter-in-law, Pamela. My friend Edna, in the days when we was speaking, said you could hold the poor girl up to a light and see right through her."

The thought of my being reduced to a waif had a certain appeal for me. All this rushing around had played havoc with my diet, which I had planned to start after lunch. Or, rather, after the box of chocolates I had eaten after lunch.

"Speaking of Lady Kitty," I said, "you've reminded me I have to speak to her about the tents for the fête. I understand she gave last year's chairperson a real drumming for not consulting her. And rightly so, I suppose, considering the event is held on the grounds of Pomeroy Manor."

"The woman's a bloody tyrant," Mrs. Malloy said vehemently, wiping the complacent smile off my lips. "You have only to look at her to see that. And no one ever gets a look at Sir Robert. Edna says the poor old bugger hasn't been off the grounds since he went hunting without permission twenty years ago. But some would say as compared to your mother-in-law, her ladyship is a prize. Mark my words, the old girl won't be in this house five minutes before she has you in tears, insisting the cat be put down."

"This isn't helping, Mrs. Malloy." I looked around the dining room for some telltale sign that my darling feline, Tobias, was listening in on our conversation from under the sideboard. "My mother-in-law and I have had our differences in the past, but I see now they were mostly my fault. I've been too quick to take offence. But no more. This dinner party is to be a new beginning."

"Whatever you say." Mrs. Malloy heaved a disbelieving sigh. "But if she asks to have *me* put down, Mrs. H., I hope you'll make it quick and painless."

"Let's talk about the flowers," I said firmly. "I'm having second thoughts about those peonies."

"They look all right to me."

"Are you sure?" Suddenly I was wondering if marigolds wouldn't have looked better in the bowl, which is the size of the church font, on the sill. The sunlight foisting its way through the leaded glass window did rather clash with all that pink. Thank heavens for Ben. His classic good looks are always complementary to any decor. Jonas is another story. Our resident gardener takes pride in looking as grungy as possible, from his hoary moustache to his clumping boots. A good thing Lady Kitty didn't have him in her clutches, or Jonas might have found himself stashed away with the Hoover under the stairs.

But who was I to throw stones? The mirror above the overmantel did not reflect a pretty sight. My hair was scraped back in a hangman's noose; I was wearing a pair of horrible old shorts, and my shirt had been rescued from the duster bag. If my in-laws caught me looking like this, they couldn't be blamed for thinking their Ben could have done a lot better for himself. But, happily, that catastrophe was not in the making. I had a luxurious two hours, at least, in which to take a bath, wash my hair, and slip into my party frock.

Mrs. Malloy put it another way. "In two shakes of a cat's tail, unless this place is taken over by the Red Cross for emergency bandage practice, we'll have Mum and Dad leaning on your doorbell. Better snap it up if you hope to lose that two stone you've been going on about all week."

"Thanks for the moral support," I said frostily.

"And you still have to get the twins dressed up in their pretties," she reminded me.

"A mother's privilege." I beamed, trying not to imagine what Abbey and Tam might now look like after an hour with Cousin Freddy. The man who looked like the local hit man was putty in my babies' hands.

"And what about St. Francis?" Mrs. Malloy tapped fingers loaded down with rings on a folded arm. "Is he still missing?" Honestly! The woman should work for Scotland Yard. I'd removed the statue that had been Mum's wedding present from its niche in the hall to give him a dusting, and I'd put him down somewhere or other.

"I'll find him," I said confidently.

"Course you will, duck!" She gave one of her gusty guffaws. "Come nightfall you won't have no trouble, seeing as how he glows in the dark. A nasty turn he gave me that time I was baby-sitting for you and the electricity went out. I thought I was having one of them visions Roman Catholics like your mother-in-law are always jabbering about. Believe you me, I got busy repenting me sins and was all done with the A's and had started on the B's when the lights came on." Mrs. Malloy shuddered at the memory.

To my shame, I was in complete sympathy with her. During childhood I had read about the visions of Bernadette and promptly forfeited any desire to become a saint. For a long time afterwards I had made sure I did something naughty before going to bed just to increase the odds that I wouldn't be singled out for the favour of a heavenly visitor rising up out of the shadows between the wardrobe and the window. Even so, I would sometimes waken in the dead of night and think I heard a voice whispering, "Ellie . . . Ell-ie, come down to the grotto." The objective, I decided, was to be neither too good nor so bad that the devil got me. And early in my marriage I had determined I could never become a Catholic, even to please Mum; not without plugging in a night-light, which wouldn't have pleased Ben.

"A rum sort of marriage, wouldn't you say?" Mrs. Malloy broke into my thoughts.

"Whose?"

"Your in-laws. There's her—an R.C. what makes the Pope look like a goof-off—and him as Jewish as they make 'em. Must have been a real turn-up for the book when they tied the knot."

I had often thought the same thing. Times have changed in thirty-eight years, but when Mum and Dad took the plunge, they must really have been going against the flow. And knowing Mum, I could only assume that the lure of forbidden fruit . . . and vege (Dad ran a greengrocer's shop) had proved irresistible.

"We tend to forget," I said, "when looking at a couple close on seventy that theirs may have been one of the truly great love affairs."

"Don't go getting all misty-eyed on me, Mrs. H." Mrs. Malloy pursed her purple lips.

"My point is they deserve this little anniversary party, with the surprise reunion with Beatrix Taffer being the icing on the cake."

"Says you! And now if it's all the same as makes no difference"— Mrs. M. gave her apron a tug that signalled business—"I think I'll go and make meself a cuppa while you amuse yourself putting out them doilies."

"Thanks for reminding me," I said with genuine gratitude and, accepting my dismissal, headed out into the hall.

Mum, who was a whiz at handwork, had given us so many lacy little mats that had I put them all out at once it would have looked like the year of the crochet hook. That morning I had unearthed four drawer-loads and piled them on the trestle table in the hall, ready to be laid out on every available surface from the Queen Anne bureau to the ironing board. Picking up one of the doilies now, I acknowledged its museum quality and wondered a little wistfully whether Mum and I might have been closer had I shared her talent.

The *bong* of the grandfather clock was not the only reason I dropped the doily. Jonas stuck his head over the banister to growl, in what was supposed to be a whisper, "Ellie girl! I can't find my Choco-Lax."

"What?"

"That stuff as keeps me regular."

"Well, don't look at me like that!" I said defensively. "I didn't sit down and make a pig of myself with a couple of Choco bars. Try and remember where you put it."

His answer was drowned out by the ringing of the telephone. When I turned back with the receiver in my hand, he had vanished up the stairs.

"Hello!" I chirped, expecting to hear Ben's voice asking if I needed him to come home and clean out the gutters, which isn't as silly as it sounds, because Mum was just as likely to climb a ladder to check them out. She's a meticulous housewife besides being such a character!

"Mrs. Haskell?"

Seeing that Ben and I had never picked up the habit of addressing each other like characters in a Jane Austen novel, I figured he wasn't the caller. Besides which, it was a woman speaking. I recognized the voice. My heart dropped to my tennis shoes. Frizzy Taffer. Oh, no! Don't tell me her mother-in-law, Beatrix, wasn't up to an evening out!

"Hello," I said weakly.

"I hope I'm not catching you at a bad moment?"

"Not at all."

"I know how it is when you're rushing around at the last minute trying to get a million things done at once," Frizzy said sympathetically. "Last week I had a thirteenth birthday party for my daughter, Dawn." Breathless laugh. "And just when the doorbell was ringing, my four-year-old slipped and cracked his head, and the minute I got him sorted out, I found the toddler had taken bites out of all the fairy cakes."

Hardly liking to boast that I was one hundred percent organized, I said it was lovely to hear from her.

"I thought I'd better give you a ring to let you know we've arranged for the taxi to bring Ma over to your place, and pick her back up when she's ready to come home."

"Then, she is coming?" I could have kissed the receiver.

"Why, yes!" Frizzy's voice turned all panicky. "You haven't changed your mind, have you?"

"No!"

"It's just that she's *so* excited!"

"Oh, I am pleased!"

"She's like a teenager going to her first grown-up do!"

"How nice!"

"Will there be any games? Ma is very fond of games."

I hadn't planned on anything of that sort, but I hastened to assure her that we might be able to work in a game of Scrabble after dinner.

"That'll be nice," Frizzy said brightly. "Ma does rather have her heart set on Postman's Knock, but look—she's lucky to be having a night out."

Oh, dear! I thought. From the sound of it, Beatrix Taffer was entering her second childhood: all the more reason to get her and my mother-in-law together while they could still enjoy each other.

After telling Frizzy I hoped to meet her too, one day, I returned the phone to its cradle as gently as if it were a baby. Filled with goodwill to mankind in general, and to myself in particular, I scooped up the doilies and went into the drawing room. Lately it had become something of a museum, cordoned off against the day when the twins could sit on the Queen Anne chairs or on one or other of the ivory silk sofas without taking bites out of the cushions, or bouncing fragile ornaments on the floor.

The peacock-and-rose Persian carpet which, like much of the furniture, was a gift from the past, dated back to the days when Abigail Grantham was mistress of Merlin's Court. Her portrait hung above the mantelpiece and I reached to straighten it. Sometimes my organizational acumen amazes me. In the midst of depositing doilies around the room, I came up with the idea of having, at some future date, my in-laws renew their marriage vows here at Merlin's Court. Suspecting that theirs hadn't been the splashiest of weddings, I couldn't think of anything nicer. Only one question nagged at me. Should the bridal pair stand in front of the fireplace or by the window? With dreamy steps I crossed to the leaded glass bay and promptly dropped the doilies. What I beheld was so frightening, my blood ran cold. There were men out on the lawn putting up big white tents. My heavens! The scene resembled a summit meeting in the Sahara. And if that weren't sufficient cause for alarm, a taxi was zinging its way through the wrought iron gates, past Freddy's cottage, like a Black Maria.

Before I could complete my gasp, my in-laws were standing on our gravel driveway, paying off the cabbie, while their little dog, Sweetie, raced around in mad circles, yipping and yapping and tying up three pairs of legs with her lead. Smile, Ellie! Do not even harbour the suspicion that Mum and Dad had done this to catch me on the hop. There had to be a simpler explanation—such as all the clocks in the house being a couple of hours slow. Besides, what did it matter that there was no time for me to comb my hair—let alone lose five pounds—before the doorbell rang? My mother-in-law was a saint. She would love me just the way I was . . . even if it killed her.

"Never let it be said we're not punctual!"

Mum stepped tidily over the threshold while Dad and the taxi driver hobbled in behind her with the luggage. Was it the brash afternoon sunlight that made Magdalene Haskell look like a workhouse waif, with her crocheted beret pulled down over her ears and her much-washed frock two sizes too big, as if to allow room for growing? She wasn't any bigger than a sparrow. And I was a heel to be disturbed by punctuality. Had I learned nothing from my near-perfect attendance at St. Anselm's Church in the pursuit of humility, patience, and generosity of spirit? The doilies weighed heavily upon my conscience and my chest. Halfway to the front door I'd realized I still had some in my hands. With the desperation of the family dog about to be caught with the Sunday joint, I'd stuffed them down my bra.

Speaking of doggie-wogs, Sweetie came trotting in to fix me with a look that said What—you still here? But I didn't let her put me off my stride. "Mum! Dad! How lovely to see you!" I enveloped them in a huge embrace that included the astonished taxi driver.

"So where's the brass band, Ellie?" Dad roared. Elijah is inclined to bellow as if the whole world were deaf. And he gets away with it, I suspect, because he has a beard worthy of Father Christmas, and dark brown eyes that must have melted the heart of many a young girl in his day.

"Oh, you mean the tents!" I started to say that they were a mistake, when the front door slammed open, almost sending Mum into the arms of one of the suits of armour by the stairs.

"Mrs. Haskell?"

A giant of a man blocked the opening. This massive creature had a pencil behind his left ear and a crumpled green form in his meaty right hand. "We've got the lot up, so if you would be so good as to sign for receipt on the dotted line, we'll peel on out of here."

"You can leave anytime you like," I said. "*After* you take those tents back down."

"But you ordered them, lady!"

"I know." I mustered a smile. "But for St. Anselm's Fête, which is on the twelfth of July, not the twelfth of June; and they were to be set up on the grounds of Pomeroy Manor, not here." Closing the door on his wounded face, I enjoyed a brief respite, during which Mum said that she had known the tents weren't for her and Dad, not that they would have wanted that kind of fuss anyway. Before I could reply, a tap sounded at the blasted door. I opened up yet again, expecting to see some fellow with a white flag, intent on negotiating a truce in which the tents went, but the bill got paid.

"Why, hello, Mrs. Pickle!" I tried to look thrilled.

"I *do* hope as I haven't come at a bad time." She looked up at me with apology written all over her currant-bun face. Edna Pickle, unlike Mrs. Malloy, looked exactly like those charwomen you see on the telly—floral coveralls, and metal curlers bristling under her headscarf.

"My in-laws just arrived"—I cast a look over my shoulder—"but it's always nice to see you."

"I'd have gone round back." Mrs. Pickle always spoke as if allowing time for an interpreter to translate the words into a foreign tongue. "But I didn't like to take Mrs. Malloy unawares, not after our recent bust-up. She can be a little sharp, can Roxie, and I thought as I should tread a bit wary, like."

By taking the longcut through the hall? Smiling to show I understood completely, I held wide the door, and in the time it would have taken to unpitch one of the tents, Edna Pickle stepped into my home and opened up her big black bag.

"Here you are, Mrs. Haskell. I brought you a couple bottles of me dandelion wine, seeing as Roxie said you went through the last ones I sent in such a hurry."

"Why, thank you." I knew without turning my head that Mum had exchanged a questioning look with Dad. "If you'd like to take those down to the kitchen, Mrs. Pickle, you'll find Mrs. Malloy there along with my cousin Freddy and the twins."

"If you're sure it's no bother?"

"Not the least."

Aware that the taxi driver, a tough-looking bruiser, was breathing hard, as if to signal his motor was still running, I am afraid I hustled her off to the kitchen before she was properly done saying "Pleased to meet you both, I'm sure" to Mum and Dad. Coming back up the hall, I squeezed out a smile for the taxi driver. His face was fast turning the colour of a bad bruise.

"Look, lady," he was saying to Mum, "I counted your cases when I put 'em in the cab, and there they all are."

"And I tell you," Mum snipped, "that I'm missing my needlework bag. Not that anyone cares, I don't suppose; even though crocheting is my life"—she paused to cross herself—"next to Mother Church, that is."

Dad gusted a sigh that fluttered the snowy whiskers around his lips. "You know what, Magdalene? You drive me crazy. Everywhere we go for thirty-eight years, you lose something."

"Go where, Elijah? We haven't been on a day trip to the seaside in all that time."

"Here we go again." He turned to me. "Your mother-in-law's got a mind like an elephant." His voice worked its way up to a bellow. "If it isn't her handbag she thinks she's lost, it's her umbrella! And you know why, Ellie? Because every five minutes she repacks. On the train she put her crochet bag first in her small case, then the big one, then the small one again."

"I like to be organized." Mum drew herself up so that she was the height of the umbrella stand.

"That'll be two pounds twenty." The taxi driver forced a beefy smile, peeled open his wallet, stuffed in the five-pound note Dad handed him, and grudgingly made change on his way out. Closing the door and turning back to my in-laws, I heard a series of merry squeals from the kitchen.

Mum's ears pricked up above her beret. "Is that the twins?"

"Yes! My cousin Freddy has been baby-sitting this afternoon, and from the sound of it, everyone is having a good time." I could hardly contain myself from racing down the hall, flinging wide the kitchen door, and showing off Abbey and Tam. So what if my darlings needed a wash and brush-up? Grandparents see with their hearts. They would understand that I wasn't raising prize poochies. No offence, Sweetie. In my exuberance I gave Mum a kiss and she didn't flinch. What she did was peck the air two inches to the right of my cheek and cling to her handbag as if it were a life raft.

"You won't believe how they have both grown, or how dark Tam's hair is now. Abbey's is still the colour of barley sugar, and she's just as sweet." Taking hold of Dad's arm, I hadn't propelled him more than a step, when his better half called a halt.

"We'll see them when we've had a wash and rinsed off all the dirt and germs from the train," Magdalene decided. "I know things are different nowadays, Ellie! You young people aren't so particular—too busy doing your own thing, or whatever the saying is. Far be it for me to criticize, but Elijah and I are too old to change."

"Speak for yourself." Dad's roar was softened by a wink and really, it wasn't hard for me to make allowances for Mum. She had to be tired and was probably struggling to remember the patron saint of lost luggage, so she could say a thank-you for the safe deliverance of the crochet bag. For a moment I couldn't think why my heart had started ticking like a time bomb. Then I remembered. St. Francis! I didn't dare look at the empty niche on the wall. Where on earth had I put that statue? And if that were not worry enough, I felt the doilies worming their way upwards, causing me to fear I would end up with an Elizabethan ruff around my neck.

Mum's nose was probing the air with the relish of a vampire breaking into a blood bank. "Ellie, what is that *peculiar* smell?"

Immediately the humiliating thought crossed my mind that my deodorant had gone on the blink. Backing away with all speed, I bumped into the grandfather clock, which gave a *bong* of annoyance. And Gramps wasn't the only one to witness my discomfiture. The two suits of armour were falling all over their metal feet to hear more.

"I don't smell anything," roared Dad.

Mum's nose went right on twitching as though it ran on one of those long-life batteries. "Lavender, that's what it is!"

Instantly I was trembling with relief. "You're right, I polished with Johnson's Lavender."

"I always use Lemon Pledge." Mum drew herself up straight and somehow managed to look tinier than ever. "But we all do things our own way, and you'll get no interference from me, Ellie." She looked around for a place to stow her handbag. The place looked obscenely naked without a doily in sight, and I couldn't have been more embarrassed if I had been caught in the bath by Mr. Watkins, the window cleaner, without so much as a couple of washcloths covering strategic parts.

Talk about heaping coals of fire upon my head! Mum didn't mention the doilies. She handed Dad her handbag. He in turn handed it to me exactly as if we were playing Pass the Parcel. I added it to the pile of luggage by the stairs.

"As I said to Elijah the other night, the last thing we need is to make work for the young people. Every night I pray to St. Francis that we won't be a burden."

Be still, my thumping heart. The empty niche on the wall yawned huge as the gateway to hell. Any moment Mum's eyes would swivel right and I would be out of the family.

"Don't be daft, woman, Ellie doesn't find us a burden." Dad's eyebrows came down in a scowl that reminded me heart-wrenchingly of Ben.

"That's what I hoped." Mum aged before my eyes. "But when we walk in here to find she has been putting up tents on the lawn that she doesn't want, and that she's been spring-cleaning in June, it shouldn't come as any surprise that she's turned to the bottle. . . ."

My mouth hung open.

"The thing is, it takes all the pleasure out of coming." Mum continued on like an express train. "Mrs. Brown at the corner shop always says that if you pick up and polish as you go along, there's never any need for turning the house upside down. But those are *her* words, not mine. What I say, Elijah, is that we should take the next train home. The last thing we need at our time of life is for Ellie to end up in one of those rehab places on our account. Ben would never forgive us. Our one-and-only is like a lot of young people these days. He puts his wife first."

Dad rolled his eyes. "You're getting better, Magdalene. Usually it takes you a full half hour to get up to speed."

I was tempted to defend myself by saying Mrs. Malloy had done most of the work while I sat around all day chomping on Choco-Lax. And that the reason I wasn't dressed for company was because the cleaners had lost all my designer frocks. But I was saved from this cowardly display when Mum turned her attention to Sweetie. The little canine was stalking up and down the hall, giving the white-paw test to the furniture. Her muzzle wore a Bette Davis "What a dump!" smirk.

"Elijah! All this commotion isn't good for the dog."

"Now, don't go pampering her, or she'll insist on breakfast in bed."
Pa sounded gruff, but his whiskers twitched fondly.

"This clinches it." Mum dropped to her knees with the speed of one
who has spent a lifetime on church pews, and cradled Sweetie in her
arms. "We shouldn't have come. The train journey was too much for her,
and now we've walked in here to find Ellie in a state, and Ben and the
babies are nowhere to be seen. Well, I'll say it again, the best thing we can
do for everyone concerned is turn right around and go home."

So much for my grand hopes that this visit would be one of unruf-
fled familial calm. Had there been a violin handy, I might have tucked it
under my chin and scraped out a mournful melody with the bow. But that
would have been playing directly into Sweetie's paws. Her presence certainly demanded music—preferably an entire orchestra with Mozart himself at the helm. Wriggling away from Mum, she stood with her furry face
tilted left, either to show off her best profile or to catch a whiff of Tobias
Cat, who was lurking under the trestle table. To give the canine Lizzie
Borden her due, she was no longer the moth-eaten scrap my in-laws had
rescued from a wretched life on the streets. This dog looked as though
she had been crocheted by Mum and hand-washed in Fairy Liquid. My
guess was that her favourite perfume was Très Chic, her nails were acrylic,
and that she now informed her pooch friends her name was Anastasia
and her family had been forced to flee the royal kennels during that nasty
revolution.

"How about a nice cup of tea?" I coaxed as Mum got to her feet.
Unfortunately, you would think I had suggested poison. Her sparrow eyes
darkened to a terrible black. Her hair stuck out around the rim of her
beret as if raised from the scalp, and she crossed herself with a trembling
hand before directing a quivering finger in the direction of the kitchen.

Sometimes I am shockingly slow on the uptake. When I looked the
way of Mum's accusing finger, I didn't see anything to rock the old house
on its foundation. To be honest, I would have expected any red-blooded
grandma to be smiling. For my adorable Tam looked like a story-book
child as he toddled into the hall. His face was as sweet as his cherry-red
sweater and his gait was a little off kilter because he was holding a dolly
above his head as if afraid it would be snatched away at any moment. Oh,
heavens! Say it wasn't so! My heart started to _bong_ in time with the
grandfather clock. That dolly was St. Francis!

"Let me explain," I began.

"No need to go off the deep end, Magdalene!" Dad broke up the
ghastly tableau by chugging over to Tam with his hand extended. "There
now, son, give it to Grandpa."

Bless my big boy, he held out the statue. But when Dad reached for it, Tam said no with hideous clarity. Then he gurgled a laugh and stuck the plaster head in his mouth.

"How can you smile, Elijah!" Mum snapped. "You'd be singing a different tune if Ellie had given that child Moses to suck on like a lollipop."

"But I didn't give Tam St. Francis! As an animal lover . . ." I dragged my eyes away from Sweetie. Her smirk said louder than words, "Liar, liar, pants on fire!" I blundered on. "As a lover of animals, I have always admired St. Francis. I took him down only to dust behind his ears—"

There are none so deaf as those who will not listen. Mum's hands were knotted in prayer, her pinched face was tilted towards heaven. "I gave that statue to you and Ben for a wedding present."

"Very kind of you, I'm sure!"

The kitchen door slapped wide open, revealing Mrs. Malloy in all her glory. "One more knicketyknack for poor Mrs. H. to dust!" she fumed. "Because as I made plain as daylight when I first set foot in Merlin's Court, I don't do drains, I don't do ceilings, and I most certainly don't do graven images."

This blasphemy turned Mum into a pillar of salt. Not so Dad, however. He looked rather taken with Mrs. Malloy, but whether because of her heaving taffeta bosom or because his faith also prohibited plaster-of-Paris idols that glowed in the dark, only he knew.

He didn't, however, get to feast his eyes or ears for long. My cousin Freddy loomed around Mrs. M. with Abbey in his arms. My little girl looked good enough to eat, with her barley-sugar curls and rose-hip smile, whilst Freddy himself looked like something the cat had refused to eat. His ponytail had come unravelled, his beard was in disarray from being tweaked by his young charges, and there were food stains on his torn sweatshirt.

"Sorry about Tam." Freddy favoured the world at large with his most ghoulish grin. "The little blighter jumped ship."

It was hard to protest his veracity with my son and heir trying to climb Dad's leg as if it were the rigging of the H.M.S. *Victory*. Mrs. Malloy threw up her hands and vanished into the kitchen to restore her soul, probably with a nip of Mrs. Pickle's dandelion wine.

"Who is that awful man?" Mum's finger gyrated between me and Freddy like a gun about to go off.

"My favourite cousin."

"Oh! Well, it takes all sorts to make a family, as Mrs. Jones down the road would say."

Dad hid any embarrassment he may have felt by picking up Tam, who had lost interest in St. Francis and abandoned him on the floor.

Far from taking offence at Mum's words, however, Freddy looked positively chuffed as he bounced Abbey in his arms. "Gosh, that's the most sensitive thing anyone's said about me in ages. Makes me feel so wanted." My cousin batted his eyes. "Thanks, Auntie Mags. You don't mind me calling you Auntie, do you?"

Mum was speechless.

"Want me to carry those cases upstairs?" Freddy's gaze roved to where the herd of luggage was taking its ease in the dappled shade of the banister rail.

"That's awfully kind, Freddy," I interposed, "but I am sure we can manage."

"Don't get up on your high horse, coz," he soothed. "I won't charge them above a fiver. They're *family.*"

Mum managed a gasp. "Elijah, we have lived too long. I want you to take me back to London so I can make an appointment with Father O'Grady."

To see about getting her son's marriage annulled? Had I been one of those women who cry exquisitely, now might have been the moment for a good sob session. As it was, I watched dry-eyed as Dad handed Tam over to Freddy, who said that if he wasn't needed, except as an ornament, he would take both kiddies upstairs for their baths. And no sooner had he disappeared with my darlings in tow, than Sweetie decided to hog the limelight. Fed up with being upstaged, she squatted down on the flag-stones and, putting her best furry profile forward, made a puddle the size of the Atlantic Ocean.

"Damn dog!" Dad roared.

Mum immediately went on the defensive. "She's just marking her territory. You do"—she made it clear her pet's lapse was my fault—"you do still have that cat?"

"We're fond of him." I edged around the accusation while sidestepping the flood, which caused me to fear we would all be forced to seek higher ground on the stairs. No hope of Mrs. Malloy magically appearing with bucket and mop. Her job description did not include canine clean-up. Regrettably, membership in the local mothers' union did not accord me such protection.

"Sweetie doesn't hold with cats." Dad's voice, soft as his white beard, indicated he had relented towards the little snot, who was mistress of the hangdog expression and, unlike some of us, probably did cry exquisitely.

"It's not that she doesn't like them." Mum fixed me with her sparrow eyes. "She's allergic."

"What a pity." I floundered. "But let's look for the silver lining. The little . . . dear obviously feels at home, or she wouldn't have taken the trouble . . . to mark her territory, so you see you have to stay for her sake and because"—I paused to heighten the moment of anticipation—"because Ben and I love you and . . . I have a special surprise for you both. Mum, I have invited your old friend Beatrix Taffer to join us for dinner tonight!"

I should have broken the glad tidings more gently, for Mum proved to be allergic to surprises. Far from being wreathed in smiles, her face now resembled a deadly bomb about to explode.

"You did what?"

"I told you . . ."

"And I told you, Ellie, when we spoke about Beatrix, that I had lost touch with her nearly forty years ago."

"I know."

"Well, what you don't know"—Mum looked ready to shoot up in the air like a Roman candle—"what you don't know is that the reason we stopped seeing each other is that we ended on a terrible row."

"Oh, dear!" Out the corner of my eye I noticed that Sweetie had cornered Tobias Cat under the trestle table and that they were engaged in a holy war of sorts over St. Francis, who at least one of them thought was a bone to be carried off and buried where no human agency could find him. Damn! It said much about how upset Mum was that she didn't look once in the direction of the animal altercation.

"Magdalene's row with Beatrix was a real humdinger." Dad was stony-faced, but I thought I detected a smile in his voice. Past experience had led me to suspect my father-in-law thrived on contention. But I didn't. My stomach had tied itself in knots.

"After all this time Mrs. Taffer has probably forgotten the entire incident," I babbled. "From little things her daughter-in-law let slip, I got the distinct impression that your old friend is failing. So wouldn't it be nice to let bygones be bygones?"

"Not on your Nellie," Mum said.

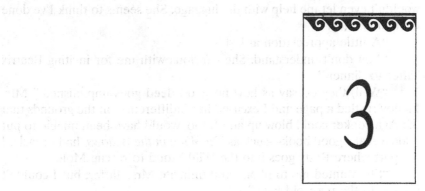

3

By way of consolation, Mum was now too despondent to stage an exit. But the moment she and Dad disappeared upstairs and Sweetie absconded with St. Francis to parts unknown, I was tempted to cast myself upon the breast of one of the suits of armour and sob out my tale of woe. Being made of sterner stuff, however, I decided to go and cast myself upon the well-padded frame of Mrs. Malloy instead.

Freddy, who thrives on histrionics, would have enjoyed the show, but he—bless his tattoos—was still upstairs, seeing to the twins' nighttime ablutions. And when I entered the kitchen after mopping up Sweetie's Atlantic Ocean, it was to discover that Mrs. Pickle had bunked off home and thus was not available to ply me with dandelion wine. Never mind. Mrs. M. was a picture to warm the cockles of your heart. Seated in a chair with her feet on the fender of the open hearth, she had a book on her lap. By no means did I object to her reading on the job. We all need time out from the rigours of the day.

Here in this room that was the heart of the house, I would unburden myself of my sorrows, along with the doilies stuffed inside my bra.

"Ah, there you are, Mrs. H." Mrs. Malloy raised her rainbow-lidded eyes but kept her nose in the book. "So what have you done with our guests?"

"They're up in their room."

"Did you lock them in?"

"No jokes, please!" I tried to smile, but felt my face crack. "Mum wouldn't even let me help with the luggage. She seems to think I've done enough already."

"A little appreciation at last."

"You don't understand. She's furious with me for inviting Beatrix Taffer to dinner."

"Well, they do say as how no good deed goes unpunished." Mrs. Malloy rustled a page and I excused her indifference on the grounds that the Aga cooker could blow up and I, too, would have been unable to put aside a really good book—such as *The Wind in the Willows,* had I reached the part where Ratty goes into the Wild Wood to rescue Mole.

"She wanted me to phone and uninvite Mrs. Taffer, but I couldn't do that to the poor old lady."

"You're bloody well breaking my heart, but could you stuff a sock in it, Mrs. H.? I'm just getting to the good part."

"Heaven forbid I disturb you."

"How would it be if I read you a few paragraphs?" Mrs. Malloy suggested kindly.

Immediately I thawed. There is always something uplifting in hearing the written word spoken aloud. Perched on the table, I embraced the entire room with my smile and said, "Go ahead, I'm listening."

Mrs. Malloy smacked her lips and intoned with a gusto worthy of the classics: " 'Lying upon the rumpled sheets beneath the mosquito netting, Sir Edward moaned the name of his lost love through passion-parched lips. "Letitia! Letitia!" The memory of how she had looked stepping out of the harem pool made him writhe with exquisite torment as he clutched his throbbing manhood to his chest.' "

"His what?" I slid off the table.

"And to think," Mrs. Malloy mused, "here's me with four husbands, give or take, and I never knew I'd been short-changed."

"You have to allow for poetic license." I moved to peer over her shoulder. "What is the title of that book?"

"Lady Letitia's Letters." She clapped it shut. "And don't go pretend-

ing you didn't know, Mrs. H., seeing as you're the one what borrowed it from the library."

"You're right," I admitted. "But what a fooler! That cover looks so demure with the single riding crop." As I spoke I was quickly stashing the vile volume among the cookery books on the shelf, where it stood out like a lady of the evening at a Sunday school picnic. "I'll think of a better hiding place later," I told Mrs. Malloy.

"Afraid Mr. H. wouldn't approve?"

"Hardly! When I first met Ben he was trying his hand at a novel whose purple prose would have made even the satyric Sir Edward blush. No, it's my mother-in-law I'm worried about. Magdalene considers Jane Austen racy and, after the set-to we just had, I would prefer not to make any more waves."

My words brought a glum look to Mrs. Malloy's face. "Seems to me you've changed some since *she*"—eyes raised to the ceiling—"walked through the front door. It's bad enough when a woman can't call her home her own, but when it's your mind what's being taken over—" She paused meaningfully.

I had to protest. "What's wrong with trying to keep the peace?"

Mrs. Malloy shed a benevolent smile on me. "That's not the real you talking. Possession, that's the medical term for what's going on here. And Edna Pickle could tell you a thing or two on that subject, seeing as how her great-great-granny was a witch."

"So you told me." A shudder passed through me, which couldn't be blamed entirely on the grandfather clock in the hall *bong*ing the hour. It was the silliest thing, but suddenly I had the feeling that I was one of those little voodoo dolls and fate was sticking pins in me to ensure that something worse than a run-in with my mother-in-law was in store. Ridiculous! My nerves were on edge. I hastened to ask Mrs. M. if she and her friend had made up their quarrel.

"We're all called upon to forgive!" Mrs. M. was given to these pious moments since joining St. Anselm's choir. "A blinking nuisance, but there it is. And when it comes down to it, I'm the only friend Edna has in this world. I keep telling her that her obsession to win the Martha gets on people's nerves. But it's like talking to the wall." Mrs. Malloy teetered onto her high-heeled feet and stowed one of the babies' squeaky toys in the Welsh dresser.

"Really?" The notion of the tortoiselike Mrs. Pickle being a woman possessed of a raging ambition seemed to me about as likely as the possibility of Mum dancing nude on a piano. But what did I know?

"To tell the truth," my faithful daily mused, "I did get to wondering if the reason the competition for them ribbons has thinned out this year is due to some of Edna's havey-cavey tricks."

"What on earth do you mean?"

"Well, not to make a big thing of it, there's that Irene Jolliffe, what always won for her jams, taking off to live with her daughter in Liverpool. To say nothing of Louise Bennett, who suddenly decides she can't grow her prize marrows no more because her arthritis has got so bad. And don't it seem funny that Mavis Appleby, whose pies could never be beaten, should up and marry that postman from London and move away?"

"Not especially," I said. "You've been saying for years that Mrs. Appleby was after anything in trousers."

"All right, then." Mrs. Malloy took this setback in stride. "What about Sarie Robertson, who done all that lovely crochet, keeling over in the market a couple of months back?"

"She was ninety-two!"

"So?"

"You can hardly say she was cut down in her prime." Brushing my hair back from my furrowed brow, I asked, "Exactly what are you saying, Mrs. Malloy? You surely don't think that Mrs. Pickle caused Mrs. Bennett's arthritis, poisoned Mrs. Robertson's denture cleaner, and set up the rumour that the other two women had left town, while all along she has them buried under her rosebushes?"

"No call to be melodramatic." Mrs. M. stuck her nose up so high, she risked having it pecked off by a dicky bird. "That sort of unpleasantness happens only to the likes of your mother-in-law. What's been at the back of my mind is that Edna may have been up to some of her great-great-granny's tricks—sticking pins in dolls made up to look like them women."

Given my thoughts of a few moments ago, this was uncanny.

"I wouldn't put it past her, that's for sure!" Spoken like a loyal friend of Mrs. Pickle's.

"Honestly!" I managed a quivery laugh.

"That's your trouble, Mrs. H. I don't suppose the thought ever crossed your mind that them bottles of dandelion wine was a bribe, to get on your good side, seeing as you're chairwoman this year of the St. Anselm's Summer Fête."

"I merely thought it a very kind gesture on Mrs. Pickle's part," I said firmly.

"There's none so blind!" Mrs. M. shook her black-and-white head. "But it don't hurt to remember that old saying about 'uneasy lies the head what wears the crown,' or however it goes." Having delivered this dire warning, she added briskly, "Well, all this gabbing won't buy me a new frock. How about"—she picked up the kettle and plonked it on the stove —"how about drowning our sorrows with a nice cuppa?"

"Not for me, thank you." The truth was, Mrs. Malloy's tea would dye your teeth black. And unlike those six-week hair rinses that wash out with the first shampoo, the effect was invariably permanent. Besides, there wasn't time. Suddenly all the things I had to do went whirling around in my head like autumn leaves. Unload the doilies, find St. Francis, put the ragout and the rolls in the oven, spend some quality time with my children, take a bath, wash my hair, get dressed . . . Was there no end? And to think that less than an hour earlier, I'd had so much time on my hands I had been thinking of giving some away to people less fortunate.

Mrs. Malloy must have read my mind, because she turned her back on the kettle and informed me she was at my beck and call.

"Don't thank me, Mrs. H., just put a little something extra in me pay packet. I'll see to wiping off the cooker while you take care of the vegetables."

"Oh, my heavens!" I clapped a hand to my face, almost knocking myself out. Turning to the window, I saw a flowerpot wobble among all the other flowerpots as a slink of tail went weaving its way among the greenery.

"Get down from that window," I ordered Tobias. "You and I need to have a little talk about your making an effort to get along with Sweetie, not that I would think it disloyal if you were to tell me where she buried St. Francis."

To my surprise, Tobias, who is a relatively easygoing chap, shot off the window ledge into a sink full of bobbing vegetables and, spraying water to the four walls, landed on the table, knocking over the jug of flowers.

Without a word of complaint Mrs. Malloy peeled off a false eyelash and dabbed at her lid before tapping the bedraggled daddy longlegs back into place. I, however, did not do so good a job of keeping my cool.

"Don't you dare raise your paw to me!" Retreating from the flash of claws that would have been better suited to a grizzly, I almost fell over a chair when my father-in-law spoke from behind me in one of his leonine roars.

"Only me, Ellie!"

Was I living in a zoo? A glance in the direction of the hall doorway confirmed this ghastly scenario. Dad stood there, holding Sweetie, whose shiny black eyes stood out like buttons on a fuzzy cardigan, ready to pop off and go pinging across the room as she yipped and yapped and strained to leap the table and be at Tobias's throat.

"Hold fast," I entreated Dad. "I'll put the cat outside."

"Oh, you mustn't go exerting yourself." Mrs. Malloy spoke to me while batting her lashes—one of which was a centimeter higher than the other—at Dad. It would appear that she had taken the peck on the cheek he had given her under the mistletoe last Christmas to mean something deeper than an appreciation of her sage-and-onion stuffing. "Leave it to me, Mrs. H., I'll put the naughty pussy outside so he doesn't scare the dear little doggie."

This noble offer was more easily made than kept. Tobias resisted arrest, first by jumping back into the sink and sending a deluge my way as I went to grab him, then by lunging onto the topmost shelf of the Welsh dresser. There he assumed an indifferent mein, worthy of the king of the castle.

Wondering what it would be like to wallow in a nice hot bath, I dragged up a chair and, after a couple of false starts, managed to descend to terra firma with Tobias clawing at my arms. "No pain, no gain," I gasped as I staggered over to the garden door, yanked it open with such speed that I swear it dodged sideways, and tossed my faithful feline out into the sun-baked courtyard. "All safe!" What stupidity! I should have remembered that Sweetie was a dog who would always have the last bark. Dad must have relaxed his grip a moment too soon. Before I could get the door shut, something no bigger than one of Mrs. Malloy's fur collars shot past my legs and with a triumphant "yip," the dog was out of the bag . . . I mean the house.

"Damn dog's nothing but a nuisance." Dad patted his cardigan front complacently.

"I expect she had to excuse herself in a hurry," I said magnanimously.

"That's what I brought her down for. Magdalene's very particular that Sweetie do her business at set times."

"What a good idea! Is Mum having a rest?" Ask a stupid question, get a straight answer from Dad. The man is fanatical about two things—never telling a lie and never going back on his word.

"She's turning out the airing cupboard."

"How thoughtful!" I had reorganized my sheets and towels the previous morning, stacking them in alphabetical order. Almond, blue, cream, etc. But there was no point in being miffed, especially if Mum was working off some of her negative feelings towards Beatrix Taffer.

"The woman's a bloody marvel!" Mrs. Malloy exclaimed with patent insincerity.

"Yes." Dad stroked his bearded chin. "When she's done with the airing cupboard she's going to dust the top of that big dresser in the bedroom. There's a spider's web up there."

Blast! I should have known she would spot that itsy-bitsy web. The only reason I had not taken care of it was that the dresser almost reached the bedroom ceiling, and the only way to get to the top (unless one wanted to drag a ladder upstairs) was to stand on the narrow ledge between the lower drawers and the six-foot mirror and hat box shelf above.

"Now, Ellie, don't go tearing yourself off a strip." Dad patted my shoulder. "You know Magdalene and her nervous energy. She's all hot and bothered because she doesn't think the window latches properly. Says anyone could break in."

Their bedroom was in the north tower, several feet above cloud level. Only a burglar prepared to risk a serious nosebleed would go shinning up the ivy, but my guests' peace of mind was paramount, especially when the express purpose of the visit was that we grow to love each other to death.

"When I go upstairs," I said, "I'll ask Jonas to take a look at the latch. He keeps a set of tools in his room, so it won't take him a moment."

Dad scowled. "Now then, Ellie! Don't go putting the man to any bother."

"Don't worry"—I kissed his furry cheek—"Jonas will be glad of the chance to putter. He's been reading *A Tale of Two Cities* until his eyes must be ready to fall out. So why don't you go and ease Mum's mind on this little matter, and suggest she take a nice relaxing bath? I'll fetch in the dog."

"No need to beat me over the head with a hammer!" Dad turned towards the hall door. "I'm the first to agree the kitchen is no place for a man—unless, that is, we're talking about my son, who's made a career out of the place."

The moment he was out the door, Mrs. Malloy flexed her lips into a velvet smile and smoothed down her taffeta frock so that it molded over her ripe hips. "Not bad for an old codger, is he?"

I had never thought about my father-in-law in those terms; the very idea was vaguely incestuous, and I wasn't about to encourage Mrs. Malloy's girlish fancies, not when it was now past five-thirty and we would have Mrs. Taffer banging on the door at seven. Had Mum entered the kitchen, she wouldn't have smelled Johnson's Lavender Wax. Truth be told, she wouldn't have smelled anything. The air wasn't warm and toasty with the aroma of dinner cooking contentedly in the oven. The beef ragout was still in the fridge, the vegetables were still bobbing in the sink, and I mustn't forget the rolls, which from the looks of them were also beginning to lose some of their *oomph.*

"Mrs. Malloy," I ventured to say, "would you be so kind as to go and find Sweetie?"

"That dog needs a nine-to-five job!" She stalked out into the garden, leaving me feeling as if I were living inside Big Ben. Every time I took a breath, the grandfather clock gave a *bong,* purely out of the goodness of its heart, to remind me that time waits for no woman. By the time I unmolded the salmon pâté from its fluted dish, my hands were shaking, and before I escaped from the kitchen and raced upstairs, I was completely out of puff.

Freddy had the twins in their cots when I went into the nursery, and having no medal to bestow on his noble breast, I placed a kiss on his moth-eaten cheek. "Thanks, Mary Poppins! You're one in a million!"

"Tell that to your mother-in-law."

"Oh, come on!" I gave him a hug. "She didn't mean—"

"To scream bloody murder when she saw me?" Freddy faked a sob and mopped his eyes with the end of his ponytail. "To tell you the truth, Ellie old sock, that woman cut me to the quick and I don't think I'll get over it until I've poured myself a pint of bitter." With that he bent to kiss the top of Abbey's barley-sugar head and tap Tam playfully on the cheek before moving over to the window, opening it up, and disappearing over the sill.

Leaning out to watch my cousin slide down the drainpipe, I was forced to rethink my recent position on burglars. But this was not the time to plan a security system. Tam was squealing "Mum! Here!" And Abbey was attempting an escape from behind bars.

Closing the window on a last glimpse of Freddy bounding towards the cottage, I turned, arms spread wide enough to gather them both up, and cried, "Coming, my darlings!"

Oh, it was immeasurably restoring to sit in the rocking chair with my children and sing songs with nonsensical words and no melody. Ten minutes later, having seen them safely and sweetly asleep, I descended the stairs feeling restored in body and soul, with the result that I did no more than gasp when the front door opened and a strange man walked into the hall.

Shading my eyes against the brassy sunlight that came tracking in with him, I inquired: "Who are you?"

He bore down on me with imperative strides and fixed me with a fearsome stare. "My God, Ellie! Have you lost your mind or your eyesight?"

"Oh, it's you!" I sagged against his husbandly chest. "It seems an eternity since I last saw you, and I couldn't be quite sure you weren't an insurance agent. And I did find a tea leaf floating in my cup this morning, which indicated I was destined to meet a dark, handsome man eager to take advantage of me."

Ben silenced my folly with a kiss that would have done Sir Edward proud, and we didn't jolt apart until the grandfather clock, working overtime as overseer, gave an almighty *bong*. "You've been focusing too hard on the teacup readings for the fête." My spouse took the last doily from my pliant hands and placed it on my head. "How are things going in our castle by the sea?"

"Not too badly." I smiled bravely. "Your mother almost walked out seconds after walking in the door, but unless she's knotted the bed sheets and climbed out the window, she and Dad are still here."

"It is possible," my love said as gently as he could, "that they weren't too excited about this visit in the first place. I did tell you, dear, that they always made rather a point of not making a . . . point of their anniversary."

"I've been thinking about that," I admitted, "and wondering if the reason might be that their wedding day does not hold the happiest of memories. But Mum's being upset with me was very specific. It had to do with my little surprise."

"Beatrix Taffer?"

"Seems she and Mum had an awful dust-up years ago."

"Let me get this straight." Ben raised an interrogatory eyebrow. "They aren't on speaking terms?"

"Haven't been for forty years."

A chuckle escaped my husband's lips. "Do you think we can get them to communicate through knocks on the table?"

"It really is no laughing matter," I said primly.

"Sweetheart"—the mischievous twinkle vanished on the instant—"I will not have you castigating yourself. What you've done is provide everyone with a chance to kiss and make up."

Amazing how he could make me melt like candle wax so that I was molded by his hands into a woman who bore no resemblance to the externals of rag bag shirt and shorts. *Call me Lady Letitia!* my soul cried. All this because he looked at me with those Mediterranean-blue-green eyes of his, so that I was sinking several fathoms deep, to where all the wonder of a lost galleon's treasure shimmered in their depths.

"I want you . . ." he whispered in thickened accents.

"That's awfully dear of you"—I caressed his cheek—"but there are certain time constraints." No doubt I looked bewitchingly cross-eyed with half my gaze on him and half on the unrelenting face of the clock.

"Ellie, I insist!"

"Well, in that case . . ." Surely even his mother would not disapprove, it being one of the tenets of the Faith that a wife never refuse her husband.

He placed his hands commandingly upon my shoulders. "I want you to go upstairs and get into the bath. You deserve a relaxing soak after all your hard work."

"Thank you." My voice came out of my boots. The clock gave another *bong*, tempting me to throw the doily at it. Ben marched me inexorably to the stairs. I ventured to ask him why he was talking in that muffled, sexy voice.

"I must be allergic to that damn dog." He dragged a tissue from his pocket.

"That's ridiculous. Sweetie had barely put her paw inside the door, when she went back outside."

Ben's dark brows came down over his nose in the scowl he had inherited from his father and bequeathed to his son. "It may well be that my problem is psychosomatic, Ellie, born of a deep-seated resentment of an animal who has usurped my place with Mum and Dad."

"I understand that it wasn't easy for you when you found out they had given Sweetie your old room. But you can't take out your feelings on a helpless animal," I soothed with my usual hypocrisy.

"You're right." He stuffed the tissue back in his pocket and quirked a smile that informed me he had been kidding. "After all, if Mum can put up with Tobias, I can do my best to be hospitable."

"Now, just a minute! Tobias happens to live here. And residence provides certain privileges."

"Yes, sweetheart!" Ben kissed the tip of my nose. It didn't matter that his husky voice was the result of some imagined allergy. I was a weak vessel, perhaps because I had eaten only one box of chocolates after lunch. When his lips came down on mine I felt my soul soaking up the sunshine, my split ends resealing, and my fingernails turning to pearl. The chandelier was spinning very nicely on its own axis when he turned me around and once more prodded me towards the stairs. "What you need, my sweet, is to cast your cares upon the waters."

"Anything you say." I leaned dreamily against him.

"Want me to join you"—I heard the smile in his voice—"just so I can do your back?"

It was a moment as fragrant with promise as the pink flowers on the trestle table and as fragile as the vase in which they were arranged. Then a scream from somewhere above us shattered the moment and sent me spinning across the hall as Ben thrust me from him to grasp the banisters, preparatory to hurling himself up to the second floor.

"Hold on, Mum! I'm coming," he yelled.

Before I could think, let alone move, there stood Mrs. Malloy, hands on her outraged hips. "Typical man," she said indignantly. "All it takes is one scream from his mother, and he's off."

Shame on her! The words had barely left her purple lips when I saw Mum race towards the stairs as if all the demons of hell were after her. What happened then was too quick to see, but somehow she lost her footing and, arms outstretched, pitched forward with a hair-raising scream. Sick with horror, unable to watch her vain attempts to save herself, I retreated into the darkness behind my closed lids and prayed that this day would go back where it came from.

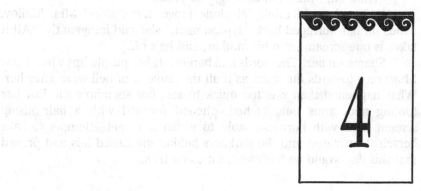

I don't like to boast, but a well-ordered household can survive the occasional mishap. Death had unleashed its claws but, cheated of its prey, had slunk away empty-handed. The evening found us gathered in the drawing room, a merry little group if ever there was one. My hair was almost dry, and I had stopped worrying whether I had put liner on only one eye and if my frock would stay zipped were I to breathe and talk at the same time. Jonas was ensconced on one of the Queen Anne chairs, nose buried in his well-worn copy of *A Tale of Two Cities*. And Mum and Dad sat on one of the ivory sofas, a full cushion apart, as if told to face the camera and not move, while Ben prowled before the marble fireplace, the better to model his cranberry smoking jacket. Unfortunately it clashed horribly with his father's fire-engine-red cardigan.

Who could blame Mum for being miffed that her spouse had not changed into something more subdued for the occasion of her survival? She had attired herself in a stiff little suit whose hem, from the telltale stitches, had been turned up almost to the waist in order to accommodate her pint-size figure. My heart was touched when I saw she had set her skimpy hair in curls that stuck out around her head like twisted paper clips.

"I couldn't persuade Sweetie to come downstairs," she informed the wallpaper. "She's in shock, poor little thing, and who can wonder after nearly being orphaned?"

"Mum," Ben said, "we all know you had a bad scare, but I was right there on the stairs to catch you when you tripped."

"My life flashed before my eyes! But don't think I am blaming Ellie for polishing those steps to a dangerous sheen. I'm only thankful that I was the one to be almost killed. At my time of life I don't have a lot of years left. I know full well that old people get to be very much in the way."

"Speak for yourself," Dad roared.

Realizing it was useless to protest that I had not polished the stairs when Mum had complained upon her arrival that the house reeked of Lavender Wax, I murmured I was glad she wasn't hurt.

"If you asks me, I do be the one as ought to be suing for't damages!" Jonas lifted his head from his book to eye Mum coldly. "There was I, fixing your bedroom window, just like I'm told for to do, and up you comes behind me screaming fit to stop an army in its tracks. If it b'aint a wonder I didn't drop dead on the spot, I don't know what is! My heart being none too sound in my chest."

Mum shrank almost to the vanishing point, but managed to rally with "I might have guessed I'd be the one to blame!"

"In future"—Jonas's voice plowed into the thick silence, breaking it up like clods of earth—"why don't you post a sign on your bedroom door saying 'Trespassers will be persecuted'?"

"Anyone would think," Mum huffed, "that I almost got myself killed on purpose!"

Ben and Dad did their part in egging the situation to a standstill by exchanging raised eyebrows. And Jonas, his moustache bristling with ill usage, slumped artistically back in his chair, compelling me to hurry over and prop his mud-caked boots on a footstool: whereupon Tobias Cat appeared out of nowhere to drape himself like a furry rug across the would-be invalid's knees.

"Perhaps it would behoove us all," I addressed the room at large, "to remember what St. Francis might say under the circumstances: 'Where there is anger, let us sow love. Where there is injury, pardon. . . .' "

The doorbell buzzed.

"That can't be Beatrix Taffer! She's not due for another five minutes." Am I the only idiot on the face of the earth who thinks that if she says something loudly enough it makes it true? That wretched mantel clock! The sundial in the rose garden was a hundred times more reliable. Given the glum state of Mum's face, I was tempted to ring for Mrs. Malloy and send her to greet Mrs. Taffer with the news that the Haskell family had not finished quarrelling. And if madam would kindly repair to the winter parlour to admire the wallpaper, or perhaps chew on a piece of celery, we would be with her momentarily.

"On your marks, get set, smile," I begged as the doorbell buzzed again. "This little outing undoubtedly means the world to Mrs. Taffer."

"I doubt that!" Mum sniffed.

"Quiet!" Dad roared at the moment the drawing room door pounced open to reveal Mrs. Malloy in all the glory of her two-tone hair and cranberry apron.

"We rang?" Ben raised a dark, inquiring eyebrow.

"All right, you lot!" When Mrs. M. forgets her place, she does so with style. "Stop that gawping and say a nice hello to your guest."

Lo and behold, Beatrix Taffer was right behind her. And what a shock! This was not the frail lady I had pictured in my mind—the one suffering through her geriatric exercise when I spoke with her daughter-in-law on the phone. This elderly woman did not hobble into the room on two canes, wheezing with every breath. She elbowed Mrs. Malloy out into the hall and rushed forward, throwing her arms wide open, in palpable eagerness to hug everyone and everything in sight. My heart sank. Here was a seventy-year-old harum-scarum if ever there was one.

"Mags! Elijah! You haven't changed a hair!"

Neither one of them moved or spoke. Indeed my in-laws looked as incapable of action as the twin suits of armour out in the hall. Thank heaven for Ben. His smile was every inch as suave as his smoking jacket as he strode towards Mrs. Taffer, looking deep into her eyes. "Welcome to Merlin's Court."

Inspired by her son's good behaviour, Mum got her act together. Extending a stiff hand, she said in a voice guaranteed to cause freezer burn, "It's been a long time, Bea!"

The newcomer beamed. "Well, if that don't turn back the clock! No one calls me Bea anymore; I'm known to young and old as Tricks."

"Suits you!" Dad stood up, looking in his white whiskers and red cardigan as if he would be quite happy to come down Mrs. Taffer's chimney any time. Not to be outdone, Jonas scrambled out of his chair with more speed than befitted an invalid.

"Pardon me muddy boots, m'lady! I just come in from digging up the veggies for your dinner."

Suppressing a quiver of unease, I said, "It's lovely to have you here, Mrs. Taffer."

"Love-a-duck, Mrs. Haskell! I'm over the moon at being invited."

Tricks was certainly something to behold. She was on the short side of five foot. Her roly-poly figure was augmented by a bosom that quite cast Mrs. M.'s into the shade and made Mum look as if she had only just graduated to a training bra. Her frock was an Indian muslin affair with three dozen dancing tassels. She vibrated energy that sent the standard lamps swaying like palm trees and the chairs scuttling out of her way.

Amazing! Her face, for all its wrinkles, belonged on a schoolgirl. A mischievous, funky schoolgirl whose ultra-red hair stood up all around her head in porcupine spikes reminiscent of a punk rocker. And . . . a thrill of shock and admiration shot through me . . . her ears were triple pierced.

When Ben's eyes met mine, I knew exactly what he was thinking. This live wire could not be a contemporary of his mother's! The very idea was idiotic. Almost as idiotic as Jonas clumping to the forefront to inform our guest that meeting her was the thrill of a lifetime.

"I've read all your books." He was shaking her hand until it almost flew off. "I know they do be for little kiddies, but Peter Rabbit and his pals has always been my heroes."

"Jonas"—unmoved by ye olde simpleton's tactics, I placed a hand firmly on his elbow—"this lady is not Beatrix Potter."

"I should say not!" Tricks gave him a playful poke in the ribs with a pudgy finger. "Mags and I are old friends, but we aren't neither of us *that* old." She beamed at my mother-in-law, who did not return the favour.

"You don't look your age . . . either of you." Dad rose gallantly to the occasion in addressing Tricks—in particular her cleavage, which was indisputably one of the scenic wonders of the world. Needless to say, Mum was not tickled pink.

"No one ever described me as mutton dressed up as lamb." Virtuous sniff. "But then, my religion teaches that the body is the temple of the soul."

It was an uncomfortable moment but, far from appearing put out, Tricks gave a snorting little laugh and appealed to the rest of us: "Same old Mags, isn't she? Always too good for the likes of us sinners. Come here, old duck, let's kiss and make up." So saying, she grabbed hold of Mum and gave her a smacking kiss on both pallid cheeks. While the men and I watched in awe, Tricks dragged Mum by the hand, almost skipping as she went, and plopped them both down on the sofa, where Tobias had retreated for a snooze. He went flying up in the air, along with a couple of cushions, but Tricks didn't notice.

"To think, Mags, it's been forty years, and all because of that silly quarrel at the seaside."

Mum hadn't said anything about where the row had taken place and, being nosy, I was curious about the rhymes and reasons, if not eager for a blow-by-blow account. Tricks's punk hair was softened from red to an iridescent pink by a stray shaft of sunlight, which also illuminated—less kindly—the ladder in her left stocking and the dirt trapped under her fingernails. "It was such a nasty grey day and no one was on the beach but the three of us." She beamed up at Dad, who was stroking his beard into a more debonair shape. "So I didn't see any harm . . ."

"In suggesting we go swimming?" My mother-in-law sat as if she were on a church pew, tiny knees together, hands primly folded; her voice was several degrees chillier than the sea could possibly have been on that faraway day.

"I know you don't like the water, Mum," Ben soothed.

"Ah"—her sparrow eyes flashed—"but what you don't know, son, is that we didn't have our swimming costumes with us. And someone"—she edged farther away from Tricks—"called me a spoilsport because I refused to—"

"Go skinny-dipping?" I quavered.

"If that is the vulgar expression."

"My word, Dad"—Ben sounded on the verge of laughter—"what part did you play in all this?"

"I took your mother's side. Had to, didn't I?"

Silence descended, threatening to engulf us, but somehow I managed to locate the salmon pâté and a tray of cheese straws while Ben busied himself rustling up drinks.

"What can I get you, Mrs. Taffer?" he asked.

"Fruit juice, there's a love." She gave a girlish giggle. "I'm quite the health nut. And do call me Tricks."

"How fitting." Mum squeezed out a mirthless laugh and accepted a glass of lemonade. She did not "drink," but on this occasion I wished she could be persuaded to indulge in something stronger. A glass of Lourdes water, for instance. Our little get-together was definitely in need of a miracle.

In the gurgling voice that was decades too young, Tricks offered a toast. "Let bygones be bygones, I say, and may the good times roll!"

Mum kept right on staring into her lemonade, but the men, my husband included, converged in a rush, and before I could get in the act, Tricks disappeared in a round of clinks and exclamations of "Cheers!" followed by an unidentified "Oops!"

Someone's drink went sloshing over the rim of his or her glass to splatter the arm of the sofa and a patch of carpet with a nice rich stain. A good hostess does not flinch under such circumstances, and I was about to say it didn't matter a tiny bit, when Tricks eased all our minds.

"Don't give it a thought, love! These modern fabrics clean up in next to no time." She patted the damp arm of the sofa. "And anyway, you can always hide the problem with one of these cuties." Suiting action to words, she lifted a doily from the oak end table and plopped it down over the carpet stain. "There!" She beamed. "Who would ever know?"

The men were struck dumb with admiration. I drank my sherry in one gulp before I could spill it. And Mum pointed a trembling finger at her life's work, the doilies that were on display throughout the room.

"Cuties!" Rounding on Tricks, Mum seized on the word and chewed all around it as Sweetie might have done a chair leg. "*Cuties!* Is that what you call them?"

"Enough, Magdalene!" Dad thundered. "She didn't mean anything."

"I might have known you would take her side."

"Parents! Parents!" Ben reproved.

Jonas could not continue at this frenetic pace. Tottering back to his chair, he hid out behind *A Tale of Two Cities*. Wishing desperately that there were some escape for me, I was tempted to announce dinner even if it meant eating the vegetables raw. Tricks started to say that she thought the world of Mags's doilies, but there was no stopping Mum. And perhaps that was all for the best. Her hostility was like a genie unleashed from a bottle after forty years of incarceration. Even were one to catch it and stuff it back in, the respite would be only temporary. We would all be waiting for the stopper to fly off again.

"*Cuties!* How very American of you, Tricks! I used to be so embarrassed when people clucked about you flirting with the Yanks at the air force base. I didn't want to believe it when your own mother burst into tears one day and admitted you accepted favours from them—sticks of gum and worst of all"—she spat out the word as if she could not bear it to touch her lips—"cigarettes."

"Be you saying she was a spy?" Jonas came back to life, his caterpillar eyebrows scurrying with curiosity.

"No, old love!" Tricks's face remained one big smile. "Mags is saying I was a slut."

Call me a defeatist, but I experienced one of those flashes of insight on which I pride myself. My splendid evening was dead. And from the looks of Ben and the other chaps, they agreed with me. But how wrong can you be? Either our guest was the mistress of the stiff upper lip, or she was incapable of taking offence (A) because she was the salt of the earth, or (B) because she was completely out of touch with other people's feelings. The thought did occur that the latter could be a real handicap— tantamount to crossing life's treacherous highways blindfolded. But as usual I did not get to wallow in philosophical conjecture.

Tricks was chirruping "Feeling better, dearie, after getting all that out of your system?" while crushing Mum in another of those pals-for-ever hugs. To which the recipient responded with her usual fervour, arms rigid at her sides. Her nose and one visible eye stared straight ahead into infinity.

I was about to extol the virtues of the cheese straws, when the drawing room door banged open, making another notch in the wall, and in came Mrs. Malloy, her fishnet knees buckling under the weight of the monstrous bouquet she carried in her arms.

The four-foot structure was made up entirely of vegetables. Obscenely oversize vegetables that looked as though they had succumbed to taking steroids. Ben was the first one to pry open his lips. "My God, Ellie! Is that your idea of an hors d'oeuvre?"

"I brought it!" Tricks leaped to her feet, sending a lamp and a couple of eminently dispensable ornaments flying, her smile radiating more light than the hundred-watt bulb. "It's my little party present—my thank-you for having me here for this fun evening."

"Give me a bunch of daffs any day!" Tactful as always, Mrs. Malloy shoved the horror at me and zipped out of the room before it could extend a green or orange paw and rip off one of the juicier parts of her anatomy to feed its insatiable appetite for human flesh.

Poor Ben. I could see him struggling to find some word of praise that would not be in violation of the chef's Hypocritical Oath. I myself was struggling to stay upright. Mum meanwhile sat there like a turnip—as if we didn't have enough of those already. And Dad and Jonas crept towards me as silently and reverently as if they were in church.

"Go on, tell me what you think!" Tricks was vibrating with excitement.

"Incredible!" Relieving me of the Leaning Tower of Veggies, Dad held it on high, while Jonas stood riveted at his side, eyes uplifted.

"You like it?"

"We love it!" The two men spoke as one. And why not? Jonas gloried in the growing of vegetables and Dad in the selling of them.

"A real prize!" one or the other of them gushed.

"Oh, you lambs!" *Modesty* was not the lady's middle name. "I'm all fired up to enter one of my Veggie Fantasias in St. Anselm's Summer Fête." I started to say I was that year's chairwoman, but Tricks talked right over me. "Everything has to be grown with the exhibitor's own wee hands." She held hers up, fingers spread wide. And I must say it was nice to know that the dirt beneath her nails was good, honest soil. "For the last five years, ever since I got into horticulture in a big way, I've won second place ribbons. But this year I think I've got a chance for the big one because Louise Bennett, who always won for her Marrow Medleys, won't be competing."

"What a bit of luck!" Ben commented.

"Isn't it? And you know what I was just thinking, Mags?" Tricks beamed at her ex-friend. "Sarie Robertson's absence this year could be *your* ticket to glory."

Mum looked black, so I explained: "There's an opening for someone else to take the first place ribbon in crocheting."

"Are you suggesting, Ellie"—Mum roused herself—"that I couldn't beat this Sarie woman if she was still in the running?"

"Of course you could. You're a *genius* with the crochet hook." I said, growing dizzy, either from hunger or because Jonas and Dad were still twirling the Veggie Fantasia in their joint hands like men possessed. "But unfortunately you aren't eligible because you're not a resident of the district. . . ."

"That's right, Mags." Mrs. Taffer spoke with her eternal good cheer. "I was forgetting you're down for only a few days. Never mind, this should be a great year. What with so many of the old-time winners having moved away or for other reasons thrown in the towel—or trowel—even the Martha is up for grabs."

Ben, who was an expert on affairs of the fête, having had to listen to me bewailing my responsibilities, started to explain the nature of this trophy, so coveted by many of the women, along with a growing number of men—not least of whom was our vicar's husband, Gladstone Spike. Gladstone made a formidable sponge cake. Alas my man about the house was drowned out by the dinner gong.

"Ask not for whom the gong bongs," I addressed the reverberating silence, "it bongs for thee."

And with that we all trooped into the dining room to embark on the dinner of a lifetime.

5

Never in the course of history had a more congenial group sat down to dine. Regrettably, my cooking was not a huge success. Which isn't to say the food was terrible, more's the pity. Terrible food has a certain credibility—an aplomb, if you will. Mediocre fare is inclined to sit there on the plate, knowing it will receive neither accolades nor the distinction of being voted the most dreadful meal anyone had ever eaten.

Bless Mrs. Malloy! She did her best to elevate the proceedings by wheeling in the trolley as if she had the head of John the Baptist in the large serving dish. But even she wasn't to be relied upon one hundred percent. You could have heard a fork drop—a whole number of them—when she slapped a loaf of sliced bread, still in its plastic wrapper, down on the table.

"Don't go making them eyes at me, Mrs. H.! You forgot to put the rolls in the oven. Poor little buggers. Their little faces beaten to a pulp, and all for nothing!" On that high note Mrs. M. departed, in a rustle of black taffeta, for the kitchen, leaving me to put my best smile forward.

"The grub's not bad, Ellie girl!" Jonas sucked gravy off his moustache and dug into his stew (which had stopped trying to pretend it was beef Bourguignonne) as if unearthing a bed of turnips.

"I've tasted worse." Dad, as always, adhered to the letter of the truth, not one word more or less. A failing for which I had been known to criticize his son—explaining that a well-chosen lie can be as sweet-smelling as a rose. But on this occasion Ben came through like a knight in shining armour.

"Everything is perfect, dear." He turned to his mother. "Wouldn't you agree that my wife has excelled herself?"

Put on the spot, Mum paused in the act of raising a not unduly laden fork gingerly to her lips to say, "You really shouldn't have gone to so much trouble, Ellie. Not when you're trying to lose weight. Dad and I would have been happy with a bowl of soup or a piece of bread and jam."

"Oh, go on with you, love!" Tricks's smile lit up her spiked hair like a halo. "I don't remember when I had such a scrumptious meal."

Mum rounded on her. "But you haven't taken two bites!"

"She's right!" Dad scolded. "If that stew sits on your plate much longer, it'll be ready for canonization."

"Yes, well . . ." Tricks flashed me an apologetic grin. "The truth is, I'm a vegetarian. I haven't eaten meat for years. But don't let that bother anyone. When I say live and let live, that goes for blood-thirsty people," she said, laughing, "as well as the poor little baa lambs and moo cows."

Splendid! My doleful little dinner party was forthwith elevated to an act of terrorism.

"So why didn't you eat your salad?" Mum pounced on her yet again. "And what about those carrots and the broccoli? Just what sort of vegetarian are you?"

"I guess you'd call me reformed rather than orthodox," Tricks twinkled across at Dad. "I haven't eaten veggies since I started growing them. You know how easy it is, Elijah, to get emotionally attached."

"I can't say as I do." Jonas mopped up his gravy with a slice of bread. "But us old bachelors b'ain't known for our sensitivity."

His reward was a schoolgirl giggle. "Oh, go on with you! Anyone can see you've got a heart of gold. Why you wasn't snapped up years ago by some lass in a tight skirt and a bunny wool sweater is a mystery to me."

Did the lady have designs on my babe in the woods? I was wondering how I felt about this possibility, when Dad said, "If I thought the way you do, Tricks, I'd be out of business. Then again, I'll admit there've been times when I've felt uneasy seeing a particularly fine cauliflower going out the door to be boiled to mush."

"You're breaking my heart, Dad." Ben speared a piece of beef. "Perhaps you should arrange for the health care visitor to conduct a spot check after each sale to ensure that living standards within the refrigerator are up to snuff."

Mum's pinched face showed disapproval of all this talk of vegetables—to say nothing of the mound of broccoli on her plate. "What I'd like to know, Bea," she said, "is what you *do* eat to keep body and soul together."

"This and that." A flutter of false eyelashes which were twice as long as the ones worn by Mrs. Malloy. "And never a day goes by when I don't take my wonderful health tonic. You should try it, Mags! Trust me, it would make you feel *forty* years younger."

"I wouldn't poison myself."

"Don't be so negative," Dad reproved. "Might do you some good with that problem of yours."

"What problem?" I asked, ever unwise.

Mum prissed her lips. "I would rather not say, Ellie. Not in mixed company. It was difficult enough to mention the subject in my letters. Not that I would expect you to remember. At my age, you learn to live with discomfort. There isn't any choice, except to go under the knife, and my doctor admits there's no promise of a cure."

"She's got bowel trouble!" Dad roared the bad news, causing the salt and pepper shakers to start up an Irish jig.

"I had no idea." Ben looked at me—the one entrusted with reading and answering his mother's letters. In excuse of my callousness I might have said that when Mum wrote anything of a highly personal nature, her handwriting became exceedingly small, as if she were lowering her voice on paper, meaning I couldn't read a word. But as it happened, I didn't get to say anything, because Mrs. Malloy came in at that moment to do the rounds with the wine bottle.

Convinced Tricks was hovering on the brink of asking if the grapes were humanely crushed, I suggested she might like to try some of Mrs. Pickle's dandelion brew. A weed's a weed for all that. The bane of the gardener's existence.

"Just a nip, love." Tricks held out her glass. "I'm forever hearing about how the lady always comes away with a ribbon for her wines at the fête."

In the wake of these praises, Ben suggested we all follow Tricks's lead. And with only one or two grumbles about being overworked and underpaid, Mrs. Malloy clacked around the table on her stilt heels, filling glasses, until she came to Mum, who flinched as if about to be struck.

"Thank you, I don't drink."

"What was that you said?" Mrs. Malloy filled the glass to the brim.

"I don't—"

"What a crying shame! But waste not want not! There's thousands dying of thirst in deserts all over the world." Moved close to tears by her own rhetoric, my trusty trench woman tossed off the wine with hardly a gulp, dried off the inside of the glass with her cranberry apron, and returned it to the table with a flourish.

"I don't know why you keep that woman on," Mum snipped as Mrs. M.'s insubordinate rump disappeared out the door.

"Don't get your knickers in a twist, love!" Tricks beamed at her. "Be a devil—drown your sorrows in a glass of water."

"If it'll make you happy" came the sullen response. And from that moment on Mum drank steadily, in teensy-weensy sips, of the fruit of the kitchen tap. A couple of times I thought of refusing to refill her glass as I watched her sink further and further into sobriety; but where does a hostess draw the line? There was also the little matter of Tricks billing and cooing at my assorted menfolk. Every time she looked his way, Jonas sat with knife and fork upended and the silliest expression on his face. Even Ben was not immune to the seventy-year-old vamp. But Dad was the worst. When he wasn't hanging on her every word, he was feasting his eyes on her superlative bosom.

"You haven't touched your wine, Tricks," he chided her in an uncharacteristically soft voice. Whereupon she did touch it by knocking the glass over with her elbow.

"Don't worry," she gurgled as the yellowish stain seeped into the damask cloth. "It'll come out in the wash."

"Without any problem," I said.

"My daughter-in-law is into all that housewife stuff. It wouldn't be for me; I've always wanted more from life. But don't get me wrong"— Tricks flapped her hands—"Frizzy's a great girl. We've not had a cross word in all the years I've lived with her and Tom, and that's a marvel in such a small house with the kiddies always underfoot."

"You could ask them to move out," Dad joked.

"I've been tempted, let me tell you, what with young Dawn getting into my makeup and the three little ones bounding about when I'm trying to do my meditation."

"That's what you get for giving up your independence," Mum chipped in. "By the way, what happened to your husband?"

"Killed in the war," Tricks responded brightly.

"The Second World War?" Ben looked puzzled.

"That's right."

"But that doesn't add up, whatever way I do my sums!" Mum stared at her. "You weren't married when I last saw you, and that was in the fifties."

"It was a stray bomb."

"You're joking!" Dad retired his fork to the side of his plate.

"Oh, all right!" Tricks threw up her hands and batted her false lashes. "So I was never married to Tom's father. These days nobody gives a hoot, but way back when I landed in the family way, I had to make up the usual cock-and-bull story about being widowed before the baby was born. I picked the surname Taffer, because I thought it was pretty, out of the telephone directory."

"Never married!" Mum shrank so low in her chair, I thought about fetching in one of the twins' booster seats for her. But once more Mrs. Malloy shattered the moment by wheeling in the trolley.

"No rest for the wicked!" Smacking her butterfly lips, she proceeded to clear away the plates as if walking a slippery deck. But if she had been imbibing in the kitchen, at least I didn't have to worry about her driving home. I had already decided to ask Tricks if she would share a taxi with her. My treat, of course.

"Anyone for pud?" Having loaded up the top of the trolley, Mrs. M. lifted the tray of chocolate mousse glasses from the bottom shelf and went around the table, plonking one down in front of each of us. "Don't anyone ask me to sit down and join the party. I might forget meself and say yes. Too late to beg, Mrs. H., I'm off to soak up to me elbows in Fairy Liquid."

Duty calling, she tottered out, never knowing how dearly I would have liked her to drag up a chair and plant herself in our midst. Mrs. Malloy could always be counted on to complicate a situation sufficiently that whatever else was going on seemed insignificant. To my surprise, Mum did not return to the cliff-hanger disclosure of Tricks's unmarried state. Instead of sticking in the knife, she dug her spoon into her chocolate mousse. I held my breath, naively hoping she would turn an awestruck face my way and say "Ellie, I've been wrong about you all these years. A woman who can make a chocolate mousse of this calibre is deserving of my one and only son."

The sad truth is, she ate as if unaware what she was doing. Her spoon might move, but her eyes didn't. They were fixed straight ahead, as if directed upon some distant shore. The men were so busy making sure

Tricks wasn't worrying her spiked red head over any misconception that her revelation had lowered her in their estimation that not one of them touched their mousse. Tricks in turn chose to stick to her dandelion wine, for which she would appear to have developed a taste—being now on her third glass. As for myself, I was (for once) not in the mood for chocolate.

"It b'aint easy being a woman with a lad to rear all on her lonesome." Jonas exerted all his rustic charm on Tricks's behalf. "Makes you a heroine in my book, it do."

"I had my struggles," chirped Florence Nightingale. "But I managed."

"Magnificently, I'm sure!" Dad raised his glass to her.

"It's hard enough bringing up children when you're married." That was Ben, who tended to think he had invented parenthood. Belatedly mindful of his responsibilities to his coworker in that endeavour, he flashed me a smile and finally tasted his chocolate mousse. Eyes closed, he touched the spoon to his lips . . . and immediately dropped it with a hideous clang.

"Ellie, there is something dreadfully wrong!"

"You mean it didn't set?"

"I'm talking about the *chocolate*! What kind did you use?"

"The regular baking . . ." The protest died on my lips and I clapped both hands to my burning cheeks.

"What is it?" demanded the Grand Inquisitor.

"I've just remembered, I hunted high and low for the box and finally found it on the shelf with the medicines."

"That wasn't no baking chocolate," Jonas growled. "That was my Choco-Lax."

"You mean"—Tricks giggled—"she made the pudding from a laxative?"

"Anyone can make a mistake." In avoiding Ben's eyes I looked towards Mum and was instantly stricken by a dose—horrible word—of remorse. "Oh, my goodness!" I snatched her spoon away. "You of all people, with your health problem, eating that stuff! Perhaps we should phone the doctor."

"She'll be all right," Dad said with husbandly conviction. "I'm always telling her she should eat more figs."

"But what if there are complications?" *Death* was the one that sprang to mind. Already I could see the headlines in the newspapers. *Woman Given Overdose of Laxative. Daughter-in-Law Accused of Murder.* There would be a photo of me hiding out behind dark glasses and a couple of paragraphs dwelling in lurid detail on *Mum's Near Fatal Fall* down the stairs tonight. Stairs that had been polished, ladies and gentle-men, to a dangerous sheen in anticipation of the deceased's visit.

"Mum, I don't know when I've felt more awful."

"That makes two of us."

This indictment cut me to the quick, but I got the feeling, which was certainly a cowardly one, that she wasn't referring to a reaction to the chocolate mousse. She sat with her hand stuck up in the air as if still holding on to the spoon I had grabbed from her, and her eyes were fixed in a blank stare.

"Mum, are you all right?" Ben half rose from his chair.

"Of course I am." She shook her wispy head, shedding her hair grips. "Where"—she glanced down at her hand—"is my spoon?"

"So tell me about your wedding, Mags love?" Tricks demanded.

"My what?" Mum jolted upright in her chair.

"What's to tell?" Dad for once offered full spousal support. "Let's talk about something more interesting. How's the weather forecast for tomorrow?"

"Now, don't be a pair of spoilsports!" Tricks beamed from one to the other of them. "If it hadn't been for that silly quarrel, I would have been your bridesmaid. Surely I am entitled to know every frilly little detail."

"All they ever told me"—Ben sat with his elbow on the table, his handsome chin resting on his cupped palm—"is that it was a private ceremony."

"So it was," Dad said with a crispness that implied "end of subject."

"And it was as lovely as a dream, I'm sure!" Tricks was not about to be silenced. "But was it held in a church or a synagogue?"

"That's none of your business." Mum was trembling so violently, the floor shook. Jonas looked dumbfounded, I didn't know how to look, and Ben looked as though he would have liked to smack both his parents for making such a mountain out of a molehill.

"Is it any of *my* business?" My spouse quirked a dark eyebrow and waited for enlightenment.

"Not from where I sit!" Dad heaved up in his chair and banged it down with awful finality.

Amazing! Tricks appeared to be the only person oblivious of the upset she had caused. Quite possibly, she had not done it on purpose; she was, I believed, too self-absorbed to be actively malicious, but sensitivity was not her middle name. Then again, who was I to talk? At that moment I wished most desperately that I hadn't invited her, or that I'd never decided upon this dinner party in the first place. Now was a fine time to realize that the words "I meant well" might well be among the most chilling in the English language. Ben had warned me that his parents did not like any fuss being made of their anniversary. The reason might be nonsensical—I suspected a registry office wedding; but what did that matter when his mother was sitting at my table with teensy tears trickling down her cheeks?

"Elijah," she said, "we have been backed into a corner and I see nothing for it but to tell our boy the unsavoury truth."

"Go on with you, Mum!" Ben's voice held both exasperation and affection. "I'm not about to cut you out of my will if you tell me you were married at Caxton Hall."

Her response was the drip, drip of tears on the tablecloth, and I found myself waiting for Tricks to glibly inform us they would come out in the wash, but it was Dad who broke the silence.

"I always said you had a right to know, son, and I wish I could have told you in private that your mother and I . . . that your mother and I were never united in holy matrimony by any legal authority."

"You're not married?" Ben turned as white as the tablecloth.

Tricks clapped her pudgy hands. "Mags, I didn't think you had it in you!"

"I do be thinking"—Jonas tried to hide his naughty amusement behind his moustache—"as how I've lived a very sheltered life."

"Of course we're married," Dad blustered. "It doesn't take a man of the cloth, or some judge, to make a marriage. What it takes is a man and a woman getting together and speaking their vows one to the other. And if that's not enough, there's the ring. Do you think, Ben, I'd have forked out four pounds ten for that one your mother's wearing if I didn't view our union as binding before God and man?"

"I'm illegitimate!" My husband raised one eyebrow after the other as if it were a juggling trick he had just mastered.

"Oh, son! Don't say that!" his mother sobbed.

"I don't blame you!" Ben gripped the arms of his chair as if on a roller coaster about to take off at breakneck speed. "You were a young, impressionable girl."

Dad thumped a fist. "She was close to forty."

"I have to try and make you understand, Ben dear." Mum raised her waif's face. "Times were different then. Elijah's parents threatened to take their lives if we married in the Church and mine said they would do the same if the wedding took place in a synagogue."

"What was wrong with a registry office?" My husband sounded a bit more mellow.

Mum let out a little screech. "I couldn't have entered one of those ungodly places."

"I still say I'm cutting you both out of my will." Ben allowed amusement to creep into his voice. Well done, my darling! He was rallying with amazing fortitude. The bar sinister loomed less large. He would not feel compelled to resign from his clubs. What surprised me was that Mum had not felt compelled to resign from the Roman Catholic Church, but she proceeded to explain how she had circumvented that calamity.

"They say you can convince yourself of anything if you want to badly enough; sort of like pasting one photo over another. So whenever I thought about my wedding day I pictured it taking place at Holy Mother Mary's Church with dear Father O'Dugal officiating . . . just the way I'd always imagined."

"But it's not too late," I cried, doing what I did best—sticking my nose in where it wasn't wanted. "You can finally have your dream wedding. Ben could give you away, Mum, and—"

"I could be the bridesmaid." Tricks didn't sound quite as enthusiastic as I would have expected.

"And I do be thinking I could do the flowers." Jonas touched his forelock.

"It would be a relief to see you respectably settled, Mum. Bear in mind, Ellie and I are getting on in years and can't expect to live forever." Ben was back in top form. "Of course I'll need to have a word with Dad to make sure he can support you and any little ones that may turn up."

Mum flushed a becoming pink, and the suspicion of a dimple appeared in her cheek. "I suppose it would be best to go to the church down here, where nobody knows us, Elijah."

"Church?" Dad sounded as though he did not believe his ears. "I'll have you know, Magdalene, that if this ceremony is to take place, it will be at the *synagogue.*"

"No squabbling, parents!" Ben told them, but his was a voice crying in the wilderness. His elders were on their feet, glowering across the table at each other.

"What a fool I've been!" His mother's face screwed up tighter than a fist. "You didn't refuse to marry me at Holy Mother Mary's because of your parents. You were putting your own feelings first. Just as you have done every day of every week we've been together!"

"If that's the way you believe"—Dad's eyebrows almost shot off his forehead—"I'll give you a wide berth from now on, Magdalene! In fact, if you would prefer it, I'll spend the night at a hotel."

It was an idle threat. The idea of his forking out good money—

when he had a bed here for free—was mind-boggling, but I felt compelled to utter a protest. "Be a dear, and you and Mum talk things over . . ."

"There is no talking to him!" His life partner included me in her glare. "If he wants to walk out on me after nearly forty years, let him! Or better yet, he can share a taxi with Bea. From the way she's been carrying on all night, that's what she's been hoping for all along."

"Mags, that's ridiculous!" Tricks managed to look demure as a virginal sixteen-year-old.

"You're a liar!" Racing across the room, Mum flung the door wide open, sending Mrs. Malloy, who was coming in with the coffee cups on the trolley, into a tailspin. "But what I say, Bea, is he's all yours. Snores and all. I wouldn't marry Elijah Haskell now if he were the last man on earth!"

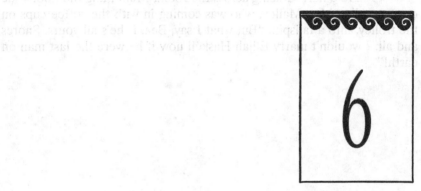

6

I was all for ending the evening by sticking my head in the oven. But Mrs. Malloy put the nix on that nifty idea in a hurry.

"Not in my nice clean kitchen, you don't." She dumped her damp dishtowel on the pile by the sink. "Now, let me see if I've been hearing straight: Your in-laws aren't married and never was?"

"There was the problem of religion . . ."

"So they went ahead and lived in sin?"

"We can't know all the ins and outs . . ."

"No need to be crude, Mrs. H. It's Mr. H. I feel sorry for, poor lad —the product of a broken home. Put himself to bed, has he?"

"He went up to check on the twins."

"Crying himself to sleep, more like!" She reached for the dishtowel to dab her eyes. "And when *I'm* to see my bed, I'm sure I don't know."

"One of us will take you home," I promised. "You do see it wouldn't have done to send you off with Dad and Mrs. Taffer?"

"The poor man could have done with a chaperone, if you ask me! He'll be in a vulnerable state, and that woman's a barracuda if I ever saw one. I wonder you didn't feel you was contributing to the delinquency of a pair of senior citizens, lending them Mr. H.'s car."

"What else could we do? Mum ordered Dad out of the house. It was clear they both needed time to cool off. My hope is that he'll come back tomorrow morning with his cap in one hand and a bunch of flowers in the other."

"Dream on, Mrs. H., that man is as stubborn as a donkey at the seaside. But don't you worry about taking me home. You need me around for moral support, and I'm not one to desert a sinking ship. I'll spend the night at no extra charge."

"I don't know how to thank you. . . ."

"You could start by making me a cup of tea." Mrs. Malloy planted herself on a chair and pried off one shoe with the toe of the other. "And you'd better add an extra spoonful of sugar to calm me nerves. I keep thinking about them two driving in that old crock. Ten to one it will break down out there in the back of beyond. Mark my words, he'll be forced to spend the night with *that woman* in the backseat. And being a gentleman of the old school, he'll feel morally obliged to marry her come morning whether or not her father comes after him with a shotgun."

"You and your lurid imagination." I managed a feeble laugh. But I must admit that while waiting for the kettle to boil, my mind concocted a Technicolor scene of Dad and Tricks driving down Cliff Road in Ben's pride and joy, Heinz, which for years had been held together with Super Glue and threats of the Great Scrap Yard in the sky. It was a convertible whose top at one time wouldn't close, until Mr. Fixit remedied the problem, so that afterwards it wouldn't open. Heinz was like a faithful old dog who knew only one master. Ben had only to climb aboard and it was off and running, but Dad might have trouble getting it into second gear without one or two of the wheels falling off.

Over the shrilling of the kettle I could hear Tricks's cooing voice asking Dad if he couldn't go faster so she could feel the wind racing through the crack in the window to ruffle her stubble hair. I pictured her turning towards him, her eyes—along with the tassels on the Indian muslin dress—dancing. Dad would do his best to keep his eyes on the road as they chugged around one hairpin bend after the other, prickly with hedgerows on the right and open-ended on the left to the rocky incline that sheered off to the sea below. By the time the road straightened out again, night would have unloosed its shadows in the manner of a woman letting down her hair. Nothing would be cozier than that old car, nuzzled in darkness, perhaps silvered by a glimmer of moon and scented with rose. Tricks might even be stirred to poetry—such as John Masefield's "Sea Fever." Good heavens! I switched off my imagination along with the kettle, at the point where I heard her suggesting to Dad that he might like to take a walk on the beach before taking her home.

Mercifully, the prosaic task of brewing up got me back on track, and I had just handed Mrs. Malloy her cup when a tap sounded at the garden door. So much for my evil mind! That would be Dad now! Returned full of contrition and fully prepared to negotiate the wedding ceremony. Wrong! The person who came barging in was Cousin Freddy, his eyes soulfully uplifted, his hands steepled in prayer.

"Any leftovers?"

"Only me!" Mrs. Malloy bared a fishnet knee in crossing her legs.

"She's spending the night," I explained. "We've had a spot of bother and things are rather at sixes and sevens."

"Don't spare me!" Freddy took a seat on the table, his skull-and-crossbones earring quivering with excitement. "Is somebody dead?"

"Worse than that!" Mrs. Malloy took a restorative slurp of tea. "Turns out Mrs. H.'s in-laws have been living together these near forty years without benefit of clergy."

"No!" He slapped his knee so hard, his ponytail danced.

"It takes a bit of getting used to," I conceded.

"I'll say! What with the old girl looking like she still thinks babies are found in the cabbage patch and, from what I gather, dancing down to church every chance she gets!"

"She'll be drummed out of the Legion of Mary, that's for sure." Mrs. M. heaved a sigh that inflated her bosom two cup sizes. "Very strict about some things is the Catholic Church, as I've heard time and again from Mrs. Pickle, who was R.C. herself before she went to work at the vicarage and decided if she was to advance in her job she'd better turn C. of E."

"Talk about hypocrisy!"

Understanding Freddy to be speaking about Mum, I hastened to her defense. "She put up a mental block in order to convince herself she was in good standing with the Church."

"And I suppose you've let her sleep in the same bed with her boyfriend with no thought to the moral welfare of your little children. Ellie, I ask you, where is this world headed?" My cousin fixed his eyes on me in sorry bemusement.

"Don't ask me! *I* am headed for bed."

I was nearly out the door when he stopped me with a question that happily had nothing to do with my errant in-laws.

"Still want me to help out with the summer fête?"

"What? Oh, yes! I did ask if you would go out collecting money for expenses such as the tent rental, didn't I? You'll find a list of potential donors on the study desk. And if you could get started this week, I would appreciate it. Good night, Freddy. Good night, Mrs. Malloy."

"If Ben needs a shoulder to cry on, I'm here!" My cousin's magnanimous offer floated after me as I mounted the stairs to the bedroom, where my husband was not waiting for me with bated breath.

He was positioned on the four-poster, feet together, hands folded on his chest, as if the district nurse had just finished laying him out. The funereal aspect of the room was heightened by the twin vases bulging with flowers on the mantelpiece. Never had the wine velvet curtain and wallpaper with its grey and silver pheasants looked more falsely festive. But I must admit that even in his state of rigor mortis Ben looked very fetching. I have always found him irresistible in his black silk dressing gown, with that hint of midnight stubble emphasizing his good bones.

"Is that you, Ellie?" He sat up, eyes squeezed shut, and swung his feet off the bed as gingerly as a hospital patient being accorded bathroom privileges following surgery.

Averting my eyes from the tempting V of hairy chest, I said sternly, "You've had a difficult evening, I'll admit, but you have to think about your mother."

"I sat with her until she fell asleep."

"That's my brave darling!"

"I'm trying, Ellie, but none of this is easy." He drew me to him, unplaiting my hair as he talked. "You see, I've always looked up to my father."

"Rubbish! He's a good three inches shorter than you."

"I thought it was only two." Ben looked momentarily chuffed. "But that doesn't alter the fact that I always viewed him as the guardian of the truth, and now—"

"Don't do that!" I pulled away to look deep into his blue-green eyes. "Don't speak as if their lives, and yours too, have been one long lie."

"Are you suggesting that I think of them as star-crossed lovers?"

"Exactly! Rather than dwell on the past, we must focus on getting the two of them back together. Their story *must* have a happy ending."

"They can both be extremely obstinate."

"Can't we all?" I moved away from him to get undressed. "But there has to be a way to sort them out."

"For their sakes and ours," he said. "Because much as I love Mum, Ellie, I don't know how well it would work if she were to stay on here indefinitely."

"I see your point." My hollow accents were muffled by my pulling my nightdress over my head.

"You don't think I should saddle up and go after Dad tonight?" Ben paced to the door.

"No. They need time away from each other. And tomorrow we will come up with a plan. At the moment all I can suggest is that tomorrow we start telephoning around to see if we can get a rabbi and a priest to perform a joint ceremony."

"My darling!" Ben swung me up and carried me over to the bed. Lying down beside me, he took my hand and raised it to his lips. "If you could only cook worth a damn, I would be putty in your hands."

"The dinner was a flop, wasn't it?"

"Yes, but being the typically insecure male, I would hate it if you could cook half as well as I do. May I suggest you concentrate on your other talents, which are infinite in their variety and"—he kissed me—"excellence."

"You know what I was just thinking?"

"Tell me, my angel." He was leaning over me, hands moving up my arms to draw down the shoulders of my nightdress.

"William the Conqueror was a love child."

"As are all he-men."

"Are you telling me that you have made a full recovery and will not have to work through the five stages of grief, or however many there are?"

"I'm afraid not, Ellie. Given the way I'm feeling at this moment, I'm going to need a *lot* of therapy."

He reached out a hand to turn off the bedside lamp, and even that momentary withdrawal seemed unbearable. After the day I'd had, nothing could have been more blissful than being with Ben on our own little island. He kissed my eyelids, then my cheeks, before taking possession of my parted lips. I inhaled the tantalizing scent of the he-man soap he used. I felt the tension seep out of my pores as his body came down lean and hard on mine. With trembling hands I parted the silk of his dressing gown and let the delicious lassitude overtake me. His supple fingers were woven into my hair, which was unfortunate, because when he suddenly sat up he almost yanked my head off my shoulders.

"Ouch!" I yelped—seductively, I hope.

"Shush!" Pressing a macho finger to his lips.

"The twins?" Sitting up, I snapped on the light and tossed back the bedclothes, ready to race out to the nursery. I hadn't heard a peep out of the intercom, but Ben's ears do tend to be sharper than mine.

"It's not them." Ben thumbed towards the ceiling. "It's Mum walking the varnish off her bedroom floor."

"You told me you saw her asleep."

"I know! But I didn't drug her milk!"

"She's probably looking for her watch or something," I said as the footsteps trudged back and forth, within inches, it seemed, of our heads. A lifetime of misery was stamped in every step. But, even more unsettling, she was talking to herself in a sort of rhythmic drone.

"She's saying the rosary!" Ben said. "The sorrowful mysteries, I expect."

"Seek ye comfort where ye may."

"She'll go on all night."

I was about to say I would find him a set of earplugs, when there came a shrill yip from Sweetie.

"Great!" My husband made a heroic attempt at sounding chipper. "Now we have the dog saying the amens."

"And if we can hear them, they can hear us."

"No need to spell it out." He grimaced, and together we gripped the bedclothes so as not to make a rustle. Silently we slid back between the sheets, only to be bounced back upright by a series of full-scale barks.

"What now?" I lamented.

"Listen!" Ben held up a hand, and then I heard it too, the throb of a car motor and the sputter of gravel as the vehicle pulled to a stop not more than two inches from the front steps.

"The Prodigal Father returns," proclaimed the dutiful son.

"You see, Mum's prayers have been answered!" With a joyful heart I leaped out of bed, whipped on a dressing gown, and followed my husband down the gallery, flipping on lights as we headed downstairs. Was my mother-in-law in a flutter too, with her ear edged up against the keyhole of her turret room?

Ben was crossing the hall, when the bell buzzed with sufficient vigour to announce a fire drill. It would seem our prodigal was not returning in a particularly chastened mood.

"Hold on!" Ben scraped back the bolt. Horrors! He opened up to reveal a policeman standing on the step in the glare of the exterior lanterns. Uniform, helmet, the works.

"Mr. Bentley Haskell?"

"That's right."

Oh, my God! There had been an accident! A bad one, from the man's bleak expression. It was one of those moments when everything comes into heightened focus. I was aware of footsteps moving along the upper gallery and knew without turning my head that Mum was stationed at the banister rail, wearing the dressing gown that had seen better days. I knew that her mousy hair was poking out of the net she had crocheted from embroidery silk. I knew that Jonas was with her and that the kitchen door had peeked open to give Freddy and Mrs. Malloy a view of Ben's rigid back.

"It's my unpleasant duty to bring you some disturbing news." The policeman produced a notebook but did not look at it. "Approximately one half hour ago I was patrolling the footpath leading from Cliff Road to Smugglers Cove Beach, when I came upon a stationary vehicle, which I subsequently ascertained to be your registered property, sir."

"I lent the car to my father and a friend of the family." Ben reached for my hand as I moved to stand beside him. "Is he . . . is my . . . ?"

"We'll get to that, sir." The policeman, whose demeanour was that of a man who had been on the job for thirty years without once requesting a day off, was not to be budged from going by the book. "I proceeded over to the aforementioned conveyance, and was attempting to determine what the make might be—it being something of a patchwork jobbie —when I was approached by two persons who claimed to have left the keys in the ignition and subsequently locked themselves out."

"I'd like to know why they got out of the car in the first place." Ben shook his head over the vagaries of the older generation. "But you'll be here for the spare key. Much appreciated, and if you'll be so good as to step inside, I will get it for you at once, Constable . . . ?"

"Sergeant Briggs, and I'm afraid there's a bit more to the matter than I have heretofore indicated." Not budging from the step, the sergeant lowered his eyes to his notebook and folded back a couple of pages. Was he about to tell us that he had booked Dad and Tricks for unlawful parking on a public footpath, or for abandonment of a motor vehicle?

"So what's the upshot?" Ben asked without fear or trembling.

"It's not a pretty story, sir, but I will try to make it as straightforward and painless as I can." Our man in blue stood eyes forward, helmet held high. "When I was approached by Mr. Elijah Haskell and Mrs. Beatrix Taffer, neither party was wearing any clothes."

"You're joking!" Ben's hand gripped my fist so tightly, I was afraid he would inadvertently arm wrestle me to the ground.

"I'm not paid to amuse the public, sir" came the wooden response. "According to Mr. Elijah Haskell, he was invited by Mrs. Taffer to take a moonlight dip in the altogether. And when the parties returned to the beach they couldn't find their clothes left by the water's edge, and reckoned they must have been washed out to sea."

"No!" I wrapped my arms around Ben for fear he would swoon and crack his head on the floor. It was imperative that he keep his wits intact for his mother's sake. A gasp was heard from the gallery above, and I feared tears would come raining down on us at any second. Stifled laughter, sad to say, was the contribution from the onlookers at the kitchen door.

"Where are our Adam and Eve?" Ben inquired through gritted teeth.

"I was able to open your car, using a little police know-how, and drove the parties over here after issuing a verbal warning about public indecency. If they'd been a couple of kids I'd have marched them down to the station"—the sergeant did have a heart beating under that uniform—"but having parents myself, sir, I know how it is."

"You need have no qualms about remanding Mr. Elijah Haskell to my custody." Ben's eyebrows came down over his nose like an iron bar.

"I get you, sir, no hope of leniency from this end." The notebook got clapped shut and tucked away. "I told the lady and gentleman to remain in the car while I had a word with you—let them sweat a little, was my idea."

"Come on now, love! You couldn't expect us to stay cooped up while you dillydallied!"

That was Tricks's voice. For shame! A bundle made up of two people wrapped up in one blanket hobbled out of the shadows to mount the steps with the gait of participants in a three-legged race. I recognized the blanket. It was the one Ben kept on the backseat of the car to disguise the rips in the upholstery. "Wasn't it lucky finding this?" Tricks enthused. "Elijah was getting goose bumps all over."

Poor Mum! It was a wonder she didn't jump over the railing. The brazenness of the Taffer Woman! There she stood in the doorway, fairly bubbling over with merriment. She even risked her hold on the blanket to raise an obscenely naked arm and poke the sergeant in the ribs.

"My knight in shiny silver buttons. We were never so glad to see anyone in our lives, were we, Eli?"

Dad didn't answer her. Shuffling over the threshold with his Siamese twin, he put his case to Judge Bentley T. Haskell. "Don't stand there, son, like you're looking at some two-headed freak straight out of the circus. All men make mistakes in their time, and there's lots of excuses for me. You have to give me that!" His brown eyes were certainly soulful, and it was apparent his bald head had paled along with his face. "That dandelion wine I drank, at your request, was powerful stuff, and then there was that business with your mother. After thirty-eight years she drives me out of the house, drives me to ruin and public disgrace."

"Threw him right in my arms." Tricks's sigh ruffled the blanket. "But bless her heart, Mags doesn't have anything to worry about. We were just having a bit of fun is all, going skinny-dipping like a couple of kids."

"Speak for yourself!" Dad roared. "I felt a hundred years old getting into that water, and I aged a couple of hundred more when I got out."

"I don't have time to suffer with you, Dad." Ben patted his dressing gown as if expecting the spare key to the Heinz to materialize inside the pocket. "If Sergeant Briggs will kindly wait while you and Mrs. Taffer put on some clothes, you can drive him back to the police station, preferably after taking Mrs. Taffer home, then book yourself in at the Dark Horse. While I'm trusting you to stay out of jail, I will be looking in on Mum to see if by some miracle she hasn't gotten wind of what's happened."

My poor darling. Little did he realize she had heard every word. Ah, how my heart ached for him, as well as for Mum, when she made her presence known.

"Thank God for you, son. At least something good came out of my unholy union with that . . . Judas!" We all looked up to see her standing at the bars, this woman for whom love's song had turned into a dirge. "But don't anyone go thinking I'm upset. Far from it! Elijah and Bea can carry on to their wicked hearts' content. After all, they're both free as the wind. So if you'll all excuse me, I'll go back to my bedroom and rearrange the furniture. I could put up with it the way it was for a few nights, but now it's settled that I'll be living here permanently, so I'll want the place looking halfway decent."

A hush descended upon the hall when she vanished from the scene. For several moments Sergeant Briggs stood with his helmet clapped over his heart, and then Jonas—a sight to behold in his nightshirt and Wee Willie Winkie cap—leaned over the railing to proclaim the words that brought tears to my eyes and a sob to my throat: "It is a far better thing that she does than she has ever done, it is a far better rest she goes to than she has ever known."

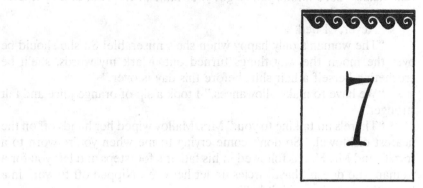

7

"Don't go asking me to weep buckets for her." Mrs. Malloy stood her ground in the middle of the kitchen. "Some people earn every hard knock they get."

"How can you be so callous?" Still in my dressing gown, my hair piling down my back, I staggered over to the sink and poured myself a strong slug of water. After a sleepless night I was as bleary-eyed as the morning, which was as close to rain as I was to tears. "What," I asked, "did my mother-in-law ever do to you?"

"She came into my bedroom last night and ordered me to turn down the radio. What's more, she brought that dog of hers along, for intimidation purposes, and it cocked its leg"—Mrs. M. sucked in an outraged breath—"on the chair where I'd put me undies."

"Sweetie's been taking male hormones to help her through a difficult menopause."

"If I'm upsetting you, I'm sorry." Mrs. M. showed her contrition by removing my empty glass and filling it with orange juice. "Here, take this to steady your nerves. If you must know, the real reason I can't stand the woman is the way she treats you. Think about it! She wouldn't even come to your wedding."

"I thought at the time it was because I was Church of England. But now I realize the ceremony would have brought back too many memories of the wedding she never had."

"She never appreciates a *thing* you do." Mrs. Malloy shook her two-tone head. "Lord knows you've got your faults, Mrs. H., but do you ever hear me complain?"

"Never," I lied.

"The woman's only happy when she's miserable! So she should be over the moon the way things turned out. Mark my words, she'll be crocheting herself a hair shirt before this day is over."

"We have to make allowances." I took a sip of orange juice and felt stronger.

"There's no talking to you." Mrs. Malloy wiped her hands off on the nearest dishtowel. "So don't come crying to me when you're worn to a frazzle and Mr. H. has followed in his father's footsteps and left you for a woman who doesn't have circles under her eyes. Nipped off to work in a hurry this morning, didn't he?"

"There was an emergency at the restaurant."

"A likely story."

"He was upset at having to take my car and leave me at the mercy of the buses. As soon as he has a free moment Ben is going over to the Dark Horse to have a talk with his father about patching things up all around."

"Or you'll have your mother-in-law with you for the rest of your life. For it'll be you who goes first, see if it isn't! By the bye, where is Mrs. Sunshine, if I may be so bold as to ask?"

"Upstairs, giving the twins their baths. She said she would take over that job in future along with giving them their religious instruction and—"

I broke off when a *rat-tat-tat* came at the garden door and a horribly distorted face peered through the pebbled glass.

"No need to jump out of your skin," Mrs. Malloy scolded. "It'll be that Freddy come to cadge breakfast."

Brightening considerably, I went to open up. My cousin would listen to my tale of woe, make his usual ribald comments, and I would get things back in proportion. Only one problem! The man on the step wasn't Freddy. He was a neat little man with hair parted down the middle and a pair of owlish glasses.

A new milkman perhaps? Caught off balance by this further disruption in the cosmic order, to say nothing of being caught in my bare feet and dressing gown, my smile may have promised more than I intended. Say, six pints a day—instead of the usual four.

"Mrs. Haskell?"

"Yes!" A glance at his pinstripe suit forced me to reevaluate his profession.

"I am Peter Savage."

"You're selling something?"

"Unfortunately not." He was studying me as if I were a painting in the Louvre.

"Then who . . . ?"

"I'm a vagrant," he replied, very much in the way that someone might have announced he was a bank manager.

On closer inspection, I saw that Peter Savage's suit could have done with a pressing and he was wearing one navy sock and one grey with brown shoes, but he was clean-shaven and his teeth were as white as the kitchen sink. Humanity demanded that I ask him in and provide a hearty breakfast. Common sense insisted I do nothing of the sort. Merlin's Court was set well back from the road, a good ten minutes' walk from its nearest neighbour, the vicarage. And upstairs I had two babies, a mother-in-law, and Jonas, who would unhesitatingly defend my honour, to the death, with an umbrella taken from the hall stand.

"I'm looking for odd jobs."

"Are you?" I said.

"Your cousin Freddy Flatts kindly provided me with a letter of recommendation." Mr. Savage dug a hand into his pinstripe pocket and produced a folded sheet of paper.

"I'll bet my bloomers it's a forgery," contributed Mrs. Malloy from the rear. But I recognized Freddy's writing when I unfolded the note, which did indeed ask me to extend the man a helping hand.

"Please come in." Beckoning him inside, I closed the door, racking my brains for something for him to do.

"I could mow the lawn," he suggested.

"Sorry," I said, knowing Jonas would pack his suitcase if I let anyone touch his lawn mower. "We're letting the grass grow."

"I'm good at windows."

Perfect, I thought. And then remembered that Mr. Watkins, the window cleaner, was due to come that very morning. And from what he had told me last time, Mr. Watkins had already lost Lady Kitty Pomeroy as a client on account of her fault-finding.

"If he really wants to make himself useful"—Mrs. Malloy sized up the applicant through narrowed rainbow lids—"he could murder your mother-in-law, Mrs. H. I'm sure you'd pay handsomely."

"Always one for her little joke," I told Mr. Savage. "Why don't you sit down and have some breakfast before we plan your workday?"

"How kind you are!" He might have been addressing an angel floating down from heaven as he seated himself on a chair, feet together, hands neatly folded in front of him on the table. "Porridge will do very nicely, with perhaps a couple of rashers of bacon to follow. Only one sausage, and the egg not too well done, thank you so very much."

"Fried bread and tomato?" Mrs. Malloy's voice was sweeter than a bowl full of sugar.

"I mustn't be a bother."

"What, you? Never!" *Bang* went the frying pan on the stove, *slap* went the bacon onto the working surface, *crack* went a couple of eggs into a bowl. Talk about actions speaking louder than words. Mrs. M. was telling me in no uncertain terms to goof off, take a pew, rest my feet while someone else did the work. In order not to feel like a complete parasite, I smoothed out the tablecloth and laid out the cutlery before sitting down across from Mr. Savage.

"I suppose you'll want orange juice?" Mrs. M. bumped the refrigerator door shut with her rump and came at us with the glass jug.

The gentleman cocked his head. "Is it fresh squeezed?"

"I stomped the fruit with me own bare feet." *Plonk* went the jug in the middle of the table; a tidal wave of juice foamed over the lip and Mr. Savage nervously gripped the arms of his chair.

"Thank you, Mrs. Malloy." I darted her a look as she returned to her frying pan, which was spitting and hissing as if flaming mad.

"So how do you know Freddy?" I asked our guest.

"We met in the course of my business, Mrs. Haskell."

"You mean before . . . ?"

"Oh, no! In my former life I was a schoolmaster living in Harold Wood, Essex, and I don't know that your cousin was ever in that vicinity. We struck up a friendship a little over a month ago when I was busking—"

"What?"

He removed his glasses to polish them with his serviette. "Doing my song-and-dance act outside the bus station. Freddy stopped to toss some change in my cap. He told me I sounded as good as the original recording artist."

"A nice compliment."

"Not really." Mr. Savage rearranged his knife and fork. "He had spotted me as a fraud. And I trust that you, who are so beaut—benevolent, will not think too badly of me. I had, you see, a radio in my pocket and was lip-syncing."

"That must have taken a certain skill."

"Only courage, in standing up to the hoots and hollers whenever I cut from a song for a late-breaking news bulletin, or an advert for fish fingers. But your cousin couldn't have been nicer. He agreed to give me singing and guitar lessons."

"Here's something to keep your vocal cords going!" Mrs. Malloy planted a steaming plate in front of him. The bacon was pink in the middle and golden around the edges. The fried egg resembled a little mobcap, white and puffy with a pretty edging of lace, the fried bread was done to a golden turn, and the tomato sent up little rosy wisps of steam. When my plate arrived—Mrs. Malloy is the old-fashioned sort who believes in ladies last—I would have been tempted to offer her a job if she hadn't already worked for me.

"You forgot the sausage." Mr. Savage tempered this criticism with a forgiving smile. "Never mind. I can fill up on toast if you'd be kind enough to make some. And lemon marmalade, if you please. My mother made me eat orange marmalade as a child, and I've never liked it."

"Will there be anything else?" Mrs. M.'s voice came down on his head with the force of a frying pan.

"I think we are ready for tea, aren't we, Mrs. Haskell?" From the sound of him, we might have been an old married couple sitting in a tea shop with our menus propped up against the sugar bowl and our shopping bags blocking the aisle.

"Here's the pot." Mrs. Malloy plonked that down, complete with one of Mum's crocheted cozies. "I'll let you pour your own! I'm off to relax for half an hour, scrubbing the bath."

"She's one in a million," I said, absently doing up the top button of my dressing gown as the hall door slammed with such force it practically blew the tablecloth over our heads.

"As is your cousin Freddy." Mr. Savage polished off the last grease spot on his plate and uttered no more than a token protest when I offered to trade him my full platter.

"Freddy understood completely when I told him I had always hated teaching arithmetic to children who shot spitballs at me and set off stink bombs in the classroom, and how one day, just like that, I decided to pack it in, pack my bags, and set off to follow my dream of becoming a rock star. I planned to hitch rides, but realized after the first ribald toot that a hitchhiker's thumb, like a green one, is something you either have or you don't. So I hopped on a bus, took it as far as it went, got on another, and ended up in of all places Chitterton Fells."

"Do you have a family, Mr. Savage?"

"My mother." He sliced into my tomato, sending up spurts of red. "There's no denying I took the coward's way out in leaving a note on the mantelpiece and creeping out of the house at dead of night. But you'd have to know Mother. She still walked me to school every morning and picked me up afterwards."

"A little overprotective" was all I could say.

"She made me hand over my paycheque and gave me just enough pocket money for essentials."

"So you weren't able to bring much cash with you."

"I thought I was headed for fame and fortune, but since my radio scam was uncovered I haven't picked up enough loose change to buy new strings for my guitar, let alone eat enough to get my daily allowance of vitamins and minerals. So this morning I came to see Freddy and he was so kind as to send me here. But when he described you, I never guessed, never dreamed that you would be such a vision of . . . kindness. Dammit!" Mr. Savage blushed and washed out his mouth with tea. "I'm stammering like a sixteen-year-old. But that's the way I feel sometimes—as if my whole life is opening up for me. Did I tell you that your cousin has offered to give me music lessons so I can get back on the road?"

"For a lifetime cut of the take, I suppose."

"He told me he is himself a musician and had played with several reputable rock groups."

"Did he mention that they had all gone under?"

"What's that?" His expression put me in mind of Abbey's and Tam's when I went to shut off the nursery light.

"I said"—I cleared my throat—"that they were all from Down Under. Has my cousin offered to put you up at the cottage?"

"He talked about it, but very kindly pointed out my practicing would keep him awake at night. He suggested I might be more comfortable in the rooms over the old stable."

What could I do but assure him he was most welcome and hope that Ben wouldn't have my head when he got home?

Mr. Savage's spectacles glistened. I swear there were tears in the grey eyes that matched his suit when he said, "I will serenade you in the very first song of my own composition."

"That would be nice." Ben had once written a soup recipe for me, which had been lovely in its way.

"It will be a paean to your nobility of spirit and bounteous benevolence." Mr. Savage's tears were burned off by the radiance of his smile. He reached across the table for my hand and would perhaps have raised it to his lips if the table had been shorter or his arm longer. My fingers had only so much stretch. *Pop* went my dressing gown seams. *Ping* went a couple of buttons across the room. The chill I experienced when this garment parted down the middle was unsettling, but it was nothing to the icy quiver that seized me when I looked up to see my mother-in-law standing in the doorway.

"Don't let me interrupt you, Ellie." She forced a brave smile even as she sagged against the wall. "And don't worry that I will say a word about your goings-on to my poor son. Doesn't he have enough to suffer with his father deserting him?"

How could I come across as anything but fast when I informed Mum that my acquaintance with Mr. Savage was barely an hour old and he followed up this unwise confession with the news that I had invited him to move in? It being expedient to get rid of the man, I sent him off to inspect his quarters, and the moment the garden door closed on him I set about clarifying matters with my mother-in-law.

"The man was living at the bus shelter."

"I'd rather not know all the gory details." Mum tottered to a chair and covered her face with her hands.

"He will be staying only until he becomes a successful rock star."

"This is all my fault! The sins of the mother shall be visited upon the child."

"You mustn't talk like that," I soothed, dragging a chair around to sit beside her. "I know things look bleak at the moment, but you and Dad have thirty-eight years invested in each other."

"Don't mention that man's name to me."

"Mum, he went for a swim—"

"An *illicit* swim."

"Agreed! But he didn't go to bed with Tricks." I tried to put my arm around her, but she flinched as if struck. Eyes bright with tears, she stared through me as if I were a pane of glass.

"I should have listened to my parents when they begged me not to marry Elijah."

I started to say that she *had* listened, that she *hadn't* married him, and that *this* was the root of the entire problem, but I bit down on the words.

"You can't turn back the clock." I risked touching her hand, remembering with a bitter pang how she had said the exact same thing to me in connection with her friendship with Tricks. "But perhaps you could talk to a priest about your situation?"

"I'm too ashamed. Being the True Faith, Catholicism has to maintain its standards. No, I don't expect you to understand"—*sniff*—"seeing as I hear the Church of England will take just about anybody these days."

"If you think it would help"—I began gathering up the breakfast plates—"I could take you to see Reverend Eudora Spike. She's extremely nice and a wonderful listener."

"A woman priest?" Mum shuddered.

"At the moment she's a deacon, but that will in all likelihood alter now that there's been a change in policy regarding women in the priesthood. But it was only a suggestion. I don't want to push you into anything against your will. . . ."

"I'd much rather not, but by all means *you* go and have a chat with her. Far be it from me to hold you back from your faith, such as it is, Ellie."

"Perhaps I should pop in at the vicarage. I do need to talk to Eudora about the St. Anselm's Summer Fête." That was true enough, and if I could get some spiritual guidance at the same time, all the better. But first things first. I was crossing the kitchen on my way to fetch the twins down to breakfast, when Mrs. Malloy walked in with Abbey, followed by Jonas holding Tam. Oh, to look at the world through their guileless blue eyes!

The next ten or fifteen minutes vanished in the happy business of getting my darlings into their booster chairs and breakfast into their mouths. Jonas had made the chairs with detachable trays that fitted neatly over the edge of the table. The man was so handy it really was a crying shame he had never married. It wasn't until I was unclenching my daughter's paw in order to wipe it off so that it wouldn't stick like glue to everything it touched that I mentioned not having seen Sweetie since the previous night.

"She's taken to her bed," Mum said, stony-faced.

"Probably indigestion," Mrs. Malloy consoled me. "I saw her, bright and early, under the hall table, chewing on that statue you made so much fuss about yesterday."

Abbey, sensitive little soul, let out a shocked squeal, but Tam applauded the disclosure by pounding his cup on his metal tray, and shouting, "That funny!" The male mentality! Or so I unjustly thought until brought up short by Jonas.

"I b'aint a religious man, but I always reckoned that St. Francis a right 'un, what with him leaving his father's palace to live in a potting shed and take care of his furred and feathered friends." Clomping over to the hall door, he turned to look at Mum, his eyes kind under the un-pruned, wintry brows. "So if it'll put a smile on your face, I'll go find him and put him back where he do belong."

"Thank you." Mum gaped at his retreating back.

"Typical!" Mrs. Malloy traded Tam his cup for a piece of toast. "Men are all alike when it comes to a damsel in distress."

Shooting a load of dishes into the sink and creating another Niagara, I was pondering the veracity of this statement, when the window facing me cracked open and a surreptitious voice spoke.

"You in there, Mrs. Haskell? Front and back rubdown, same as usual?"

"That'll be lovely," I said, and upon catching Mum's eye, made haste to add, "It's Mr. Watkins. He's the window cleaner."

"If you say so, Ellie."

In dire need of occupational therapy, she fetched down her crochet work from a shelf of the Welsh dresser. From its size, I could guess only that the article-in-progress was destined to be a swimming pool cover. Sitting down at the table, Mum said, "You get dressed, Ellie, and go and see your woman priest. You don't have to worry about the twins, I'll take proper care of them." The glance she fired at Mrs. Malloy made clear she would not welcome any assistance from that quarter. She did add, however, upon picking up her crochet hook, that she would make Jonas a hot drink for elevenses.

Did this suggest a change of atmospheric pressure within the house? Possibly. But the outside world did not look so promising when I set out to walk to the vicarage half an hour later. The clouds were massing, dark and threatening overhead. An occasional spatter of rain got me in the eye, the sea gave a distant roar like a lion at the zoo ready to devour the first piece of meat dropped its way, and Mr. Watkins on his ladder looked none too happy. But I didn't need blue skies and sunshine to experience an exuberant urge to spread my arms wide and soar like a gull. I was free! Free to run down Cliff Road and fantasize about Dad being brought to his senses when he discovered Mum was making hot drinks for another man. A bachelor, no less!

All I needed was a talk with Eudora to put me back on track. Our vicar was a sensible woman. And the vicarage was an equally straightforward house, without fuss or furbelow. Its windows smiled a gentle welcome as I passed under the lych-gate. And the front door was flung wide as I traversed the mossy path, as if to let me know I was welcomed with open arms.

"Is that you, Mr. Watkins?" inquired a voice as I mounted the time-worn steps. Behold Mrs. Edna Pickle in slippers and floral apron. She was minus her curlers, but her hair did not look as if it had been combed that morning, and her figure sagged comfortably as if taking a holiday from its corsets. "You'll have to forgive me, Mrs. Haskell. We was expecting the window cleaner yesterday and he didn't turn up. No ambition, that's his trouble. If it's not too cold for him to turn out, it's too sunny." She frowned dolefully.

"He's at Merlin's Court, doing our windows." I followed her into the narrow hall with its dark brown varnish, faded strip of carpet, and the portrait of the Archbishop of Canterbury hanging from the picture rail.

"You're lucky he showed; but he'll soon be packing it in now it's come on to rain. Anyone would think the man had a private income." Mrs. Pickle shook her head in slow motion. "Then there's the rest of us, that if we wants things to happen in this world have to go ahead and make them happen."

"So true."

She then set about closing the door in almost as much time as it would have taken the average person to vacuum three rooms and get going with the polishing. "How did you like the dandelion wine, Mrs. Haskell?" she asked.

"Delicious. We served it at our dinner party last night and even Mrs. Taffer, who doesn't normally drink wine, had several glasses." My praises brought a triumphant gleam to Mrs. Pickle's eyes, but I didn't get to ramble on.

"I *thought* I heard voices." The sitting room door to our right opened and out came Eudora. She was smiling and I tried to do likewise. But, so great was my shock, all I could do was stare. It was several weeks since I had last seen my spiritual adviser and the change in her appearance was extraordinary. Her figure had gone from substantial to spare, her glasses were askew, and her hair had lost its structure. Once it had fitted her head like a felt hat. Now it drooped in dispirited waves about her haggard face.

"Ellie"—her voice was as faded as her cardigan—"did we have an appointment?"

"No."

"Then you'll be here about the fête." She rubbed her forehead as if trying to increase the bloodflow to her brain. "Lady Kitty Pomeroy phoned yesterday . . . or it may have been the day before . . . to talk about the stalls. And she said she would be getting in touch with you."

"I haven't heard from her ladyship and it wasn't strictly speaking about the fête that I came, although if you have any instructions for me, that's fine." I was getting flustered. "There's a problem—a family matter I wanted to discuss with you."

"Something wrong with Ben or the children?"

"Nothing like that. It's my in-laws. They had a major bust-up at Merlin's Court last night. And the upshot is my mother-in-law has moved in with us. But if this is a bad time for you, I could always come round tomorrow."

"Nonsense. I've always time for a fellow suf—parishioner."

"I'll get myself down to the kitchen and make some coffee for you ladies." Mrs. Pickle headed down the hall. I had no doubt the beans would be well and truly aged before she plugged in the percolator.

"You'll have to work around Mr. Spike," Eudora called after her. "He's in the middle of making a sponge cake, so tread carefully." She turned and smiled wanly at me. "Being married to Ben, Ellie, you know all too well how men are when they're cooking. And things aren't always easy for dear Gladstone. People tend to view him as my shadow and . . . well, never mind, come along and sit down."

Ever since my first visit to the vicarage, I had loved that well-worn sitting room with its overstuffed easy chairs, in which you could plant yourself and take root. One set of windows gave a view of the churchyard with its weary regiment of tombstones, some standing heroically to attention, others staggering to maintain their balance in the face of eternal cannon fire. The back windows looked out on a raggle-taggle garden, where clumps of bushes and flowers grew wherever the mood took them. The room had a sense of peace that seemed to emanate even from the wallpaper, whose only remnant of pattern was the seams.

The two handsome pieces of furniture were the library table, which did duty as a workmanlike desk, and its companion leather chair. This chair had its back to us as we came in, but there was nothing to that. Who could blame it for preferring a view of the garden to the confessional?

While Eudora removed a pile of papers from the brown plush sofa, I noticed two things. The place smelled of cigarettes, and a tray with toast, butter, and marmalade sat on the coffee table.

"There now"—she straightened up—"why don't you sit down and tell me what's been happening?"

"Thank you." At a loss where to begin, I absently reached for a piece of toast and spread it with butter and marmalade. Could the physical changes in Eudora be blamed on her having taken up smoking? "Delicious!" I mumbled.

"What?"

"This marmalade is the best I've ever tasted."

"It *is* rather wonderful!" Eudora attempted a smile, then straightened her glasses in an attempt to focus on the purpose of my visit. "You were saying that a crisis has developed within your family."

"And I'm to blame," I said, resorting to another piece of toast and marmalade. "Against Ben's advice, I invited his parents to celebrate their thirty-eighth wedding anniversary with us. Nothing overboard, you understand, just a dinner party. But I put my first foot wrong in asking a friend of Mum's, Beatrix Taffer, whom she hadn't seen in forty years, to join us. The evening was not a success from the word go. And it took a decided turn for the worse when it came out that Mum and Dad are not legally married."

"We all have sinned and fallen short of the glory of God." This textbook answer was not typical of Eudora, but I plodded on with my tale of woe.

"Mum and Dad appeared on the verge of making an honest man and woman of each other, but then they got into a row over the original problem, of who should perform the ceremony. A rabbi or a priest? After a brief snarling match she ordered him out of our house. And that wasn't the end of it. A couple of hours later a policeman knocked on the door with Dad and Mrs. Taffer in tow. He'd caught up with them after they'd gone swimming in the raw and—"

"You must count yourself blessed, Ellie." Eudora was looking absently around the room as she spoke.

"What?"

"One is never completely naked with long hair. Men are not known for their modesty, but my heart goes out to that poor woman."

"What about my mother-in-law?"

"Her also." To my surprise, this was said without marked enthusiasm. "What I suggest, Ellie, is that Ben have a word with his father and you do the same with this Mrs. Taffer. Encourage them to apologize for behaving thoughtlessly. Being a Christian, your mother-in-law will have to forgive them."

Was I imagining things, or did Eudora intend to make this sound like a punishment? Her expression was grim, but that may have been because the leather chair by the desk was swiveling around to face us, and a voice from deep within its confines now addressed us.

"A sad thing it is when we turn God into a bogeyman to scare children and little old ladies out of their wits."

"Mother!" Eudora stood halfway up before sinking back down. "I smelled tobacco, but I thought you were out in the garden."

HOW TO MURDER YOUR MOTHER-IN-LAW

"So I would have been, m'darlin', taking me banishment like a trooper." A half-smoked cigarette waved through the thickening cloud of smoke that veiled the speaker from our eyes. "But it started to rain, so here I am."

"Listening in on a private conversation."

"It was wrong, sure enough, but as I always say"—a smoke ring puffed overhead—"sin is its own reward."

"Ellie, I'm so sorry." Eudora looked completely at a loss.

"Don't upset yourself," I managed to say.

"That's right, Eudorie. *This is the day the Lord has made, let us rejoice and be glad.*" Having delivered this biblical thrust, the woman ground out the cigarette and stood up, the shadows dropping away from her like burial linen. She was in her mid-seventies, with a Roman nose even more ruddy than her cheeks and more black than grey in her hair. "I'm the mother-in-law," she informed me. "*Step*mother-in-law, to be precise; and that's noways a job for the faint-hearted. The name's Bridget Spike, m'darlin', but all me friends call me Bridey."

"Now I remember," I said, "Mrs. Malloy—my daily help—told me you were here on a visit."

"Did she now? And did she tell you I make the best marmalade in the world?"

"No, but I believe you," I said, looking down at the piece of toast in my hand.

"Ah, I thought me fame would be spreading." Mrs. Spike reached for her pack of Rothmans. "Gossip's a grand thing sure enough, and as certain as there's shamrocks in Ireland, word will get out and about that I soak me false teeth in gin of a night and scared the bishop out of his shorts when I told him the joke about one of his own and the chorus girl."

Unsure what to say, my eyes met Eudora's. In them I beheld an expression better suited to an axe murderer than a clergywoman.

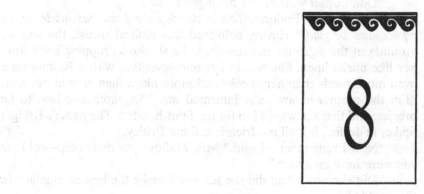

8

Were we in the midst of an epidemic? Did a woman risk having her mother-in-law move in permanently with her if she stood next to someone already afflicted at the bus stop? Seeing that I had no wish to complicate anyone else's life, it was possibly just as well I was the only person to catch the Number 39 when it pulled up a few yards beyond the vicarage gate.

I had looked up the Taffers' address in the phone book before leaving and I didn't expect any problems in finding the house. When I got off in the village square, I was still puzzling over what I would say to Tricks, but I took it as a good omen that the clouds were lifting. The bus swept away in a sun-spattered drizzle, and I sidestepped a busker's cap spilling over with change that glistened as if brushed with dew. Dropping in my mite, I tried not to feel resentment that this middle-aged urchin could sing like a yellow-cheeked willow warbler while poor Mr. Savage, who had the soul of a troubadour, couldn't put two notes together and was living in a garret above my stables, a slave to his art. As I passed a greengrocer's shop on Robert Road, I remembered that Dad had a fine voice. Immediately I began daydreaming about his returning in a fit of remorse to stand beneath Mum's balcony and serenade her.

In a spirit of determined optimism I turned left onto Kitty Crescent. Would it be out of line to tell Tricks that if she had designs on my father-in-law, she had best forget them? Surely it wasn't too much to ask that she do something productive—encourage him to return to Mum, get down on his knees, and beg forgiveness. And while he was down there—no point in wasting energy at his age—pop the question. Or should I stick to the letter of Eudora's advice and simply ask Tricks to apologize to Mum on her own behalf?

Speculation was getting me nowhere fast. I had passed Number 18 and now had to retrace my steps along the row of semi-detached houses that looked as though they had been cut out of cardboard and put up in an afternoon. Ah, here we were again. Unlatching the gate, I walked up the narrow path, negotiating the rusty tricycle and bits and bobs of hop-scotch chalk, to stand on the step beneath the corrugated porch. There and then, quite on the spur of the moment, I became so churned up, my knees turned to butter.

Frizzy Taffer could hardly be expected to welcome me with open arms after the havoc my dinner party had caused. The knocker fell with a trembling thud, and before I could pry my nose away from the side window, the door flew open and a weary voice demanded: "What now, you little pest?"

"I—"

An arm that must have been a mile long shot out to drag me over the threshold.

"Oh, crikey! I am sorry!" The one-woman welcoming committee stepped back with her hands clapped to her cheeks and her eyes brimming with embarrassment. "I thought you were Barney, my seven-year-old, he's been in one door and out the next all morning." Frizzy Taffer needed no introduction. Her reddish-brown hair was wider than it was long and positively bristled with static electricity.

"I'm Ellie Haskell," I babbled. "But if this is a bad time, I could go away and not come back."

"No." She grabbed me again, this time by the hand, and I was afraid to flinch in case it came off in her grasp. "Don't go!" she cried. "I've been hoping all morning that you would phone."

"I should have done so before barging in here."

"This is better. It's so much easier to talk face-to-face." She released me and shoved the door shut. "Believe me, I am glad to see you."

The narrow hall had that stripped-down-to-its-underwear look. The paint was a washed-out beige and there wasn't one stick of furniture, for utility or display. Which was just as well. As it was, it would have been difficult to take a step without treading on a pile of colouring books and broken crayons or mounds of building blocks or choo-choo trains. Toys on the stairs, more toys on the windowsill. And, to get the message across that Frizzy Taffer's life wasn't all fun and games, the Hoover was dragged out by its cord to stand on the threadbare strip of carpet.

"I'm afraid I stirred up a bee's nest," I said.

"You're the one I feel sorry for." Frizzy stuffed her hands in her skirt pockets and looked towards the door to our left, which had been ajar and was now inching open. A baby of about eight months came crawling, pat-pat, on its fat little hands across the hall floor. A sticky-faced baby with a riot of red-brown curls. Shrieking up behind her came a scruffy-haired boy of four or five.

"Mummy! Laura broke my puzzle."

"I'm sure it was an accident, Dustin." Frizzy scooped the baby up into her arms.

"Wasn't!" The boy bounced down on his bottom and began drumming his little army boots on the floor. "I don't want her anymore. Let's give her away." His legs stopped pedaling and the freckles on his nose seemed to light up as he spotted me.

"Are you the ice cream lady?"

"Mrs. Haskell is a friend of Mummy's." Brown eyes weary, Frizzy settled her bundle of joy on her hip. "She has twins, not much older than Laura. And I'm sure you want to tell her that you love your sister."

"No, I don't." Dustin hauled himself up to stand, toes turned in, scowling at the floor. "And I don't like that grandpa man who slept in my bed last night."

Did my ears deceive me? In a daze, I watched Frizzy brush back the baby's hair. "That's enough, Dustin! You know you liked going in the top bunk with Barney. It was fun, wasn't it?"

"Until I fell out." Understandably disgusted, Dustin stomped off upstairs.

"Did my father-in-law spend the night here?"

"Believe me, I wasn't keen on the idea."

"He was supposed to go to the Dark Horse."

"Tricks told him she knew for a fact that they were all booked up."

"He didn't bother to check?"

"You know my mother-in-law; she can be quite convincing. Don't get me wrong, any other time I would have been glad to have him"—Frizzy tried to make a joke of it—"like when the kids are grown and gone. I'm sure your father-in-law is a perfectly lovely man. But Tom and I don't have any privacy as it is. You only have to take a look at this place to see the walls are paper thin. We can hear every word the people next door say. We can hear them breathing. We can hear the towels drying on the rail in their bathroom."

"I understand." She didn't have to paint a picture of the mother-in-law in the bedroom just across the landing. "Where," I asked, "is Dad now?"

"At the Dark Horse. There was a bit of a rumpus this morning between Mum and me when I insisted he phone them and see about a room. But he was all right about it."

"I should think so."

"And I was hoping you might have a word with Tricks and try to get her to realize she's caused enough trouble for one week. I think she's in the kitchen, because she offered to fix a bite of something for Dawn—that's my oldest daughter. She always comes home to eat around twelve-thirty, because she doesn't like the school lunches. And I think"—Frizzy gave the baby a hoist—"that's her now."

A scream had erupted from the kitchen, and a girl in a bottle-green skirt and white blouse came hurtling through the door, auburn plaits slapping against her shoulders and eyes blazing with fury.

"Mummy, do something! Gran just committed a *murder*!"

"I'm sure it was an accident." Frizzy appeared in no immediate danger of dropping the baby.

"She's *destroyed* the only thing I've ever loved."

"Oh, dear—not Goldilocks!"

"I want to die too."

"Yes, dear! But don't you think you could first say hello to Mrs. Haskell?"

Ignoring this request, young Dawn stood with her chin out, arms folded, panting like a locomotive. "You don't care, do you, Mummy? It's not *your* goldfish that's been horribly done to death. She didn't even get to die in her own bowl."

"I know this is hard on you," Frizzy risked a step towards her daughter, "but I don't think you should be too hard on Gran if she accidentally dropped the bowl or rinsed Goldie down the sink in changing the water."

"I knew you would take her side." Dawn's voice dropped the temperature ten degrees. "Mummy, when will you grow up? Last night when I was putting more water in the bowl I banged it against the sink and it cracked, so I put Goldilocks in the egg saucepan and before I got home just now Gran went and got it down from the cupboard without bothering to think why it was full of water, plopped in an egg without looking, and . . . Mummy, she cooked Goldy to death for three and a half minutes!"

Frizzy winced. "I'm sure she was sorry."

"Gran's a wicked old hypocrite!" The girl kicked aside a toy car and watched it slam into the staircase wall. "She's always going on about not eating this or that, because even apples and oranges are entitled to live out their lives in peace."

"Now, Dawn, you know you love Gran."

"Mummy"—stamp of the foot—"I was *very* committed to that goldfish."

The kitchen door opened and out came Tricks in tie-dyed muslin, her hair spiked up all over her head, her triple earrings glittering, and her elderly schoolgirl face as equable as ever. "I'm every bit as upset as you are, love," she told her granddaughter, "but we have to remember that tragedies of this sort are a necessary evil on the road to spiritual enlightenment."

"Thanks a lot!" Dawn was almost bursting with fury.

"Think how nice it would be if as a result of this little accident you started a campaign to save the lobsters. People drop them in boiling water all the time, and no one calls out the R.S.P.C.A.!" Enough said on the subject, Tricks focussed her attention on me. "Ellie my love! Oh, Elijah will be sorry to have missed you. Frizzy couldn't talk him into staying, but I know without a shadow of a doubt that he enjoyed his visit. Him and me took a walk down to the greengrocer's on the corner first thing this morning. And you know, I think he might like to do some volunteer work. You should have heard what he had to say about the way the fruit and vege were set out in the window."

"I'm hoping," I said, "that he may volunteer for active duty on the home front."

"Whatever makes him and Mags happy!" Tricks radiated good nature. "But, as I told Elijah, if things aren't meant to be, it's best to find out now, while he still has his whole life ahead of him."

"There you go!" Dawn looked ready to chew on her pigtails. "Interfering again. That's what you do best, Gran—interfere and ruin lives."

"That's enough!" Worn to the bone, Frizzy set baby Laura down among the puffer trains and jigsaw puzzle pieces.

"Go ahead, take her side!" The girl took a couple of outraged steps before letting loose a piercing scream. "No! This can't be happening to me!" Pouncing down into a crouch, she fanned her hands across the floor. "Who let the kids play with *my* Barbie dolls?"

"Guilty!" Tricks shot up her hands. "But don't you fret, love, their hair will grow back."

"Gran, don't ever, *ever* speak to me again!" Leaving the four dolls where they lay, Dawn leaped to her feet, flung her arms wide, and cried, "Is *nothing* sacred?" before thundering, sobbing, up the stairs.

"Oh, to be young again!" Tricks hunched a tie-dyed shoulder.

"It is a pity about those dolls," Frizzy said. "My cousin Alice sent them all the way from America."

"Well, I'm sure she can send some more. Meanwhile, I'll get back to the kitchen and open a tin of sardines for the child."

A scream descended on us from the landing. Poor Dawn! Who could blame her for fearing that the late Goldilocks would turn up on a toast point?

"On second thought"—Tricks was still all smiles—"I think I'll get back to the garden and have a natter with the runner beans. Never any back-chat from them. Always a treat to see you, Ellie, and I send lots of hugs and kisses to Mags."

Away she went through the kitchen door, leaving me with the real-isation that I hadn't said a word to her about contacting Mum in an attempt at healing their rift. Just as well! Dawn's outburst against inter-ference had sounded the alarm that I hadn't learned my lesson. Once again I had been motivated by only the best of intentions when sticking in my oar, instead of leaving my in-laws to paddle their own canoe.

"The first thing Tom will ask when he gets home is what I've been doing all day. Dawn's a lovely girl, but she's got a wicked temper, like my aunt Ethel." Frizzy dredged up a smile when we had the hall to ourselves.

"I'll get out of your hair," I said.

"You don't have to rush off." Frizzy made the token protest as she picked up baby Laura and escorted me towards the front door.

"Thanks, but I should be getting home." The words were hardly out of my mouth when Frizzy gave a squeal and backed smack into me. A shadow blocked out the light from the side-panel window, and I saw a face, framed in a headscarf, before the knocker came down with a *plonk*.

"Lady Kitty Pomeroy!" Frizzy pressed a hand over the baby's mouth before dropping cumbersomely to her knees and signaling for me to follow suit. I obeyed. "I don't believe this!" she hissed. "Yes, I do! She of all people was bound to show up on this of all days. Quick!" The knocker landed with two thuds this time. "We have to hide. I can't have that woman catching me in this muddle. This estate was built on land that used to belong to Sir Robert's family. When the first house was built her ladyship was present to stick in the ceremonial fork. And she's been sticking it in ever since."

"Of course," I said, "Robert Road, Kitty Crescent!" The three of us —baby Laura had accepted the call to action—were engaged in a crawling race worthy of the St. Anselm's Fête, over the Snakes and Ladders board and around the Noah's Ark.

"In here!" Frizzy yanked open the door to the cupboard under the stairs and hustled her offspring and me into the cave where mops and brooms gawked at us out of the shadows. Laura gave a snuffle of delight as I popped her into the clothes basket full of sheets and towels. And people say housewives lead humdrum lives! Frizzy shoved in behind us and was drawing the door shut, when Tricks provided a delightfully heart-stopping moment by appearing in the wedge of light. No room in the air raid shelter; but Frizzy was in quivering command.

"Lie down and play dead," she ordered.

Tricks was nothing if not a sport. Down she went flat on the floor, arms at her sides, only her hair sticking up.

"Is it the insurance man, love?"

"Lady Kitty."

"Ah!" The syllable held a wealth of comprehension.

"Don't get me wrong." Frizzy spoke into the fog raised by her panicked breathing. "I don't think Lady Kitty's some sort of monster. She does no end of good with all her charity work, and no one could accuse her of being a snob."

"Well, I don't see how she could be, love!" Tricks piped up from her foxhole. "Everyone knows her mum was chief cook and bottle washer up at Pomeroy Manor and her dad was the handyman. Talk about one for the book—the lucky ducks having that windfall on the pools just about the time Sir Robert inherited the manor and all its debts. Don't have to be brainy to see why he married the meddlesome Minnie, do you?"

I fully expected Dawn's voice to screech from above stairs, "Hark, who's talking?" But we didn't hear a peep out of her.

"Aren't you worried about the children giving the game away?" I inquired into the gloom.

Frizzy shook her head which, given the breadth of her hair, put a crimp in our cramped space. "What with the mood Dawn's in, she wouldn't answer the door if her life depended on it. And, awful as it sounds, we have Lady Kitty alarm drills. If Barney's out front, he'll have ducked out of sight and Dustin will have taken a peek out the window and taken cover behind a chair. As I say, she's not a bad sort but . . ."

Silence, so thick it threatened to smother us, sifted up through the floorboards. It took me a moment to realize that, in a manner of speaking, the all-clear had sounded. The knocker had not come walloping down again. I heard the baby gurgle, I heard Tricks lift her head from the floor, and I was joining Frizzy in exhaling a relieved breath when I heard a woman's voice inquire, "Anyone home?"

My knees turned wobbly. And I was only an innocent bystander. What must the woman of the house be feeling? We hobbled out into the hall, Frizzy treading on my heels and both of us stumbling over Tricks, who was still facedown on the floor. Only baby Laura escaped the humiliation of the moment. She was left asleep in the clothes basket, like Moses cast adrift in the bullrushes.

"Your ladyship!" I stammered.

"What an unexpected treat!" Frizzy's smile kept sliding off her face.

"I was writing a note to put through the door, when I thought to try the knob." Lady Kitty gave a self-congratulatory laugh. She was wearing a fur coat which didn't go with the month of June or her headscarf. A law unto herself, this woman. Her snapping black eyes moved to Tricks lying flat out by the staircase. "A simple curtsy would do, Beatrix."

This jest, if such it were, produced a puckish grin from Tricks. "I was doing my daily meditating."

"She goes into a sort of trance." Frizzy helped her mother-in-law to her feet. "Sometimes it takes us hours . . . *days* to bring her out of it. And Mrs. Haskell"—she nudged me forward—"she and I were just checking the fuse box. The fridge keeps turning itself off."

"What?" Lady Kitty's voice conveyed disapproval. "That won't do, will it! We can't have appliances getting above themselves. And you, Frizzy, can't go sticking your head in the cupboard under the stairs every time something goes wrong."

"No, your ladyship." This response was made in a junior-housemaid voice.

"The fuse box has nothing to do with it. I'll send around my electrician. And you be sure and tell him that if he doesn't do the job in record time, I'll take his name out of the hat."

Perceiving our blank expressions, Lady Kitty was so gracious as to explain herself. "My father used that method when paying his bills. He'd put the names of the people he owed money to in the hat he wore to funerals and weddings. Every Saturday night he'd hold a drawing to see who would get paid that week. If someone annoyed him, he took that person's name out of the hat. And that went for me and my sixpence pocket money." Her eyes gleamed at the memory. "I wasn't brought up soft. And I've never taken the easy way since Father's win on the pools made me mistress of Pomeroy Manor. But that doesn't mean I look down my nose at those who never quite seem able to cope."

"I do apologize for the muddle." Frizzy's hair had lost most of its oomph.

"Makes a home, doesn't it?" Tricks beamed.

"It's my being here." I thrust myself into the fore. "I barged in just when Mrs. Tom Taffer" (sounded like something out of a nursery rhyme) "was getting going vacuuming up the toys . . . I mean the floor."

Lady Kitty favoured me with a crisp smile. "I gather you're here, Ellie, in your official capacity as chairwoman of St. Anselm's Summer Fête. Time's marching on, and it doesn't do to get behind with our responsibilities, does it? How much money have you collected so far for the tents and other equipment?"

"Fifty pence." I addressed her lace-up shoes.

"Not doing too well, are we?" She tightened the knot of her headscarf. "It strikes me, Ellie, that if I can offer the manor grounds year in year out for this event, you could put your best foot forward."

"My cousin Freddy has promised to go out collecting."

"Very kind of him. But call it delegating—call it what you will—it doesn't do to shift our responsibilities. If a job's worth doing, it's worth doing ourselves." Lady Kitty's expression softened. "What you have to realize, dear, is that charity work is not for the faint-hearted. If we are ever to make this a better world, we have to learn to turn the screws. Speaking of which"—she pointed a finger—"I see a screw is missing from the Hoover."

"Perhaps the baby ate it," Tricks said brightly.

"Very possibly, but I had hoped better care would be taken with my property."

"But I thought"—Frizzy flushed a deep orange—"I thought you gave me that vacuum."

"*Lent*, dear. Not gave." The smallest of frowns creased her ladyship's brow. "I'm always willing to help out in a fix, but we all have to assume some personal responsibility, don't we, dear?"

"Yes, ma'am."

"That's right. And to show I'm not disappointed in you, I'm going to send my Mrs. Pickle over to give this place a good turnout."

"That's awfully good of you, but—"

"No buts, Frizzy, I'm well aware that Edna Pickle is slow as treacle, but she's prepared to stay till the work is done, and as she'll tell you quite proudly, she can't read, so you never have to worry about her snooping. I'm sure if you start watching your pennies, you'll be able to afford her a couple of days a week until the house gets squared away."

"Thank you."

"That's my mission! Picking up the pieces of other people's lives. Ellie"—the grande dame of the western world turned to me—"you must come for lunch tomorrow—no, better make it the following day. Be at Pomeroy Manor at noon sharp, and we'll get you organized. We want this to be the best fête ever, don't we?"

What I wanted was to get home, but someone knocked at the front door before I could make my getaway. Frizzy opened up to admit a tall young woman with stooped posture and her hair hanging in schoolgirl ponytails on either side of her face.

"Pamela." Her ladyship's fur coat bristled as she turned to face the intruder. "I thought I told you to stay and watch the bikes."

"I know you did, Mumsie Kitty." The girl's hands were tangled into knots that would never come undone. "But when I looked at my watch I got worried that you would be late for your doctor's appointment and I didn't want your blood pressure to go up."

"I have a watch of my own, dear!"

"I'm sorry! I thought you gave it to Mrs. Pickle so that she could time herself when doing the stove."

"*Lent,* dear! Not gave. Too good-natured for my own good, that's my trouble." Lady Kitty gave a sigh that rippled the tail ends of her headscarf. "People take advantage."

"You *must* take the Hoover back," Frizzy made haste to say.

"Certainly, dear! Pamela can tie it on her handlebars. My goal is always to encourage people like you to better yourselves, not to crush initiative. But first things first. Let me introduce my daughter-in-law, the Honourable Mrs. Allan Pomeroy. She and my only son live with me and Bobsie Cat—as we call Sir Robert. They have their own room and get one night out a week. Isn't that right, Pamela?"

"Yes, Mumsie Kitty."

"There isn't a happier family anywhere. May God strike me dead if I tell a lie," Lady Kitty told us.

My father-in-law was a disgrace to the honoured Haskell name. Duty dictated that I seek him out at the Dark Horse and demand that he return with me to Merlin's Court and beg Mum's forgiveness for last night's indiscretions. But before I reached the corner where Kitty Crescent turned onto Robert Road, I knew I wasn't up to another round as peacemaker. The morning had been one big fat waste of time, and I longed to see my children again before they were grown up and ready to leave home.

I was standing at the bus stop in the drizzling rain, looking at my watch, when there came a roar of thunder so low to the ground I feared the sky had fallen. A hurricane whipped my skirts between my legs as my cousin Freddy pulled up against the curb. His lean, mean legs straddled his motorbike, and the arms of his leather jacket were pushed up to display metal bracelets that looked like handcuffs. The pavement was still vibrating when he turned off the engine and flashed me a fond smile.

"Want a lift, coz?"

"Shouldn't you be at Abigail's?"

"Lunch hour." He shook his head sadly. "The curse of the working-man. Come on"—he patted the seat of the bike—"hop aboard."

His skull-and-crossbones earring, coupled with the ponytail that looked as if it had been used to wipe up an oil spill, did not suggest someone who would hum along, up hill and down dale, at a chaste thirty miles an hour. But as I have said, I was eager to get home now, if not sooner. For all I knew, Mum was sunk in depression, Jonas was on the brink of proposing marriage just to cheer her up, and the twins were hungry enough to eat each other.

We were off in a blast worthy of Cape Canaveral. The car ahead of us took the ditch and a lorry backed around the nearest corner, leaving the road ours for the seizing. A dozen lampposts came charging at us like a troop of Gilbert and Sullivan policemen. Shops and windows gaped at us with wide window eyes, but even the traffic lights determined it was futile to try to stop us. Each one for a mile stretch turned green at our approach until the town itself took the hint and scarpered into the mist.

"Comfy?" Freddy shouted over his shoulder.

For the moment the Constable landscape hovered quietly behind its hedgerows, but who knew when a big furry cow might loom up and go "Moo!" or even "Boo!" If Mum had been here, she could have occupied herself with crocheting, but all I could do was make conversation.

"I say," I yelled, "do you know Allan Pomeroy?"

"Who?"

"Sir Robert and Lady Kitty's son."

"Oh, him!" Freddy's damp ponytail slapped my cheek. "Met him once at the Dark Horse. One of those fair, rosy-cheeked blokes who look as though they should still be in short trousers. Talked proper posh, mostly about his mother."

"Devoted to her, I suppose."

"Terrified, is more like. He was telling me and the other blokes at the bar how Mumsie arranged his marriage."

"Did what?" I almost bounced off my seat.

"You mean you haven't heard about it from your source?"

"Mrs. Malloy? She must have assumed I already knew."

"I guess! Picking your son's wife is going a bit overboard these days, wouldn't you say? The woman has to be bonkers. Get this, Ellie: She arranged a cooking contest and awarded the bridegroom to the winner."

"You're joking!"

"As true as I'm sitting here."

"And women entered this contest?"

"By the score. They came out of the woodwork. And who can wonder? With his father's pedigree and Mumsie's money, Allan Pomeroy had to be the most eligible bachelor for miles around. I tell you, coz, it makes me grateful to be a common slob."

I was speechless. The road rose up like a drawbridge as we headed for the clifftop. My hands unsnapped from around Freddy's middle, I was leaning backwards, my shoulders resting on a cushion of the air. The sky was inches from my face. Just when I thought I was to be thrown to the four winds, the world abruptly righted itself and we were buzzing down the straightaway within view of St. Anselm's Church.

"Amazing!" I said.

"What is?"

"Pamela. Have you ever met her, Freddy?"

"Don't think so."

"She's like a frightened puppy! I can't picture her getting up the nerve to enter that contest."

"Still waters run deep."

"You can say that again," I replied. We had Mum, the all-time altar girl, living in sin for thirty-eight years. Dad going skinny-dipping. Reverend Eudora Spike looking ready to commit murder. The list went on. . . . But Merlin's Court had come racing into view, its gates flung wide in welcome. Consumed with impatience, I was halfway off the bike before Freddy brought it to a sputtering halt outside his cottage.

"We must do this again sometime." I gave my cousin a hug to help steady myself. "You'd better get going if you want to fix yourself a decent lunch."

"What did you say?" Freddy tends to feign deafness when told to grub for himself. He was staring at the house. And, raising my hand to part the misting rain like an organdy curtain, I saw what had attracted his attention. Someone was standing on the corner balcony.

"Help! Somebody help me!" The wind batted the cry to us.

"Hold tight, old sport!" Freddy shouted through cupped hands as he raced down the drive, his ponytail in full flight.

Unfortunately I have never been able to accomplish two things at one time, such as run and see straight. Even when I closed in on the house I couldn't put a face to the person on the balcony. Mum? Jonas? Mrs. Malloy? Oh, God! What was wrong?

Another shout from on high brought me into collision with Freddy, who had leaped the mini-moat to reach the courtyard a good half dozen steps ahead of me. Such is my faith in the male sex, I expected my cousin to claw his way up the brick face without the aid of so much as a tooth-pick. But all the slowpoke did was place his hands on his hips and sing out, "Rapunzel, Rapunzel! Let down your hair!"

A shaky laugh drifted down and I looked up to see Mr. Watkins. His rain-darkened beret was tipped over one eye, his cheeks were deflated, and he gripped the balcony railing as if he were the captain of a ship about to go down. Stupid me! His van was parked smack in the middle of the courtyard, but I hadn't put the window cleaner on my list of suicidal possibilities. Even allowing for two or three lunch breaks, he should have been long gone.

"Whatever's wrong?" I quavered.

Mr. Watkins managed a brave smile that stretched his thin mous-tache to the limit. "I can't get down. The windows are locked and I cannot reach my rungs."

Freddy and I did an about-face, and lo and behold there was the ladder, propped up against the wall six feet away. A mere skip and a jump for Superman but an impossible stretch for Mr. Watkins, who was not known to exert himself.

"Took a hike, did it?" My cousin gave his infamous smirk.

The prisoner spread his hands in a flourish. "I went round the corner of the balcony to do the windows on the other side, and when I got back someone had moved the ladder."

"Cheer up, old cock," Freddy said. "It's a beautiful view."

"That it is, sir! I'm not one to complain, but I've been up here for hours." Mr. Watkins hacked a consumptive cough. "I shouted for help till my voice gave out."

"This house is built like a fortress. Sound bounces off the walls." Freddy flung a damp arm around my shoulders and whispered chummily in my ear, "That blighter's going to sue you for *everything* you're worth, coz."

"Rubbish!" I elbowed him towards the ladder. "We'll have you on the ground in a jiff, Mr. Watkins."

"Much obliged!" Pressing a trembling hand to his beret, he swayed against the railing. "There were moments when my life flashed before my eyes."

"Freddy will get you down while I go inside and make a pot of tea." So saying, I did a bunk towards the back door and let myself into the kitchen.

No scene could have been easier on the eyes. The Aga cooker shone, the copper bowls gleamed, Tobias Cat was taking a siesta in the rocking chair, and Mum and Jonas were seated at the table, she crocheting away for dear life while he looked on in admiration.

"There's magic in your hands, Magdalene."

"That's kind of you to say, Jonas."

So this is what they had been up to while my back was turned! Getting on a first-name basis while leaving the window cleaner playing the balcony scene from *Romeo and Juliet*!

"Are you two having a nice chat?" I asked brightly.

"It were time for a bit of a sit down, after the morning we've had"—Jonas scuffed back his chair and stood—"isn't that right, Magdalene?"

"Are the twins all right?" My eyes went from one elderly face to the other.

"Would I neglect them?" Mum rolled up her crocheting. "They've been fed and are down for their naps."

"So what's wrong?"

"For starters, Sweetie refused to come out of her room. Poor little mite! She still feels in the way. Then we couldn't find St. Francis. Too much clutter everywhere you look, but if it doesn't bother you, Ellie, and my son has adapted himself, far be it from me to criticize. We all have different standards." Mum paused for breath. "About half an hour ago I did have a very unpleasant experience, but if you don't mind, I'd rather not talk about that right now; I'm still far too upset."

Had Dad telephoned? It was hard not to pry; but I focussed on the moment at hand. "Do either of you know how the window cleaner came to be marooned on one of the balconies?"

"What's that?" Jonas's wintry eyebrows shot up.

"Someone moved his ladder."

"He'd stuck its legs in the flower bed." Mum sniffed. "In this rain! Maybe *you* wouldn't have minded the horrid holes that would have been left, Ellie, but I brought up Ben to be particular. It took some doing, let me tell you, to drag that heavy ladder onto the courtyard. Not that I'm asking for sympathy. No, that must all be saved for another."

"Serves Watkins right!" Jonas put in his twopenny worth. "Always expecting to get paid for doing nowt. It do tickle me pink, as how this time he got his wish."

Mum favoured him with a compression of the lips that was as close as she ever got to a smile.

"Born doing nothing and done nothing ever since, that's him!" Jonas ranted on. "Parading around the place in that daft beret and silk cravat like he just got out of France in a cartload of cabbages. I do be telling you there's people as what get locked up for a lot less."

At this opportune moment Mr. Watkins entered the kitchen. And if he couldn't be counted upon to seize the moment and make it worse, Freddy came in behind him.

"Feeling better?" I asked the walking wounded.

"He's in a bad way," Freddy said with a gloat.

"I'll say three Hail Marys and two Our Fathers, seeing I'm the one to blame." Mum stood, arms straight at her sides, ready and willing to be pierced through with the arrows of reproach. The look Mr. Watkins gave her was not sweet as honey, but he was clearly not up to a showdown. Pressing a hand to his beret, he swayed in the breeze stirred up by all the heavy breathing in the room.

"If I could just sit down for a moment, Mrs. Haskell. . . ."

"Of course!" I hurried over to the rocking chair, and when Tobias Cat refused to budge fluffed him up like a cushion. "How's that?"

"Thanks ever so."

Freddy, every inch the thwarted thespian, helped lower Mr. Watkins to his seat. "Don't you have a footstool for him, Ellie? The man fainted three times getting here."

Life had its moments. I managed to get rid of Jonas, who was rolling his eyes and making rude grunts, by asking him to go and fetch a hassock. Confident that he wouldn't hurry himself, I focussed on the next order of business: sending Freddy on his merry way. When he didn't take the hint that his lunch break had to be well and truly over, I held the garden door open and told him to scram.

"But Ben would want me to stay." My cousin gave me his most winsome smile. "My boss—alias your adoring husband—instructed me to buzz by the old homestead and see how things were going."

Mum had tears in her eyes, but I managed to restrain my emotion. "Then you had best hurry back and report." Before I finished counting to ten, Freddy ambled off down the steps to my amazement, and when I turned back into the kitchen, Mum, every inch the martyr, was making Mr. Watkins a cup of tea.

"Feeling any better?" I asked him.

"They say time's a great healer, Mrs. Haskell, but I doubt I'll ever be able to climb that ladder again." He gripped the arms of the rocker as it swayed backwards, his eyes brimming with terror. "You see how it is! I don't feel safe *this* far off the ground. So what's to become of me? That's the question going around and around in my head. I'd been thinking of late that it might be nice to be married. But what woman in her right mind would take on a wretched invalid?"

"I'm sure you're painting too bleak a picture." I couldn't look at

Mum for fear she was bracing herself to make the ultimate sacrifice. Then again, that might be just what was needed to return Dad to his senses.

"Between you and me and the kitchen sink"—Mr. Watkins burrowed back in the chair to the vocal displeasure of Tobias—"I've always hoped that me and Roxie Malloy could make a match of it."

"That might be a way out for her," Mum said.

"What do you mean?" I asked without fear or trembling. My mother-in-law looked so harmless standing there by the stove. She didn't drop the kettle, which in her hands acquired the magnitude of a ten-gallon watering can; instead, she dropped her bombshell. "I gave the woman the sack."

"I don't believe it!" After all the horrors of the past twenty-four hours, I was still a babe in the woods, but I did not give way to the childish impulse to flood the floor with my tears. For starters, I had no idea what Mrs. Malloy had done with the mop, unless she had cracked it over my mother-in-law's head before marching upstairs to regale the twins with the dreadful news that she was lost to them.

"What I'll never understand, Ellie"—Mum handed Mr. Watkins his cup of tea without spilling a drop—"is why you put up with that dreadful woman. I would say to Dad—in the days when we were speaking—that it stood out a mile that she *drank*." Lips on the straight and narrow, she got on with the business of wiping down the stove, as calm as you please.

"We all *drink*! The intake of liquid is part of the human condition." I flapped a hand towards Mr. Watkins, who was downing his cuppa as if a return to full mental and physical health depended on it.

"*Gin!* That's what I'm talking about." Mum folded her dishcloth and set it aside, for future darning, I suppose.

"Mrs. Malloy does not imbibe on the job!" I had to fight to keep my feet on the floor so as not to hop up and down with rage, an activity which in addition to making me look ridiculous would have jarred Mr. Watkins out of his chair. All I needed was to have him add a slipped disc to his list when suing us for damages. "Do you really think, Mum, I would leave the twins with Mrs. Malloy if I thought she would be under the sofa with a bottle? She's a changed woman since she signed up for brass-rubbing classes at St. Anselm's."

"A pity she doesn't do a bit more of that here!" Mum gave her signature sniff, but wasn't finished. "And that *hair!*"

I was on the very edge of saying that Mrs. Malloy was blessed with a full head of the stuff, albeit in two colours, but I bit my tongue. Standing before me, I reminded myself, was the woman who had brought Ben into the world.

"She looks like a prostitute." Mum screwed up her face. "Those taffeta frocks with the necklines down to the knees!"

"You wouldn't happen to have a tube of liniment handy?" Mr. Watkins piped up. "I'm beginning to ache all through my joints."

I would gladly have thrown one at him. But first things first. I mustn't miss a word of what Mum was saying.

"I suppose I shouldn't have been surprised when I caught her . . ." She dangled the unfinished sentence under my nose.

"When you caught her doing what?"

"Reading that filthy book!"

Following her sparrow-eyed gaze towards the row of instructional volumes in the art of cookery, I thought bleakly, so that's it—the one thing I missed, sponging off the batter-spattered pages of *The Way to a Man's Stomach.*

"Admittedly, there are a few dirty spots here and there. . . ."

"A few spots here and there!" Mum was in full flood. Marching over to the shelf, she pulled out a volume as if afraid of catching a venereal disease. "Every page, every line full of *smut.* I almost had a heart attack when I opened it up looking for a recipe for pork loin. There were *loins* all right, writhing and throbbing and generally carrying on in the *most* disgusting way."

Mr. Watkins was on the edge of his seat, tipping Tobias onto the floor in the process.

"Oh, heavens!" I pressed my hands to my cheeks.

"There's the most awful bit about stoking the boiler." Her face working, Mum stared me down. "Don't think for one moment, Ellie, that I am criticizing. You know that has never been my way! But how you could let Mrs. Malloy bring a book like this—with *twenty-eight* references to 'her ripe red strawberries'—into the house when you have an impressionable young husband, I will never understand."

"I'm coming over all hot and cold!" Mr. Watkins did indeed look feverish. But who had time to worry about him?

"Honestly, Mum, you've got everything back to front." I attempted a shamefaced laugh. "*Lady Letitia's Letters* is my book."

"I *knew* it!"

"Well then . . ."

"I *knew* you would defend that woman. But it's not a bit of good, Ellie. She owned up without so much as a blush the moment I showed it to her."

"Of course she did!" I had tears in my eyes. "That's the sort of person she is—loyal to the death."

Wasted words. My mother-in-law wasn't standing still for my defense of Mrs. Malloy. She marched over to the Aga, and before I could let out a howl of protest ripped the book down the middle, lifted the cover of the hot plate with the iron hook, and crammed *Lady Letitia's Letters* down onto the coals.

"If it wasn't hot stuff before, it is now," Mr. Watkins murmured.

"It was a library book!" I flung myself across the room. "My library book! I will be arrested. Librarians all over the country have banded together in demanding the return of the death penalty for books that are more than a fortnight late."

Mum flinched as if she had stuck her hand on the hot plate. "I might have known it would be like this." She gave a teensy-weensy sob. "A woman on her own is always fair game. You don't need to tell me that I'm no better than the female in that book, for it's written all over your face. But let me say this, Ellie. In all the years Dad and I were together, I never once let him"—shudder—"see my *loins.*"

Before I could respond, the hall door opened. In stalked Mrs. Malloy in all her glory, with Sweetie nipping at the hem of her frock.

"Oh, there you are!" I stammered.

"Well, if that don't warm me cockles." Mrs. M. drew on her three-quarter-length black satin gloves with slow deliberation, but I could tell she wasn't as calm as she wished to appear. The beauty spot which she usually penciled in above her lip was way up over her left eyebrow. And when I hurried over to her, she warded me off with a shaky hand.

"If it's all the same with you, Mrs. H., I've been having a last sit-down in the nursery with me precious babes. They've always loved their old Roxie, have little Abbey and Tam."

Mum stood there as if she had been stuffed by a master taxidermist; but I would gladly have dropped to my knees in full view of Mr. Watkins and Sweetie, who was herding Tobias into a corner.

"Mrs. Malloy, we have to talk this over."

"Thanks but no thanks, Mrs. H.; you could hand me Mrs. MacIvelli's"—a glare in Mum's direction—"head on a silver platter, and it wouldn't make no difference. You'll be getting me resignation in tomorrow's post."

"This is all so silly. I've explained to Mum that it was I who borrowed *Lady Letitia's Letters* from the library, and I know she's most frightfully sorry for going off the deep end at you—"

"I can see she's all choked up." Mrs. M. teetered around on her high heels, lifted her supply bag from Tam's booster chair, and cocked her black-and-white head at Mr. Watkins. "Up with you, lad, you get to take me home in the van."

I played for time. "He's feeling poorly."

"And I suppose if he sits here all day, paralysis will set in."

"He got stuck on one of the balconies." I had to raise my voice, because Sweetie was yipping and yapping as she made little rushes at Tobias in an attempt to wrest what appeared to be a bone from his tenacious paws.

"Ah." Mrs. M.'s butterfly lips softened into a smile. "Mr. Watkins couldn't find his ladder with his little footsies, poor lad."

"Blame me for that." Mum came back to pinch-faced life. "Another case where I went wrong thinking I was doing right—"

"I'm still in shock." The victim's beret fell off when he hung his head. "Every bone in my body aches from the drenching I took."

"What a shame." Mrs. Malloy's smile spread. "You come with me, there's a dear, and we'll stop at the chemist's to pick up a tube of nice smelly ointment."

"I don't know as I can stand up." Mr. Watkins stared hopelessly up at me, his right hand protruding at a peculiar angle, but it took a moment for the penny to drop.

"Goodness! I haven't paid you!" Reaching for my handbag, I went to give him a twenty-pound note, saw him fade before my eyes, and hastily produced a fifty. Undoubtedly I was making a mistake admitting liability, but surely this would be the end of the matter.

Pocketing the money with no trace of a smile, Mr. Watkins struggled to his feet, saying in a terminally weakened voice, "I'll have to be careful of this few quid, for who knows when I'll work again."

"Cheer up, duck!" Mrs. Malloy gave him a *whop* with the supply bag. "You and me will plot our revenge on the way home."

Someone let out a squeal. It could have been Mum, but in all probability it was Sweetie. The dear little doggie kept getting underfoot as my former daily half dragged, half carried wan Mr. Watkins into the alcove where we kept the Wellington boots.

"Is it asking too much for someone to get the door?" Mrs. M. asked in awful accents.

"Coming!" With leaden steps I went and opened up. Too choked up to say good-bye, I couldn't bring myself to close the door on the two figures heading for the van. Arms dangling at my sides, I stared into a future without Mrs. M. giving me her orders for the day.

"Say it," came Mum's voice from behind me. "You blame me for the lot. But don't worry yourself, Ellie, I've never been one to cause trouble and I'm not about to start in my old age. I'll go upstairs and pack my suitcases."

Tempting as this offer was, I couldn't let things end this way. I would feel like a villain, and Ben had enough to contend with, given the bar sinister. Prying myself away from the open door, I went over to Mum and tried to give her a hug. She fended me off, declaring she couldn't take any more, and Sweetie greedily seized upon the notion that I was attacking her mistress. Leaping two feet in the air, she took a yank out of my skirt. I yelled. Mum squealed and Tobias, with a meow to waken the dead—to say nothing of the twins in the nursery—hurled himself into the fray. Jaws snapped. Teeth flashed. Eyes rolled until only the whites showed like boiled eggs. And when the fur settled, dog and cat were heading out the door.

"Sweetie! Stay!" Mum pressed a hand to her throbbing lips.

Obedient to her command, the little dog rushed back into the kitchen, all the way into the corner by the Welsh dresser, to retrieve the bone of earlier contention with Tobias. Only it wasn't a bone, it was the much-put-upon St. Francis, and nothing—not a bolt of lightning nor a heavenly voice thundering "Stop that dog"—could have stayed Sweetie's racing paws as she vanished into the great green yonder.

"She's not thinking clearly, poor little poppet" was Mum's verdict. "Who knows what she may do in her state of mind!"

"Eat St. Francis?" I asked.

"No! Take her own life! Don't think I am blaming you, Ellie, but I will never get over it if my darling, in a fit of despondency, throws herself over the cliff."

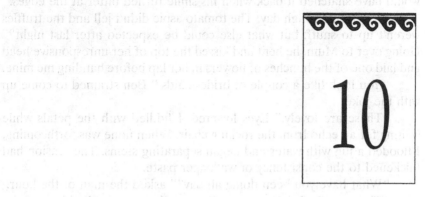

10

I was tempted to have Ben arrested for breaking and entering when he waltzed through the door that evening. Any fool knows there is a time and a place for everything, including husbands, and this was neither the hour nor the venue. I had put Abbey and Tam to bed, fed Jonas a make-shift meal of leftover cottage pie, and packed him off to the parlour to sleep it off. But I was still at a loss as to what to do with Mum. My mother-in-law's face, as she sat hunched in the rocking chair with Sweetie clutched to her makeshift bosom, was enough to send me right up the wall. But did her sonny boy notice?

No.

"How are my girls?" He whipped his hands out from behind his back and with a conjuror's flourish produced two identical bunches of sweet Williams. "Don't I get any welcome-home kisses? I'll have you know there are women starving in remote corners of the world for such an opportunity."

He was right, damn him! Never had he looked more diabolically handsome, with his dark hair crisped by the misting rain and his eyes almost the teal blue of the mixing bowl on the Welsh dresser. His innate elegance was apparent in the set of his shoulders and the turn of his trouser cuffs. And to think I hadn't had time to wash and starch my hair! Really, it was enough to make a woman pine for the convent. Mum did not lift her eyes from her dog.

"Home from the wars?" I bestowed a peck on Ben's cheek and would have snatched it back when his smile turned bitter at the edges.

"It's been a rough day. The tomato aspic didn't jell and the truffles weren't up to snuff, but what else could be expected after last night?" Going over to Mum, he bent and kissed the top of her unresponsive head and laid one of the bunches of flowers in her lap before handing me mine.

"You look like a couple of bridesmaids." Ben strained to come up with the joke.

"These are lovely." Eyes lowered, I fiddled with the petals while waiting for an echo from the rocking chair. When none was forthcoming, I flooded a jug with water and began separating stems. The tension had thickened to the consistency of wallpaper paste.

"What have you been doing all day?" asked the man of the hour.

"The usual"—I snapped a stalk savagely in two—"looking out the window to see what the neighbours are doing."

"We don't have any neighbours."

At that I lost my composure. A case of delayed anger, I suppose. Flinging the flowers into the sink, I whirled to face him. "*Thank* you for setting me *straight* on that one." I was about to say I'd had enough of everything and everyone, but Mum forestalled me.

She rose from her chair, and said, "I'm sorry, son, you've made your bed and will have to lie on it, but I can't live like this and won't subject Sweetie to constant hysteria"—she held the smirking dog closer—"she might make another attempt." And on that dismal note, the mistress and mutt vacated the room.

When the saucepans had stopped bouncing up and down on the stove, Ben availed himself of the rocking chair, flattening the abandoned sweet Williams in the process. Head flung wearily back, he addressed the ceiling. "We can't go on like this, Ellie."

"You don't say."

"What was all that about the dog?" He pried a finger under his collar as if I, along with his silk tie, had him about the throat.

"According to Mum, Sweetie threw herself in front of a bus coming past the gates. She was forced to administer mouth-to-mouth resuscitation."

"But the dog is fine."

"It's debatable. I have spent the last hour listening to your mother ponder aloud whether to take heroic measures should the need arise. Quite frankly, at this moment I am the one who needs to be on life support."

"Sweetheart, you need to relax." Ben got up and began pacing the length and breadth of the kitchen. After lap three, and barely winded, he placed a gentle hand on my shoulder. "Today of all days you could have let the housework go. Be damned to routine."

Who was this monster hiding inside my husband's body? Blinking back tears of fury, I lashed out at him. "See those dishes in the sink? See the twins' washing piled up in that basket? Does it look as though I couldn't tear myself away from the daily grind?"

"I'm not saying any of this has been easy on you"—Ben rubbed a hand across his forehead—"but the day hasn't been a piece of cake for me either. I went to see Dad at the Dark Horse this afternoon and got absolutely nowhere with him. He's still smarting from having been caught with his pants down, and the only way out of his embarrassment is to blame Mum for the whole affair. I had Freddy pick up my car and drive it back here, meaning I won't have to use yours again tomorrow, but otherwise we are no further forward."

"Well, I feel sorry for your father. To hell with Sweetie! Dad is the one liable to end up under a bus. Everyone makes mistakes, and I'm sure he is consumed with remorse."

"I can't believe you're taking his side." Ben brought a hand down on the working surface with such force that the cups and saucers in the sink chattered with fright. "I'm beginning to feel I never knew the man."

"Because he went for a nude swim with Beatrix Taffer?"

"No! Because he did not have the courtesy to marry my mother."

"She was a grown woman when they set up housekeeping."

"Ellie, you are not being sympathetic."

"You're right!" My voice went spiralling up to the ceiling. "For your information, your mother *sacked* Mrs. Malloy this afternoon. Yes!" I held up a shaking hand. "I can tell myself that Mum reacted with such virulence due to a deep-rooted fear that she and Lady Letitia might be sisters under the skin, but—"

"Lady who?" Ben looked completely at sea.

"Letitia. The wanton heroine of the library book Mum consigned to the flames of the Aga. And if it isn't bad enough that she refused to apologize to Mrs. Malloy when I explained that I was the one who had brought the book into the house, she stranded Mr. Watkins, the window cleaner, on a balcony for several hours, she accused me of driving her dog to suicide, and . . . she criticized my cottage pie."

"Ellie, I am not defending her, but I do think you could make allowances. Haven't I put up with assorted members of *your* batty family over the years?"

This was a low blow considering my sensitivity on the subject of Freddy's mother, Aunt Lulu, who shoplifts for a hobby; Aunt Astrid, who believes she is the reincarnation of Queen Victoria; and Uncle Maurice, who can't be left alone with any woman this side of the grave.

"You . . . you bastard!" The foul words were out of my mouth before I could call them back.

"So!" Ben curled his lip and retreated to the farthest reaches of the kitchen. "I should have known it wouldn't be long before you threw my illegitimacy in my face."

"Oh, for heaven's sake!"

"Whatever is going on in here?"

Mum burst into the kitchen with Jonas hard on her heels. Her wispy hair stuck up all over the place as if she had spent her time away from us pulling it out, and her nose twitched like a divining rod. "I had just tucked Sweetie up for the night when I heard the most fearful disturbance. I know, son"—her voice left me right out of the picture—"I know it is none of my business—"

"You're right." The cruel words slipped past my lips. "It is absolutely *none* of your business."

An appalled silence descended, but I refused to drop dead even though Mum stood there looking as small and lost as the statue of St. Francis. The situation could not be solved by the simple expedient of dusting her off and putting her back on the shelf. More's the pity. "I've known this was coming," Mum said in a tired little voice. "It was only a matter of time before I was driven out into the streets. . . ."

"Now then, lass"—Jonas placed a gentle hand on her shoulder—"b'aint no call to go upsetting yourself. Ellie here is a mite impetuous like most young'uns. She don't mean the half of what she says."

"Is that so?" I met Ben's stony expression unflinchingly before turning on my heel, and, without missing more than a few beats when my foot skidded out from under me on Tam's miniature fire engine, swept out into the hall and up the stairs. No sound of the cavalry headed by Rin Tin Tin in hot pursuit assailed my ears. Not that I cared. One minute to the second later I returned to the kitchen wearing my outdoor togs and carrying a brown suitcase. Unfortunately I was not possessed of a pair of arm-length black satin gloves to pull on with awful finality. But, then again, I don't claim to have Mrs. Malloy's style.

"I checked on the twins and they're sound asleep," I informed the assembled faces. "There's mediocre cottage pie and some salad in the fridge, so if you will kindly excuse me, I'm off."

Jonas's eyebrows went up and didn't come down; as for Mum's reaction or that of her son, what's-his-name, I did not waste time taking inventory.

"Wait!" Ben followed me out into the grey gauze of rain. We faced each other across twenty paces of courtyard like participants in a duel that must inevitably end in one of us being carried away on a stretcher and the other being bundled into a coach and driven hell-for-leather to the coast, where a boat would be waiting to set sail for France. We were lacking only our seconds. But doubtless Mum and Jonas would momentarily appear to stand beside Ben and hand him the requisite brace of pistols, along with informing him when to duck.

"I hope this isn't about your misplaced cuff links or something equally inconsequential." Staring coldly into my husband's fierce blue-green eyes, I stoically refused to be distracted by the wistful tendril of raven hair clinging to his damp brow.

"I can't let you go like this, Ellie."

Now we were talking.

"Just try and stop me!" Suitcase firmly in hand, I headed for the square of courtyard in front of the stables, where his car, old Heinz, was parked—courtesy of *my* cousin Freddy. A wry, bitter smile touched my lips in anticipation of Ben's next move. He would catch up with me in one masterful stride, spin me around to face him, and when he crushed me to his worsted wool chest, I would feel the anguished pounding of his heart and the hot rush of his breath upon my eyes . . . my face . . . my creamy neck, before his lips seized mine in a kiss that would bring both of us to our knees.

My steps slowed. But the earth didn't move and neither did my husband. His voice caught up with me as I reached the moat bridge. "As I was saying, my dear, I can't let you go without satisfying my curiosity on one subject."

"Which is?" I kept my back to him.

"Who is the chap camping out in the stable loft?"

"Do you mean the one who looks like a schoolteacher?"

"Is there more than one?"

"Not when I last looked." I turned wearily to face him. "But what with one thing and another, it has been one of those days. Anyway, there's no need to hide your straight razor. Mr. Savage is quite harmless."

"He told me he was a rock-and-roll singer, when I collided with him on my way to the house."

"So he will be when he learns to carry a tune."

"And just where did you dig him up?"

"He's a friend of Freddy's."

The former love of my life did not ask why my philanthropic cousin had not offered Mr. Savage a room at the cottage. He knew the answer to that one. What he said was "Ellie, this is madness. We cannot turn our home into a hotel."

We were now eyeing each other with the venom that only two people deeply in love can display.

"You don't say!" Standing with a hand on my hip à la Joan Crawford, I feigned a smile. "Excuse me, but I thought that was exactly what we're doing." I was a viper. And the best part is I felt not a whit of remorse. I even gave the knife a twist when adding, "On Mr. Savage's behalf, let me say he isn't living *in* the house, turning it upside down and everyone against me." Head down, I pawed the flagstones with my hoof, and when I looked up it was to see the garden door close behind the dark shadow of my husband's back. How could he let me go without a backwards glance?

Having successfully put myself out in the cold, I immediately wished there was some way out of the situation other than returning to the house, suitcase in hand, or heading for the open road. Reminding myself without much enthusiasm that blessed are the persecuted, I took a couple of steps back towards the garden door, but could not bring myself to mount the steps. All things considered, I would have preferred to drink weed killer rather than swallow the required dose of humiliation.

My decision to take Ben's car instead of my own wasn't entirely due to its being conveniently parked outside the stables. The Heinz was a temperamental beast liable to break down if another vehicle looked at it cross-eyed. With a bit of luck I wouldn't get beyond our gates before it began sending up smoke signals in an attempt at summoning assistance, thus forcing my husband to come charging to the rescue, remorse flowing from every pore as he prayed he would reach me while I still had my eyebrows.

Serve him right! The rain had let up, meaning it wouldn't put a damper on things, and there was still enough of a breeze to fan the would-be flames nicely. Somewhat cheered, I tossed the suitcase in the backseat and climbed behind the wheel. With the wind breathing down my neck through the open window I turned the key in the ignition. My reward was an ominous grunt and grind, and when I pressed the pedal to the floor, all hell broke loose under the bonnet—everything from *ping*s and *thump*s to what sounded like an official explosion. So far no smoke, but you can't have everything—including, it would seem, a husband hot-hoofing it to save his beloved car, if not his wife, from extinction.

Who would have believed it? Ben had been known to wake up in a cold sweat if he thought the Heinz in danger of catching a chill from being left in the stable with the door open a crack. He would race outside to tuck a couple of woolly blankets over the torn seats when the temperature dipped to dangerous lows. I even suspected he had made provisions for the car in his will. So where was Sir Galahad? Twisting my head almost off my neck, I looked back to the house. Not a curtain twitched. Not a door peeked open. Nothing but the blank-eyed stare of the tall windows and a glimpse of Mr. Watkins's ladder propped up against the balcony on which he had been stranded.

Sadly, he had not had the stamina in his depleted state to move it to his van, but I was made of sterner stuff. There had to be a way for me to remove myself from the home turf, even if I could not take my own car because the Heinz blocked its exit from the stable. . . .

"Having a spot of bother, Mrs. Haskell?" The kindly voice nearly did me in. Mr. Savage stood beside my open window, having appeared out of nowhere like a genie bent on granting me three wishes. It had been several hours since we last met, but time had been kind to him. His grey pinstripe suit had not picked up any wrinkles, his hair was neatly plastered down, and his smile was that of a true troubadour. It banished the clouds that had descended upon my soul, causing me to do the unthinkable—confide my troubles to a man who owed me nothing but the roof over his head.

"Nothing's wrong of any major importance." I blinked to ward off tears in the duly ascribed manner of the damsel in distress. "I was about to run away from home, but the wretched car won't start."

His bespectacled eyes begged me to say it wasn't so; then they spotted the suitcase in the backseat and hope fled like a wayward dove.

"Has there been trouble"—his chin quivered—"over my being here?"

"Of course not." I smiled bravely up at him.

"Did I eat you out of house and home at breakfast?"

"Now, stop that! My husband"—nobly giving the devil his due—"my husband is not one to count the eggs."

"Then . . . if I may be so bold"—Mr. Savage cupped a hand

around his mouth to prevent his words being transported by the wind back to the house—"is the problem your *mother-in-law*?"

"She's going through a difficult time," I hedged.

"But that's no excuse for her to make your life a living hell." Mr. Savage blushed at the profanity. "You don't deserve such treatment, Mrs. Haskell. One has to know you for only a few hours . . . minutes . . . seconds even, to know that you are deserving of the utmost ador—respect."

"That's life!" Bending my head over the steering wheel, I willed him to pour more balm over my wounded spirit, and he came through like a trooper.

"Were I ever to be blessed with a wife such as you"—his hand touched mine with gentlemanly restraint—"I would wash my mother's mouth out with soap if she said one cross word to you. To me you're a goddess, Mrs. Haskell."

"You mustn't exaggerate."

"You took me in out of the storm."

"It wasn't raining that hard." I mustered a smile.

"For you, I would slay dragons!"

A mother-in-law by any other name! My spirits were rising by the second.

"I'd move mountains for you." His spectacles had misted up.

"That's awfully kind," I said, "but what would really help would be for you to help me get this car running."

"More than happy!" Mr. Savage positively beamed as I moved over for him to climb aboard. Life was certainly looking up. Out of the corner of my eye I saw the garden door crack open a full half inch. Good! Let the nosy parker wonder what was going on in the front seat of his car. Mr. Savage clearly had a way with motor vehicles. And when Heinz gave the soft-throated purr of a pussycat being nudged awake by its owner's foot, I could think of only one way to reward my knight in a pinstripe suit.

"Mr. Savage?"

"Yes, Mrs. Haskell?"

"Would you care to chauffeur me into the village?"

"I . . . I . . . regret I must decline the privilege." His pale face flushed.

Properly snubbed, I told him I quite understood.

"No, you don't." He caught himself in time to eliminate any suggestion of a rebuke. "A woman of your incomparable gifts would be unlikely to suspect the brutal truth."

"Which is?"

"That I can't drive. Mother would never let me learn."

"What a dreadful waste," I said with absolute sincerity. "You are a natural if ever I saw one, Mr. Savage."

"Do you really think so?" With a smile like his, who needed headlights?

Feeling happier than I had in minutes, I impulsively asked if he would like to embark on his first lesson.

"That would be super."

"Only one small caveat." I wagged a warning finger. "Do not, if you value your life, touch any of those knobs."

"Whatever you say." He jerked his hand from the danger zone and fixed his bewildered spectacles upon my face. "Would the wheels fall off?"

"That innocuous-looking panel is the radio, and my husband does not look kindly upon anyone who changes the station."

"Entirely his prerogative," Mr. Savage replied sanguinely. "Not a word of criticism shall pass my lips." Heaving up in his seat, he leaned out the window, his head straining on his neck as he looked first right, then left. "Your mentioning the wireless, Mrs. Haskell, was a timely reminder that I had my little tape recorder with me when I came from the stables and that I set it down on the ground before speaking to you. Oh, super-duper! Here it is!" Up he came for air, holding the small plastic box with its hundred and one buttons, for all the world, as it were, our last hope of sending out a distress signal to the mainland. "I was hoping I would see you"—head bent, Mr. Savage buffed away at fingerprints, imagined or otherwise, on the shiny black surface—"I wanted to tell you that I wrote my first song this afternoon."

"Congratulations."

"It's titled 'The Fair Maid of Chitterton Fells.' "

"How catchy!" Trying not to look as though I harboured any suspicion that I might be the inspiration behind his little ditty, I smoothed back my tousled tresses and looked at him through rain-darkened lashes. The shadows painted pinstripes on his face to match his suit as he hugged the tape recorder to his sunken chest.

"It is a paean to love at first sight."

"Lovely!"

Was I guilty of a grave error in judgment? The precariousness of my situation hit home when Mr. Savage, with an exuberant "Toot! Toot!" set the car in motion with a backwards lurch and a forward thrust. Away we went in leaps and bounds. The iron gates came rushing at us as if this were the local gymkhana and they were the first obstacle to be sailed over before our horses took the water jump.

"Brake! Brake!" I shouted.

"No problem!" That ticking sound wasn't a bomb; he had inadvertently yanked on the signal indicator.

"Hit the pedal!"

"Right!"

"No! The one on the left!" When I pried my hands away from my eyes, it was to discover that Mr. Savage had brought the Heinz to a standstill three quarters of an inch from the cliff edge. From below came the disappointed sigh of the turbulent sea.

He beamed at me. "How's that?"

"Wonderful! But don't even think about trying to cross the finish line." While he was making his eight-point turn, I clung to the edge of my seat, along with the hope that Ben would put in an eleventh-hour appearance.

He did not do the husbandly thing, but the remainder of the drive into the village was reasonably sedate. No more playing vehicular hopscotch. A single foray up the embankment, and only once rearing up on our hind wheels to chase a squirrel up a tree.

"Think I'm getting the hang of it?" Mr. Savage's smile penetrated my closed lids like strong sunlight.

"You should take up driving professionally."

"I may look into it if my career in rock and roll doesn't take off." We were going the wrong way down a one-way street. But why be a spoilsport! The lampposts had the good sense to dodge out of the way, and Barclays Bank and the town clock could give as good as they got. Besides which, we were within swinging distance of the sign heralding the Dark Horse.

"This is it, Mr. Savage."

"You mean . . ." He peeled his hands off the wheel to stare at the pub with its ye old oak timbers and leaded windows.

"We have arrived at my destination." I had to raise my voice over the crunch of metal on metal as the Heinz nosed onto the pavement to collide with a disposal bin, rocking it on its cement socks. "Do you want to wait while I go inside, or . . . ?" I left the question ajar, along with my door, as I climbed out.

"I would be honoured to join you in a lemonade." He turned off the engine as if he had been in the habit for years.

"That's awfully kind of you." I closed the car door on his hopes of thumbing a metaphoric finger at his mother. "However, I came here only to deliver the suitcase in the backseat. It belongs to my father-in-law, who is putting up here."

"You aren't really running away from home?" Spectacles agog, Mr. Savage followed me onto the sidewalk.

A sigh feathered the hair back from my brow. "Only for half an hour or so." I was about to suggest that we could take the longcut home in the interest of putting the wind up my loving family, but I was not a complete jade. The poor, susceptible man must not be subjected to prolonged proximity with my charming self. The scent of Pine-Scrub emanating from my skin might lead him to do something foolish, such as offer to buy me a bag of potato chips. I would see the prodigal father, give him a quick talking-to, and tell Mr. Savage that I would drive home.

What he lacked in brute strength he more than made up for in gallantry as he proceeded towards the etched glass door of the Dark Horse, practically on all fours, dragging the carcass—I mean the suitcase —along the ground. When we were blocking the path of a couple of decidedly merry blokes who appeared uncertain whether they were coming or going, he remembered he had left the tape recorder in the car, where anyone could steal it.

Rather than watch him hobble back to the curb like Caliban, I did the honours this time. Then without much more ado we entered the saloon bar to be blinded by the dazzling array of copper warming pans and ornamental horseshoes. Elbowing our way through the crush of local yokels, we crossed in front of the gas log fire to reach the bar with its two-inch coat of varnish and enough brass handles to steer a rocket ship.

"Out on a date, madam?" The woman at the helm paused in mopping up spills to look from me to Mr. Savage and back again.

Taking a deep breath of malt-liquor air, I hugged the tape recorder to my chest. "Whatever are you doing here, Mrs. Malloy?"

"Earning a living." Pride inflated her considerable bosom. "I'm the new barmaid. It's me life's calling." She picked up a glass, blew on it, gave it a buff with her cloth, and set it down with exaggerated care. "Sad to say, I didn't get to answer the summons until this evening, after I was given the heave-ho from me job at Merlin's Court. But as they say, Mrs. H., when one door closes, another one opens. I had a word with me old chum Edna Pickle after I took Mr. Watkins home. She suggested this might be a good career move."

"How is Mr. Watkins?" I flustered.

"Not long for this world, from the sound of him." Shooing my hand off the counter with her cloth, Mrs. Malloy buffed fiercely away at the unsightly fingerprints. "But we have to bear in mind that only the good die young." A sigh ruffled her purple eyelashes. "What goes to explain why your mother-in-law is still numbered among the living. As for you, my lad"—she pointed a finger that made Peter Savage jump—"the least you could've done to earn your keep was make the old girl a cup of tea and stir in a couple of spoons of arsenic."

Mr. Savage, far from looking shocked, produced a smile as untarnished as any of the brass. But some of us still had a sense of what was fitting in civilized society.

"Life will get back to normal at Merlin's Court one of these days," I said firmly. "And you will come back to us, Mrs. Malloy."

"Don't count your chickens."

"Meanwhile, you have this job." I held on to the tape recorder as if it were a life preserver that would enable me to keep my head above water. "It was good of Mrs. Pickle to suggest you apply."

"One in a million is Edna," returned Mrs. M., conveniently forgetting that she had routinely kept me abreast of her pal's shortcomings.

"There's nothing like a woman friend." Mr. Savage looked dreamily into my face.

"I shall be spending the night at her house." Mrs. M. folded her arms, hefting her taffeta bosom up to her chin. "Wouldn't take no for an answer, would Edna. She didn't want me to be alone. Not under the circumstances. Being reduced to a charity case don't suit me, but I've ways of making it up to her." Gimlet stare. "I've decided to leave her me china poodle, the one I always promised would be yours after my day."

"That's as it should be." I endeavoured to sound suitably crushed.

"Well, let's cut the cackle. It won't do me no good to get the sack twice in one day." She reached for one of the brass taps. "A pint of bitter for the gent, and what about yourself, Mrs. H.?"

My response never made it past my lips because we were in that instant hemmed in by an influx of stein-hefting, tongue-lolling imbibers, one of whom gained the advantage of added height by standing on the suitcase Mr. Savage had set down on the floor. This brief respite was not wasted on Mrs. M., who clasped a heavily ringed hand to her throat.

"Where's me brains, Mrs. H.? You haven't come down here for a belt of lemonade; you packed your bags and walked out of that hellhole you call home, didn't you now?"

"No! I'm here on behalf of my father-in-law."

Either my voice was lost in the roar of the crowd, or she didn't believe me. No doubt about it, she had brightened considerably. "There, now, ducky! What you don't want to do is go from the frying pan into the fire." She looked at my companion and pursed her damson lips. "Mr.

What's-his-name here could be a prince, I'm not saying he isn't, but he's getting you on the rebound."

"Am I?" Mr. Savage swallowed his Adam's apple.

"Of course not!" I thumped the tape recorder down on the bar for emphasis.

"You can come and live with me," offered my Lady Bountiful. "You can even bring the twins if you're one hundred percent set on it."

A man in a tweed cap and knitted waistcoat asked for a pint of mild in a voice that was anything but, and was roundly told to bugger off.

"That's awfully kind of you, Mrs. Malloy," I said, "but the only reason I came here was to bring Dad his suitcase. He's staying here until things sort themselves out."

"So I heard. Room 4, top of the stairs, first on the right." Wiping her hands on her apron front, she began pulling on the taps and foaming up the glasses at a furious rate. To my mind the day was wearing thin, but by the expedient of putting one foot in front of the other I made my way, with Mr. Savage in tow, past a pair of settles with tapestry cushions and through an open doorway into a narrow hall with the Ladies and Gents to our left and on our right a flight of stairs with more twists and turns than a gothic novel. It wasn't until I was nearing the top step that I realized I had left the tape recorder on the bar. Luckily, every ounce of Mr. Savage's being was concentrated on dragging the suitcase onto the landing, which was no bigger than a handkerchief. While he took a breather I knocked on the door of Room 4.

Dad took his time opening up. Even then all that came poking through the crack was the tip of his white beard.

"I don't want more towels. What do you think I'm doing up here, running a Turkish bath?"

Understandably unnerved by the lion's roar, Mr. Savage's spectacles fogged up, but I managed to remain calm.

"Dad, it's me—Ellie!"

"Never rains but it pours!" Grudgingly, my father-in-law removed his foot from the crack and granted admittance. Behind him on the chest of drawers was a television with the sound turned off but the picture going full blast.

"Very nice," I said, looking around. Truth be told, the radiator was the handsomest piece of furniture in the room. The wardrobe had *not* seen better days, the walls were boring beige, the bedspread hospital-green, and the exposed pipes of the wash basin were unpleasantly reminiscent of someone who had ended up on the wrong side of Good Queen Bess and been hung, drawn, and quartered. As for Dad, he was not himself. His bald head was more in need of a shine than his shoes, and his attempt to brighten up the place with an artful arrangement of fruit and veggies on the windowsill made my heart ache. Was he hearkening back to his shop in Tottenham, or laying in provisions for a long siege?

"We brought your suitcase."

"So I see." Dad glared at Mr. Savage, who was dragging the leather carcass over the threshold. "And he'll be your mother-in-law's solicitor, I suppose."

"Don't be silly." I sat down on the bed and felt it sag to within an inch of the floor. "He's a rock-and-roll singer. A friend of Freddy's, who—"

"Is that right?" To my surprise, Dad's brown eyes showed interest.

"I'm just starting out. Local gigs, that sort of thing, until the job market opens up." Mr. Savage cleared his throat and took a couple of steps towards the windowsill. "Would you mind if I had an orange? I've been falling behind in my intake of vitamin C." He had said the magic words.

"Help yourself." Dad tried to sound gruff and failed, which encouraged me to get down to the nitty-gritty of my visit.

"We do wish you'd come home," I told him.

"Who's we?" He went right on watching Mr. Savage peel his orange.

"Ben and I, and . . . . Mum." My voice could have done with some oil to cure the squeaks. "There's no doubt in the world that she misses you desperately. All it would take from you would be a teensy-weensy apology"—I crossed my fingers behind my back—"and a carefully worded assurance that you have no romantic interest in Tricks Taffer. Come on, Dad." I leaned towards him. "Surely it would be worth it in the interest of salvaging a thirty-eight-year relationship."

"Did Magdalene say she wanted me back?"

"Not in so many words, but . . ."

"But me no buts!" His face turned so red, I was afraid it would set his beard on fire as he stomped up and down in front of the bed. "Magdalene was the one who turned me out on the street, so if there's any running to be done, she'd better be the one to get her legs in gear."

"But think of all the good times," I implored him.

"Like when?"

"Like when you were first in love."

"In what?" This bellow almost caused Mr. Savage to swallow the apple he had raised to his lips, but when Dad next spoke, it was in a curiously flattened voice, as if all the air had been let out of his lungs.

"Speaking of rock and roll, I had a decent singing voice myself once upon a time."

"Did you?" I sat absolutely still.

"Would you believe that back in the early days I once wrote a song for Maggie?" Incredibly, he was smiling, faintly but surely, and his eyes looked past me to the days when he and Mum were young and life and love were filled with promise. And suddenly, as I watched Mr. Savage reach for a banana, an idea popped into my head that made just as much sense as the notion of Dad doing volunteer work at a local greengrocers.

11

Absence does not always make the heart grow fonder. When I approached the bench—I mean the bar—and asked Mrs. Malloy if she had put the tape recorder behind the counter for safekeeping, she produced it with a wallop that would have given a woman with stronger insides than myself a prolapse.

"Anything else I can do for your majesty?"

In case she was on commission, I ordered a large gin and tonic. Then, horror of horrors, when she rang up the price I remembered I had not brought my handbag with me. The car keys were in my raincoat pocket, but no matter how far I pulled out the lining, I couldn't come up with a penny in loose change. Asking if she would kindly keep a running tab, I looked around for a table that wasn't under her eagle eye.

All were occupied except one, bang up next to the bar, so there I retreated with a drink that was almost as tall as I, which I couldn't drink because I would have to drive home. Even if Mr. Savage should abandon his newfound musical collaboration with Dad and return to me this side of morning, I wouldn't feel comfortable letting him drive in the dark.

Under different circumstances I could have asked Mrs. Malloy to let me write her an IOU. But given her present miffed state, the best I could hope for was to be ordered out back to do the washing-up. For a doleful few moments I sat twiddling the knobs of the tape recorder before depositing it on the floor in hope that it would be mistaken for a black leather handbag. I knew I was being silly. All I had to do was go upstairs to Room 4 and borrow some money from Dad. But on that particular night I balked at the thought of looking like a helpless female. If the shoe fits, you don't *have* to wear it.

A woman had come into the pub. A woman wearing a headscarf and a furtive expression. Not only did I recognize her, I presumed on our brief acquaintance to stand up and hail her over to my table.

"Hello! It's me, Ellie Haskell." The welcoming smile died on my lips. Frizzy Taffer's response wasn't one of unbridled enthusiasm. She actually backed into a couple of people, a bald man in a loud plaid jacket and a woman in black leather, before moving with lagging steps towards me.

"What a nice surprise." Her nose should have grown at voicing this blatant lie. It was already red and puffy, as were her eyes, suggesting either a bad cold (which she hadn't had that morning) or a prolonged bout of crying. Frizzy's face was as drab as her raincoat. Not knowing what else to say, I told her I hadn't expected to see her again so soon.

"I never come here." Frizzy checked the knot of her headscarf. Not a single hair escaped onto her forehead, making her look like a nun who, though prepared to humour modern times by wearing civvies, would not forgo her wimple.

"This isn't one of my usual haunts," I assured her.

"Really?" Her red eyes shied away from my double gin and tonic.

"Just a prop." I gave the glass a *ping* with my finger, almost sending it toppling over. "I came to bring Dad his suitcase and am still here because I can't face going home yet."

"I know the feeling." Frizzy shed her reserve but not her scarf, and sat down, elbows on the table, hands under her chin, to support its tremble.

Resuming my own seat and trying not to notice that Mrs. Malloy was hanging over the bar, eavesdropping as if her job depended on catching every word, I said, "You were a brick letting Dad stay at your house last night. I do hope none of this has caused an upset between you and Tricks."

"She'd have liked Mr. Haskell to stay with us until he settled things with his wife." Frizzy reached absently for my gin and tonic. "But you know Tricks, nothing ever gets her down." This was said with surprising venom.

"How about a nice bag of crisps, on the house?" Mrs. Malloy gushed.

For once my frown had the desired effect, and my former daily retreated behind the bar in the manner of the Oracle of Delphi subsiding behind a cloud to bone up on his lines in readiness for the next supplicant.

Downing the gin and tonic in one swallow, Frizzy stared at the glass as if unsure what it was or where it had come from. "This can't be happening," she said softly. "I'm a nice person."

"One drink isn't wicked."

"What?" She looked at me as if I were no more real than the now-empty glass. Then she started to cry as if her insides were being put through the wringer and her tears squeezed out with every turn of the handle. It was awful, so awful that I couldn't speak, let alone reach out a hand to her in her misery.

"I had to get out of that house or I would have torn her hair out. That would have been a case of the punishment fitting the crime." Frizzy placed a hand on her headscarf. "Because of my mother-in-law's carelessness," she told me dully, "I'm bald as an egg."

I couldn't believe what I was hearing.

Frizzy continued with a sob. "Tricks lost the cap to her bottle of Nake-It—"

"That's the stuff you use on your legs and under your arms instead of shaving, Mrs. H.," explained Mrs. Malloy, who tends to think I just got off the Ark. "My third, or it could have been me fourth, husband used to say I had the loveliest armpits of any woman he had known, but don't let me keep you from your story, Mrs. T."

Frizzy trembled. "She poured the Nake-It into an empty bottle of Bright and Breezy Cream Plush shampoo. Not a word to anyone about what she had done. I never thought twice when I went and washed my hair this evening. Why would I? And I gave the beastly stuff plenty of time to work, because I didn't rinse it off my head for at least fifteen minutes. While I was massaging my scalp—trying to get the stuff to sudse, the baby started fussing and Dawn was carrying on to her dad about the goldfish that got cooked to death. So I wrapped a towel around my head to go and sort things out. When I did get a moment to stick my head back under the tap, there was my hair all over the towel, ready to be shaken out into the dustbin."

"Your lovely curls!" I could have cried for her.

"My one claim to looking halfway decent." She wept.

"Whatever did your husband say?"

"Tom was livid with his mother. And I know I shouldn't have gone off the deep end when he told me it would grow back. He was just trying to make me feel better."

"Men don't have our sensitivity." Mrs. Malloy poked at her own black-and-white confection with unwonted nervousness as if afraid it would come away in her hands.

"Was Tricks upset?" I asked my table companion.

"She said we should look on the bright side, that now I could stop worrying about my dandruff." A faraway look came into Frizzy's eyes, and it took a moment for me to realize this was because she was watching the entrance door, or, rather, the young woman who had just walked through it. "That's Pamela Pomeroy," she said in a frozen voice.

"Why, so it is!" Under the circumstances, I didn't know whether to wave frantically or feign poor eyesight. Too late for debate. Pamela had spotted us and was heading our way, her ponytails waggling like spaniel ears and her brown eyes brimming with enthusiasm. Was this the same person who had stood with slouched shoulders and hangdog expression in Lady Kitty's shadow that morning at the Taffer residence?

"Thank goodness I've found you both!"

"You were out looking for us?" Considering I had met her only that once and hadn't received the impression that she and Frizzy were fast friends, I inevitably concluded that Pamela was one of a search party sent out to comb the hills and dales around Chitterton Fells for the missing wives. Was there a bounty on Frizzy's poor bald head along with mine?

"No, I had no idea you would be here." Pamela gave a schoolgirl laugh as she sat down on the third of the four chairs. "But I had been thinking about how sweet and nice you both seemed, so it has to be fate! I was beyond desperate when I got up from the dinner table and ran out of the house. If the pond hadn't looked so grotty, I swear I would have thrown myself in. That would have served Mumsie Kitty right, don't you think?"

Misery does love company. Frizzy brightened perceptibly and I immediately lost interest in my own troubles.

"Whatever happened?" I asked before Mrs. Malloy could take a dive off the bar.

Pamela bit her lip, looking for all the world like a fourth former

who, having hung her hockey stick on the wrong peg, now waited in dread
of a summons to the headmistress's office. "Mumsie Kitty invited Reverend Spike and her husband, Gladstone, over for dinner to talk about the
St. Anselm's Summer Fête. We were all at the dining room table, because
with it being a special occasion, my father-in-law, Bobsie Cat, my husband, Allan, and I got to eat with the grown-ups." Hiccupping sob. "And
right in the middle of the treacle pudding, Mumsie Kitty asked me if I
had remembered to take my temperature to see if this was the day for the
big O."

"The what?" Frizzy's jaw dropped an inch or so lower than mine.

"You know." Pamela was knitting her fingers together. "My time to
ovulate. I've never been very regular, and Mumsie Kitty always carries on
as if it's my fault for not being better organized. But I couldn't believe it,
and Reverend Spike almost dropped the jug of custard when Mumsie
whipped out a thermometer and stuck it in my mouth."

"I would have died," I said.

"I nearly did! I was so surprised, I almost choked on the thing."

"See if this will drown your sorrows!" Mrs. Malloy materialized with
a loaded tray and would have availed herself of the vacant seat if some
inconsiderate oaf hadn't summoned her back to the bar for a double
martini on the double.

"I haven't reached the worst part yet." Pamela took a reviving sip
from her glass. "When Mumsie Kitty pulled out the thermometer, she
said all systems were go and not a moment was to be lost if there was ever
to be a Pomeroy heir. She ordered Allan out of his chair and told him to
rush me up to the bedroom and get busy."

"Did your husband flare up?" Frizzy had almost finished her drink
and was eyeing mine.

"He couldn't speak. The poor darling suffers from asthma, and a
confrontation with his mother always brings on an attack. I know the
Spikes must have misinterpreted his heavy breathing. It was all so humiliating. Bobsie Cat tried to speak up for me. He's a dear, but like always he
didn't get out three words before Mumsie Kitty ordered *him* to his room.
I don't suppose he minded. He would get to play with his trains in peace.
But something inside me snapped. Right in front of the vicar and her
husband I told my mother-in-law she was an old battle-axe."

"Good for you," I said, passing Frizzy my glass.

"I just couldn't bear it." Pamela's eyes grew as big as the cardboard
coasters on the table. "The thought of Mumsie Kitty sitting there in the
dining room, watching for the chandelier to start rocking like mad, was
the last straw. I've always told Allan his mother would be in the bedroom

with us if she could, cheering him on from the sidelines. But before tonight I never dared stand up to her. When I said I was leaving, she called me a worthless, ungrateful girl. She said I wasn't to dare take the bike she lent me. Would you believe it? That bike has to be thirty years old, and she *gave* it to me; I swear she did. The woman is a monster!" Pamela looked from Frizzy to me. "I'm sure you both know that I got to marry Allan as a result of winning the pie-baking contest Mumsie Kitty organized so as to find him a suitably domesticated wife."

I was about to tell her that I had married Ben after renting him for a family reunion weekend, but Frizzy interjected, "It doesn't matter how you got fixed up if you love each other."

"And we do!" Pamela gripped the edge of the table. "We're crazy about each other and have been ever since we met as teenagers at the St. Anselm's Summer Fête. It was luck"—a rosy blush made her look more than ever like a schoolgirl—"the most brilliant luck that out of ninety-seven women I baked the best pie and won my darling Allan's hand in marriage. It was as much for his sake as mine—to give him some breathing space—that I walked out tonight, but wonderful as he is, it does bother me a bit that he didn't try to stop me."

"Join the club," I said glumly. "Ben didn't give his mother the sack when she had words with me."

"And come to think of it, Tom didn't get down on his hands and knees when *I* headed for the door," supplied Frizzy.

"You mean we three are in the same boat?" Pamela no longer looked as if she had been dropped from the hockey team.

"Sad but true," I informed her.

"And room for one more." Frizzy toasted the vacant chair. "Usually I don't believe in fate and all that stuff, but . . ." Her voice wobbled to a fade-out.

A shiver crept down my spine, the result no doubt of the entry door being subjected to a prolonged series of openings and closings; anyway, I heard myself saying in rather an insistent voice that it wasn't a mind-boggling coincidence, this being a one-pub town, that we three fugitives should meet up here.

Mrs. Malloy did her best to make our collective woes a paying proposition for the Dark Horse as she scuttled out on her stilt heels with yet another round of gin and tonics. I was still reluctant to indulge, but I felt compelled to offer a toast. "Down with mothers-in-law!"

"Oh, I do feel better," Pamela sighed as the three of us clinked glasses, "even though I don't know how I'll ever face Reverend Spike again."

"Well, speak of the devil!"

At Mrs. Malloy's outburst we all turned, some of us a trifle woozily, to see St. Anselm's presiding clergywoman enter the unhallowed portals of the saloon bar. Amazing, how quickly the place thinned out. Several ladies I recognized from the Hearthside Guild swiftly vacated by the back door, and a grey-haired gentleman in country tweeds, who had petitioned that fruit juice be substituted for wine at communion, shot past Mrs. Spike like a pointer, nose to the ground.

To add to the confusion, my heart started to thump. Not because I minded Eudora seeing me with a glass in my hand—the reverend lady had on occasion taken a glass of sherry at my house—but because it was no longer possible to deny that something beyond the realm of chance was happening here. Deep in my soul I knew that this day had by seconds and minutes been leading inexorably up to the moment when the circle would be complete.

Surprising the world did not stop spinning and Eudora did not stop dead in her tracks when I experienced this mind-boggling revelation. She walked up to the bar just like any other customer.

"What'll it be, a half pint of best bitter?" Mrs. Malloy flexed her purple lips into an ingratiating smile.

"Nothing to drink, thank you. I stopped by on the off chance that you might remember an elderly lady coming in for a packet of cigarettes."

"Does she have blue hair? White hair?" Mrs. M. replied with the wariness of a lawbreaker sniffing out an undercover cop.

"Dark, with silver streaks. A bit on the shaggy side." Eudora ran an agitated hand through her windblown locks.

"Oh, *her*! Why didn't you say right off the bat that you was talking about your ma-in-law, instead of making a sermon about it?" Chuckling at her little joke, Mrs. M. turned sideways to wipe off the counter and give me, Pamela, and Frizzy a here-we-go-again wink.

"You've seen her?" Eudora gripped her handbag with both hands.

"I should say I have! These last few weeks I haven't once been over to the vicarage to have a cuppa with Mrs. Pickle and to give her a few pointers on how to get her work done this side of Christmas without that old lady buggering about the kitchen, looking for her fags." Elbows on the bar, Mrs. M. leaned forward in patent hope of having a fiver pressed into her hand in return for this information.

"Yes, but have you seen her in here tonight?"

"Can't say I have." Having given vent to an irritated toss of the head, Mrs. M. remembered she was a member of the reverend's flock and asked the lanky young man working the other end of the bar if he had recently served an elderly woman with an Irish brogue and a nose like a parrot.

"Not me!" He kept right on manning the brass taps.

"Thank you anyway." Eudora extended a hand to Mrs. Malloy, who, instead of shaking it, made the assumption she was about to receive a blessing. St. Anselm's is very High Church. Indeed, the ugly rumour persists that a photo of the Pope hangs in one of the vicarage bedrooms. Eyes closed, purple lips pursed, Mrs. M. humbly lowered her receptive head.

A woman of the cloth does not punch a time clock. Duty done, Eudora turned to leave and in so doing came within inches of our table. Pamela was seated with her back to her, but it was she Eudora focussed on first.

"My dear, I was so worried about you. How are you holding up?"

"I didn't throw myself in the pond."

"We've been telling her there are better ways of drowning her sorrows." Frizzy raised her glass in wobbly salute.

"Well, don't overdo." Eudora's worried glance included me, and with some justification. For reasons I didn't delve into, I had decided to let the Heinz cool his wheels outside the Dark Horse, when it was time to leave—with or without Mr. Savage—and I was now on my third sip of Mother's Ruin.

"I couldn't help overhearing your enquiries about your mother-in-law," I said. "We're all a bit keyed up on that particular subject."

"So things aren't any better with Ben's mother?"

"Worse!"

"And life at my house isn't all sunshine and flowers." Frizzy nibbled on her slice of lime as if intent on sucking out the last drop of alcohol. "This isn't like me, you know. I haven't drunk anything stronger than lemon squash in years."

"Desperate measures for desperate times!" Her spaniel-ear ponytails wagging, Pamela hoisted her glass and cried, "Down the red lane!"

"Is there anything I can do to help?" Eudora by now looked extremely concerned, and without doubt it was in her ministerial capacity that she pulled out the fourth chair and sat down. But we three musketeers were all eager to hear about her mother-in-law troubles, and halfway into her sorry tale she became a fellow victim with no easy answers to an age-old problem.

"I've always tried to be sensitive to the fact that Bridget is Gladstone's stepmother. I never wanted her to think I would have treated his own mother differently. That's the reason I tried not to fuss overly about her smoking, although Gladstone hates it worse than I do. The dear man tends to be chesty and Mrs. Pickle is always offering to make him up one of her potions."

"Don't go wasting your money." Mrs. Malloy stuck her nose over the bar yet again. "If Edna had the power, she would have come up with a brew years ago as would have made sure she got her heart's desire."

Was she talking about Jonas? I wondered. Did Mrs. Pickle have serious designs upon his virtue?

"If I thought she could work magic, I would ask her for something to make my hair grow back, or better yet . . ." Flushing a deep orange, Frizzy said quickly, "Is your mother-in-law's smoking the biggest bone of contention?"

"I'm afraid not." Eudora shook her head. "Even worse is her way of talking about the Bible." The rest of us grouped closer around the table as she lowered her voice. "She *will* go on about it being even spicier than *Lady Chatterley's Lover.* But enough said, I shouldn't be running Bridget down, especially when she's not here to defend herself."

"Oh, go on, ducks!" Mrs. Malloy set down more drinks before gathering up the empties. "Have a gin. Anyone watching will think it's holy water."

"Thank you." Perhaps to resist the temptation of reaching for the glass, Eudora fingered the bracelet at her wrist as if it were a set of rosary beads. "Yesterday the bishop called on me to discuss church business, and I couldn't get Mother out of the room. Within five minutes she had started in on St. Paul being a frustrated old bachelor who would have been better occupied improving his golf swing than poking his nose into other people's married lives."

"If I'd been you," Pamela offered by way of support, "I would have rushed over to the church to drown myself in the font."

Eudora smiled wanly at her. The vicar had lost weight, even in her nose, and her glasses kept sliding off. "I didn't know where to look when she laid into St. Peter, saying he should have thought about his husbandly responsibilities—such as taking out the dustbins and helping the kiddies with their homework—before bunking off to become a saint. But the absolute worst part"—Eudora had to struggle to continue—"was the bit about the circumcision. Mother said it was the funniest part in the whole Bible and how anyone could keep a straight face at the idea of Abraham summoning all the men and telling them that God had spoken to him, so if they would all meekly drop their drawers he would wield the knife and get busy with his cropping. She actually asked the bishop if he would have stood still for that, or run like hell."

"Did you have a row with her after he left?" I asked.

"I told her I wasn't pleased." Eudora took an inadvertent sip of gin and immediately pushed the glass away. "The whole thing was extremely upsetting for Gladstone. He had a sponge cake in the oven at the time I told him what had gone on—he's so hoping he'll win a ribbon this year at the fête—and when he remembered to take the cake out, it was burnt to a cinder. And speaking of burnt offerings"—she drew a shaky breath—"when we returned from the hall this evening, it was to discover there had been a fire in my study."

"No!" Frizzy's hands started to shake. She reached for another glass.

"Only a small one, thank God! My desk was hardly damaged, but next Sunday's sermon had gone up in smoke. Accidents will happen, I know, but what upset me was Mother's calm announcement that she had been smoking and had left the room to make herself a cup of tea. She hadn't even bothered with an ashtray—just left her cigarette dangling off the paperweight, the one Gladstone won for flower arranging at our last parish. I lost my temper, and by the time I had cooled down, Mother was nowhere to be found."

"Did your husband give her an ear full?" I asked.

"Gladstone was beyond words. He went to bed with a migraine. And I probably overreacted by setting off in the car to look for her. On a couple of other occasions Mother has hitched a ride down to the village to buy cigarettes. With the shops being closed, the pub seemed a logical place to enquire after her."

"I expect she's home by now, setting fire to the rest of the house." Pamela had trouble focusing her big brown eyes on Eudora's wan face. Her glass sat empty, as did Frizzy's, and, realizing I had some serious catching-up to do, I took a huge swallow from mine. Either the gin had floated to the top, or I had previously failed to notice the stingy measure of tonic.

"Dawn told her dad she wanted a contract put out on her gran for poaching the goldfish and I said I was all in favour"—Frizzy tugged her headscarf down over her ears—"but Tom put his foot down."

"Stick-in-the-mud!" Pamela giggled.

"I confess thoughts of murder did cross my mind a few times today," I admitted.

"We all have those moments." Eudora pushed her glasses back on her nose. "But we have to set them aside and get on with the business of reestablishing harmony in our lives."

"Why?" Frizzy banged her glass down on the table, sending the copper warming pan on the near wall swinging to and fro like the pendulum of a clock trying to make up for lost time. "Why can't we bump off our mothers-in-law and live peacefully ever after?"

"Sometimes it does pay to break the rules." Pamela looked as if she were about to say more but didn't.

"The tricky part," I said with a perfectly straight face, "would be getting away with it."

"Now then, ladies"—Eudora glanced uneasily around the pub before gathering up her handbag and pushing back her chair—"I suggest we call it a night."

"Oh, go on! Be a devil, Vicar," said Mrs. Malloy.

"Yes, do be a sport, Mrs. Spike," urged Pamela tipsily.

"Do stay!" cried Frizzy, reaching for another glass.

"Deciding how to murder them all *would* be highly therapeutic." The gin was doing the talking for me.

"I really don't think—" Eudora hesitated on the edge of her seat.

"Surely even a clergywoman gets to let her hair down once in a while," said Frizzy somewhat thickly.

"And it's just a bit of fun." Pamela almost nodded her head off.

"A time for every purpose under heaven!" Folding her hands piously, Mrs. Malloy leaned over the bar as if mistaking it for St. Anselm's pulpit.

"I hope I don't present myself as not of this earth." Eudora eased back into her chair. Her eyes, behind the thick lenses, brimmed with vulnerability.

"So how do we do it?" Pamela demanded. "Push them down the stairs, or is that too corny?"

"It worked for my aunt Ethel." Frizzy ran a finger inside her glass, then licked it thoughtfully. "True, she stuck to her guns that Herbert—her bully of a husband—tripped over the cat, but no one in the family believed her. Aunt Ethel gave herself away putting up a wacking big headstone with the inscription SORELY MISSED. Don't worry, Mrs. Spike—she isn't a member of your parish. She goes to the Methodist church around the corner from my house."

When Frizzy had mentioned her aunt's temper that morning, I had naturally supposed the woman's tantrums were of the more socially acceptable sort, such as holding her breath until she passed out. Under different circumstances I would have responded with well-bred consternation to the revelation of Auntie's unladylike excesses, but as it was, I found myself wanting to get back to the game afoot.

"Perhaps pistols?" I suggested.

"I don't know anything about guns." Eudora was making a worthy effort to get into the spirit of the thing.

"What I think"—Pamela's face shone with glee—"is that we should administer justice of the poetic sort."

"What do you mean?" I tried not to look dim-witted.

"The murder method should be directly connected to whatever our particular mother-in-law does to drive us barmy."

"Such as Mother's smoking?" Eudora shook her head. "Are you suggesting I make a bonfire out of her cigarette butts and lash Mother down on top?" The absurdity of the idea made the vicar laugh with her old heartiness. "I'd never get away with murder that way."

"Give me a minute and I'll think of something really nifty." Pamela was nothing if not undaunted.

We all sat and stared at each other until Frizzy said, "You make it sound so easy . . . like putting Reverend Spike's mother-in-law out on the ice floe."

"That's it!" I straightened up to sit stiff as a board. "Eudora, you tell her that after tonight's inferno you must insist she smoke outside, whatever the time of day or night, come sunshine or hailstorm. Afterwards, you make patience your accomplice. And one night when the snow lies cold and cruel on the ground—"

"What if we have another mild winter?" One of Eudora's few faults might be an inability to suspend disbelief.

"Then you would make do with a pea-souper fog," I said firmly. "The premise is still the same. When she picks up her ciggies and heads out into the night, you race around, locking all the doors and windows, before bundling your husband off to bed and turning the radio on full blast so he can't hear his stepmother kicking up a racket in her attempts to be let back in."

"Then what?" Head bent, Eudora sat twisting her wedding ring around on her finger. "My dear, I hate to burst your bubble, but Mother is definitely not one to die of fright."

"That would be much too tame anyway." Pamela spoke as if reading from a schoolgirl adventure story. "Think how much more novel it would be if Mrs. Spike wandered around and around the exterior of the house, growing more giddy and disoriented by the minute, in the ever-deepening fog. Poor little old lady! Thinking she was still in the garden, she would blunder out onto the road and go bouncy, bouncy over the cliff edge."

"Oopsy daisy!" Frizzy turned a hiccup to good account.

Pamela smiled pridefully. "The verdict would be death by misadventure."

"It's a bit iffy." Mrs. Malloy broke a marathon silence to pontificate from on high. "But then, as I've said time and again to Edna Pickle, you've got to take chances in this life if you want to get where you're going. Of course in Edna's case I'm usually talking about switching to a new kind of brass cleaner, which doesn't take nerves of steel but . . ." Unfortunately a customer claimed her attention.

"Now my turn!" Pamela pressed her hands together in prayer. "Someone please tell me how to do Mumsie Kitty in."

"How about grinding up the thermometer and putting the glass in her food?" Frizzy signaled for another gin.

"That wouldn't work." Pamela's ponytails drooped on her shoulders. "The woman has insides of steel."

"What about the bicycle, the one she told you not to take tonight because it was only lent?" This from Eudora, making a noble effort to be one of the gang. "You could fiddle with the brakes and let a steep hill do the rest."

"Oh, happy day!" Pamela recovered her bounce. "What a super payback for all the times Mumsie Kitty has given with one hand and taken back with the other. I would have to hide her new bicycle to make sure she took the old crock when setting off on one of her lady-of-the-manor visits. . . . But what's a little extra effort in such a good cause? I'll even give her back the nightie she gave me so she will have something pretty to wear when they lay her out."

"If she got flattened by a steamroller, they could put her in a pajama bag and be done with it." Mrs. Malloy dabbed at her eyes, then generously gave us another round. "This conversation is breaking me heart, but then, I always was a softie."

"My turn!" Frizzy, giddy with alcohol or the opportunity to work off her anger, brought the meeting back to order by banging her glass on the table in lieu of a gavel. "Someone please tell me how to do away with Tricks."

"That's easy." I was ready and eager for this one. "She cooked her own goose—or should I say goldfish?—when she put the Nake-It in the shampoo bottle. You are a walking testament to her ability to make royal blunders. Meaning no one would suspect you, Frizzy, if you put poison in her food or drink."

"What sort of poison?" Frizzy did not look overwhelmed by my brilliance. "I don't think chemists are keen on selling you half a pound of arsenic these days."

"You could use weed killer," Eudora suggested. "I remember reading some time ago of a woman who died, according to her husband, of an accidental overdose of the stuff."

"A case of reckless herbicide." Pamela covered her mouth to restrain a giggle.

"I don't want to be a wet blanket," Frizzy said, "but wouldn't it taste nasty?"

"No problem," I told her. "Tricks mentioned at dinner last night that she supplements her diet with a health tonic. All you would have to do is tell her that you had found a better one, and not to be put off by the taste, because it is guaranteed to take twenty years off one's age in twenty minutes."

"She would go for that, all right!" A smile spread over Frizzy's face, but before she could fall all over me with thanks, Mrs. Malloy stuck in her oar.

"Very nice, I'm sure! But I can't stand here all day, sending me customers away with a flea in the ear, waiting for you lot to get to the juicy part."

"She means *my* mother-in-law," I translated.

"Now, don't go thinking you have to go all out on my account, Mrs. H." came the magnanimous rejoinder. "Just because the woman gave me the sack the moment your back was turned don't mean I want her to suffer a lingering death. Something quick and easy would suit me down to ground. Nothing with too much blood, if it's all the same with you. I don't want to be swabbing floors till kingdom come when I return to me old job."

"Would you care to be so bold as to suggest a means to her end?" I inquired sweetly, if somewhat sloppily. The alcohol was making my head spin.

"Well, if that don't warm me cockles." Mrs. Malloy folded her purple lips and assumed a pensive mein. "We can't push her off the balcony where she had Bill Watkins trapped all afternoon; that would be too much of a muchness after her close call on the stairs last night. And we can't feed her funny mushrooms—that wouldn't look too good for you, Mrs. H., after that business with the chocolate that wasn't proper chocolate in the pud."

Eudora, Frizzy, and Pamela all looked at me with slightly startled expressions.

"A pity, but there it is." A sorry shake of the head from Mrs.

Malloy. "You haven't painted a pretty picture of yourself, Mrs. H., so you'll have to be extra cunning if you hope to get away with finishing off the job."

"Oh, for heaven's sake," I fumed. "This is just a game."

"Of course it is," she soothed, "and I think I've got the answer, ducks! Think about it, Mrs. H.—from the moment you invited your in-laws to come and visit, you was all of a panic, dusting and polishing and alphabetizing the towels by colour in the airing cupboard, all for fear *she* would go nosing about, sniffing out cobwebs and the like. So what I say is—"

"She's right," I informed the others. "I wouldn't put it past Mum to climb on the roof and check under the tiles for dust. She accused me of looking exhausted when she and Dad arrived. And she was right. Every time she comes, it's the same. I bolt up in bed at night in a cold sweat, remembering something I've missed."

"What a strain," sympathized Eudora.

"Oh, no!" I clapped a hand to my mouth. "The tall dresser in her bedroom! I never got around to giving it a dusting. Did you, Mrs. Malloy?"

"No good looking at me with them puppy dog eyes, Mrs. H.! If I've told you once, I've told you a dozen times, I wouldn't touch that Tower of Babel with a barge pole let alone me feather duster. Just let anyone look at it cross-eyed and down it would come; and that brings me back to what I was saying before you went and interrupted. All you'd have to do is empty out the bottom drawers and load up the ones high up so as to make it nice and top-heavy and Bob's your uncle. Unless your ma-in-law wanted to drag a stepladder upstairs, the only way to get a good peek at the top of that dresser would be to climb from a chair onto the middle ledge. Something that wouldn't be all that safe at the best of times. Well, ladies, what do you think?"

"Super," enthused Pamela.

Eudora looked deeply reflective.

"It brings to mind the practice of crushing to death religious dissidents during the Reformation."

Frizzy—as a result of this tidbit of information or the booze catching up with her—swayed silently in her seat.

"There you are." Mrs. Malloy's taffeta bosom swelled with pride. "What's good for the history books is more than good enough for the likes of us, Mrs. H.; think of it this way—your ma-in-law likes nothing better than to be a bloody martyr."

"You have a point," I said, a trifle flatly. I felt a little tired, which I

often find puts a crimp on maintaining a high level of anger or resentment. No longer could I remember with burning clarity every word, look,
and gesture that Mum had used to drive me around the bend. Oh, I
hadn't forgotten that she had sacked Mrs. Malloy, burned my library
book, accused me of driving her dog to attempted suicide, won Jonas over
to her side, and capped off all these misdemeanours by instigating a
quarrel between me and my one and only husband. But what must also be
remembered was that she had been suffering undue stress.

Whatever, the thought of Mum lying pop-eyed under that dresser,
waiting to be scraped off the floor with a spatula and flipped over like a
pancake, was enough to put me off gin and tonics for life, to say nothing
of murder. That having been said, I felt the need for my friends to like me
and think me a good sport. Tying on a bright smile, I said, "We've certainly written a new chapter in the life and crimes of Chitterton Fells."

"I suppose we have." Frizzy managed to sit up straight by dint of
holding on to the table. "But if we weren't playing Let's Pretend and
really and truly had to get down to the business of murdering our mothers-in-law, I think we'd all be shaking in our boots."

"That's what I was thinking." Pamela stared down at the coasters
she was stacking into a little mound. "So maybe the thing to do would be
to take the coward's way out and hire a hit man."

"And where would we find such a person? I don't imagine they're to
be found queuing up at the unemployment office." Eudora's face seemed
to plump up as she smiled so that she looked like her old self. For her, the
homicidal therapy appeared to have produced benefits.

"Speak of coincidences." I was back in the game, playing conspira-
tor for all I was worth. "Who should be staying in the rooms above the
stable at Merlin's Court but Mr. Peter Savage, a self-described vagrant,
who only this evening proclaimed his appreciation for my hospitality by
vowing he would gladly kill for me." To have added that said person had
been speaking about the slaying of dragons, not the human animal, would
have spoiled the effect. So, too, would the said gentleman's arrival on the
scene. But, fortunately for me, his rock-and-roll session with Dad was
running long.

"Mr. Savage!" Pamela knocked over her coasters in her excitement.
"I can see him ever so clearly in my mind! He has long hair, a grungy
beard, possibly a tattoo, and definitely an earring—a silver one in the
shape of a skull."

Amazing! We had been looking for someone to read tea leaves at
the St. Anselm's fair, and it would seem we had found her. So what if she
had missed Mr. Savage by a mile? Pamela had described my cousin

Freddy to a T, and I was about to tell her so, when the door of the saloon bar burst open as if kicked in by the spurred boot of a gun-toting bad guy in a B western and in strode my own personal black-browed villain.

"Ellie!" Ben roared in a voice that—the bar sinister be damned—proclaimed him once and always his father's son. His eyes roved the cowering occupants of the room before lighting on my lily-white face. In two fell strides he reached me, and before I could bleat "Don't you dare!" the blackguard swooped me up in his arms of steel and headed for the door.

The only one to utter a protest was Mrs. Malloy. Her voice came at us like a shot in the back. "I'll have you know, Mr. H., this is a *respectable* establishment, but if you must make off with a defenseless female, take *me!*"

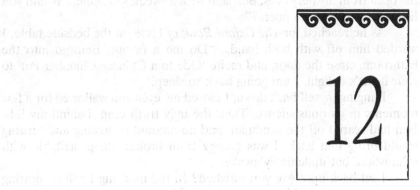

12

Talk about a rude awakening! I dragged open my eyes in the grim light of predawn, when the pheasants on the wallpaper still had their heads tucked under their wings and the mantelpiece clock was still a merciful blur, to see Ben up on one elbow, his handsome face looming over me.

"I adore you, sweetheart," he whispered huskily.

"That's nice." I moved to turn over, but it would have taken a mattress rammed down the man's throat to shut him up.

"I feel a responsibility to show you how desperately I love you and how sorry I am for not being more supportive over your difficulties with Mum."

"Your silk pajamas speak louder than words." I patted his face with a sleepy hand.

"Are you sure I can't get you something?" His breath buzzed about me like a worrisome fly. "How about a cup of tea or some eggs Benedict?"

"No thank you." I ducked under the sheet. "If I diet while I sleep, I can eat pretty much what I like during the day."

"Whatever you say, my darling." He picked up my hand, thereby preventing me from clobbering him with it, and worked his way from pinky to thumb, bestowing a trail on it of itsy-bitsy kisses. Driven to frenzy, I sat up with a flurry of bedclothes. But instead of faltering under the blast from my fiery orbs, Ben said with a sweet, sad smile, "Would you like me to read you a poem?"

As he reached for *The Oxford Book of Verse* on the bedside table, I warded him off with both hands. "Do me a favour, Ben, go into the bathroom, close the door, and recite 'Ode to a Chinese Chamber Pot' to your heart's delight. I am going back to sleep!"

Flinging myself back down, I closed my eyes and wallowed for a few moments in glorious silence. Then the ugly truth crept behind my lids. Ben had scared off the sandman, and no amount of tossing and turning would bring him back. I was groggy from broken sleep, irritable with exhaustion, but undeniably awake.

I sat back up. "Are you satisfied? In the morning I will be putting nappies on the twins' heads and the envelope with the gas bill into the toaster."

"You're still angry with me for the way I acted." Combing his fingers through his ebony hair, Ben leaned back on the pillow and studied the ceiling as if seeking answers to winning me back.

"I am not angry," I told him angrily. "Didn't I prove, exhaustively, when we got back last night that all was forgiven?"

"My darling, you did everything a woman could do."

"Think about it. Did I say one word about your kidnapping me from the Dark Horse? Did I make an issue about your leaving poor Mr. Savage stranded? True enough, we left the Heinz parked right there by the curb, but the keys to it were parked in my raincoat pocket."

"Ellie." Ben gathered me into his arms, his laughter tickling my cheek. "Don't worry about him, Dad will have let him stay the night."

"I'm sure you're right," I conceded grudgingly. "And we can always hope that the experience of sharing a single bed with a member of the hairy-kneed sex will bring your father to his senses."

"I hope so." Releasing me gently, Ben flopped back down and pressed a hand over his eyes as if trying to block out more than the light stippling the furniture and ceiling. "But by the time he comes crawling back to Mum, it could be too late."

"Don't be a pessimist." All irritation gone, I snuggled up close.

Ben sighed. "There's something I haven't told you, Ellie."

"Oh?"

"After you left last night, Jonas and Mum went off to the sitting room alone, and when they came out . . ."

"Go on." My heart was suddenly beating like a drum.

"Mum took me aside. She told me Jonas had asked her to marry him."

"No!" I almost fell through the bed.

"Ellie, I couldn't believe I was hearing correctly when she said she was considering accepting his proposal."

"In heaven's name, why?"

"They're both on their own and she thinks she can make something of him."

"He's over seventy! Does she really think she can get him to join the army or take night classes to become a stockbroker or"—I chewed on a finger—"join the Catholic Church?"

Ben shuddered. "He's getting her on the rebound. And I suppose if I were any sort of son, I would go after him with a horsewhip."

"Hush!" I silenced him with a kiss. "It's as plain as the nose on your face that Jonas came up with this ploy as a means of getting your parents back together. And you can't blame Mum for wanting to make Dad jealous."

"You're right." Ben sounded as if he could have kicked himself for his stupidity. "I don't know why you are being so nice to me, Ellie."

"Niceness is seditious," I said. "One kind word leads to another and becomes a vicious circle."

"I shouldn't have let you leave last night."

"My being gone gave us both a chance to cool off. And Dad did need his suitcase."

"I'm glad you met up with your friends." Ben kissed first one eyebrow, then the other. "Did you have a good chat?"

"Oh, the usual stuff."

"What, knitting patterns and that sort of thing?" My love spoke with mounting affection and hopefully took the pounding of my heart for wifely reciprocation. It was silly to feel guilty about what had occurred, but I felt like Judas when I planted a kiss on Ben's lips. "Did your mother say anything about my abrupt departure?"

"She didn't get the chance. I did all the talking, Ellie, and I think she got the message that this is your house and she is to stop taking over and sacking the help."

"There's only Jonas left and, if we are to make his efforts pay off, I suggest you see your father, sow the seeds of jealousy, and do your best to make them sprout."

"Easy said as done, sweetheart! I'll let slip that Jonas has taken up weight-lifting and is thinking of dyeing his hair."

"Is he?" I was seized by unreasonable alarm.

"Of course not!" Ben switched position with breathless haste so that his eyes—blazing into mine—became a kaleidoscope of shifting blues and greens. The fictional Sir Edward had nothing on my husband when it came to grand passion, and I soon realized without too much regret that we had taken the subject of his parents to its natural conclusion.

"Darling," I heard myself say, "if you kept a harem, would I be your favourite wife?"

Afterwards took its own sweet time coming, but eventually the room came back from fade-out and we lay holding hands until Ben drifted back to sleep and I started thinking about Mum alone in her tower bedroom. Surprisingly I didn't focus on whether she had been roused from her slumbers but on the possibility that the lofty chest of drawers would come crashing down if she did decide to scale its narrow ledge to check along the top for dust. A case of my conscience getting the better of my common sense; but as I thumped my pillow and turned over, I did wonder if Eudora, Frizzy, and Pamela were embarrassed by what we had talked about at the Dark Horse. Oh, for heaven's sake! I burrowed deeper under the bedclothes. Our behaviour might have been immature, but so long as our mothers-in-law never got wind of it, where was the harm?

Daylight banished any lingering unease. By the time I had taken my bath, put on a maidenly print frock, and rescued my young from the imprisonment of their cots, I was eager to make a fresh start with Mum. Having completed his morning makeover, Ben met up with me on the landing to take Tam, sporting a sailor suit, from my arms. Off father and son sallied to conquer the kitchen, where Abbey and I soon joined them.

The chairs stood four-square around the table; the plates and bowls stood to attention on the Welsh dresser. From the window I could see Jonas working in the garden. Everything and everyone was in its rightful place . . . except Mum. I was surprised not to find her at the sink, dismantling the taps in order to give the washers a polish.

"Ben"—I turned from seating Abbey in her booster chair—"have you seen your mother?"

"No." He poured a sample measure of freshly brewed coffee into a cup and applied his nose to savour the bouquet before taking an experimental sip which, after much rolling around the tongue, was found to be of suitable vintage, and duly swallowed. "She's probably still in bed."

Rubbish! We both knew the only time Mum would agree to a lie-in was when the coffin lid closed. What could be wrong? A particular piece of bedroom furniture loomed large in my fears, even though it was lunacy to picture her being pressed to death like the Blessed (or was it Saint?) Margaret Clitherow. Ben and I couldn't have failed to hear if that chest of drawers had come tumbling down, unless . . . my blood ran cold . . . it had happened when we were making love and the trombones and clarinets were at their zenith.

Leaving the twins in their booster chairs under the watchful eye of Daddy, who promised not to feed them eggs Benedict, I raced upstairs to tap on Mum's door.

"Hello, it's me, Ellie!"

No answer.

I knocked again. This time, to my relief, I was rewarded with a tiny invitation to "Come in."

When I timidly complied, I found Mum stretched out in bed with the sheet up to her chin, looking as if she were only waiting for a well-wisher to close her eyes and drop a couple of pennies on her alabaster lids.

"Don't worry about intruding." She didn't so much as turn her head my way. "As my poor boy made plain last night, this is your home, not mine."

"Aren't you feeling well?" I hovered by the bedside while the skyscraper dresser mocked me from the wall.

"I'm as right as can be expected." The ghostly words were spoken without a flicker of expression or eyelash.

"Good!" I looked around for someone to come to my aid, but the Grecian nymphs on the mantelpiece had their hands full holding up their bronze skirts. "Ben just made coffee and I could bring some up, or if you would prefer to come down . . ."

"That's very kind of you, Ellie." I heard a sigh so weak, it wouldn't have fogged a mirror held to her lips. "But if it's all the same with you, I'll stay here out from underfoot. That way I can't be accused of causing trouble and you can get on with whatever it is you do all day. All I want is my son's happiness."

"He won't be very chipper if you put yourself to bed for life." I tried to soften the words, but my patience was wearing as thin as Mum's hair, which stuck out from her face in forlorn wisps.

"There's no need to be sarcastic, Ellie; but when all's said and done, I don't suppose you will have me cluttering up the place for long." It was pure chance that her eyes fixed upon the dresser, which to my nervous gaze appeared to be on the point of keeling over, with or without outside help.

"Please, Mum." Sitting gingerly down on the bed, I said with all the firmness I could muster, "You mustn't talk about dying."

After looking blank for a second, her face cleared. "I meant you wouldn't have to put up with me if I went ahead and married Jonas; he was talking last night about buying a little cottage with a thatched roof and roses around the door."

"And I suppose you'd have Miss Marple living next door?" I am ashamed to say I let my irritation get the better of me.

"Who?"

"The village busybody. But don't get me wrong," I added quickly, "it all sounds extremely romantic and I am sure Dad will be sick with jealousy. Not that you give a fig bar what he thinks."

Mum's sniff was somewhat ambiguous.

"Jonas is a dear, wonderful man"—I sat pleating the corner of her sheet—"and I'm sure you would quickly adjust to his sleeping in his gardening boots."

This wicked fib did not fall on fertile ground. Squaring her birdlike shoulders, Mum managed a courageous smile. "After nearly forty years with Eli, I can cope with pretty much anything."

"I'm sure you can," I soothed, "but I don't know that you will be able to wean Jonas away from the Church of England. He's a *pillar* of our little congregation." This at least was not a complete fabrication. To my certain knowledge, Jonas had attended St. Anselm's on two occasions— my wedding and the twins' christening.

Finally! I had scored a bull's-eye. Mum blinked uneasily and murmured, "I must have heard what I wanted to hear. The way I understood it, he was C. of E. in name only. Are you telling me"—she shrank down in the pillows—"that he *passes* the collection plate?"

"And changes the numbers on the hymn board," I assured her without a blush. "You did know he's an elder?" At seventy-odd, surely no one could deny Jonas that distinction. "Oh, well, diversity is the spice of life. I'm sure you will be able to work things out—perhaps one Sunday at his church, the next at yours. After all, you and Dad coped with your difference all these years. . . ."

"That's not the same thing at all!" Mum bobbed up like a jack-in-the-box. "It wasn't the Jewish people who destroyed our monasteries and pinched our holy relics!"

"To say nothing of a few nuns' bottoms in the process," I agreed, with a sorry shake of the head.

"What my parents refused to see when I told them I wanted to marry Eli"—Mum's sparrow eyes filmed with tears—"is that Catholics and Jews have a *lot* in common."

"Of course they do," I concurred. "There's the Old Testament and—"

"And more important"—*sniff*—"is that I grew up with the mass in Latin while Eli attended services in Hebrew, so neither one of us understood a *word* of what was going on."

"That would make for a strong bond."

Mum looked at me in amazement bordering on shock. "Are you telling me, Ellie, that you understand why I did what I did?"

"Absolutely. In respecting Dad's religious convictions you couldn't insist that he marry you in a church any more than he could have demanded that the wedding take place in a synagogue, and neither of you could have accepted a heathen registry office."

"So you don't lump me in the same category as other fallen women . . . like Tricks?"

"Of course not," I said firmly. "You're much prettier."

"Am I?" A smile wavered on her lips, and I wondered with a pang of guilt if this was the first compliment of a personal nature I had ever paid her.

"You put Tricks completely in the shade." I laid my hand on hers. "Which doesn't mean you shouldn't gild the lily. Have you ever thought" —I was getting really daring—"about putting a rinse in your hair and using a smudge of shadow to bring out the sparkle in your eyes?"

She lay so still against the pillows that for a moment I thought I had gone too far, but then she said softly, "That's one thing I've missed in life —having a daughter to help keep me smart."

"We could have a beauty session today." I gave her hand a squeeze. "I was looking at my hair this morning and thinking I need two inches cut off the ends."

"You want me to cut it for you?"

"If you wouldn't mind."

"Well, if you're sure you have a decent pair of scissors . . ." Sitting up, Mum pushed back the bedclothes and reached for her dressing gown at the foot of the bed. "I must say, Ellie, I'm not usually in favour of women your age wearing their hair long, but on you it looks better than most."

"Thank you." Picking up her slippers and handing them to her, I thought, Is that where I've gone wrong? Had I been guilty of never asking for her help or advice because my own insecurities necessitated I present myself as the model wife and mother when in the company of the woman whose son I had appropriated? While Mum was buttoning up her dressing gown I moved casually over to the dresser, which had figured in my idle little plot to murder her and, upon a hands-on inspection, realized that guilt had made an idiot of me. That piece of furniture was as unbudgeable as the Rock of Gibraltar.

"You go on down, Ellie"—Mum was plumping up the pillows and spreading up her sheets—"I need some time to sort things out in my head."

"Take all the time you want." I moved towards the door. "By the way, where's Sweetie?"

"Under the bed."

"And we haven't heard a peep out of her." Hope reared its naughty head that the doggie would dig her way to China and chew up *their* Oriental rugs.

"She had a bad night. Not, of course, that you should feel guilty about that, Ellie."

Hand on the doorknob, I said, "Perhaps she would like a magazine." On Sweetie's last visit she had devoured several copies of *Woman's Own.*

"That's all right, she took one of my crocheting patterns under the bed with her." To my delight, Mum smiled as if she really meant it, and I heard myself asking if she would mind doing some ironing for me sometime.

"I know Ben misses the way you do his shirts."

"Since you mention it, Ellie, I did notice that you press the creases in instead of out, but we can't be good at everything and I'm sure you could teach me a thing or two." She was clearly racking her brain. "I've got it, you could show me how to defrost frozen dinners."

"It's a deal," I said, and headed downstairs convinced beyond a shadow of doubt that everything was coming up sunshine and roses.

On reaching the kitchen I found Ben draining a cup of coffee, one eye on the clock.

"How was she?"

"Fine. We kissed and made up." I bustled him towards the garden door. "It dawned on me that incredible as it sounds, I may have been to blame for part of the problem. But I don't want to hold you up doing a rehash. What are you going to do about the cars—take mine and worry about getting yours later?"

"I'd better hurry," he said, shrugging into his jacket, "if I'm to have my meaningful talk with Dad, before setting down to Abigail's."

While the twins fussed in their booster chairs, I retrieved his car keys from my raincoat pocket, placed them lovingly in his hand, and waited for both his well-shod feet to clear the step before closing the door firmly behind him.

"Daddy's all gone bye-bye," I carolled at my impatient twosome, but before we could get down to a serious game of patter-cake on this, the fifth day of the tournament, the door banged open and Jonas came stomping into the kitchen with a big bunch of dahlias in his hands.

He shoved them at me. "Here you go, Ellie girl. Thought you might like something to brighten your day."

"You're a dear!" I gave him a peck on his grizzled cheek and received a grunt in return. The window showed a square of rheumy-eyed morning which promised to turn into a day of fretful rain and whining wind. But Jonas, as I understood it, was talking about the atmospheric pressure inside the house. His eyes under the shaggy brows were worried and his moustache had more of a droop than usual when he said, "You done wandering off, lass?"

"I'm back in harness," I promised. Avoiding Abbey's grab for the dahlias, I went over to the Welsh dresser to get down a vase. And when Jonas next spoke, I sensed he was glad I had my back to him.

"Did you hear tell, girl, as how I asked Magdalene to marry me?"

"Word leaked out." I was about to say I was wise to his little game and thought it might just do the trick where Mum and Dad were concerned, when a knock came at the garden door. Bunging the flowers in the vase, I opened up, fully expecting to see Freddy on the doorstep with an empty porridge bowl in his hands and a hopeful smile on his lips.

"Mr. Savage," I cried. "So you're back safe and sound!"

"I had to see you." His spectacles sparkled and his smile broke through the mist to drive back the threat of rain. "I had to come and thank you for last night."

"How kind!" Without looking around I knew that Jonas's eyebrows were lodged in the middle of his forehead and that Abbey's and Tam's rosebud mouths were opened wide.

"It was the best night of my life, and it only heightened the pleasure to know that my mother would have been appalled. What matters is that I learned more in one evening—"

"Good."

"I couldn't believe it when you let me start your motor!"

"And afterwards"—I hurried him along before Jonas could rush to the phone and ask Reverend Spike to make an emergency house call— "did you have a productive session with my father-in-law?"

"Between us we composed four new songs and added a new verse to 'The Fair Maid of Chitterton Fells.' "

"That's wonderful." I was genuinely pleased for him and sorry I had to break the news that I had left his tape recorder at the Dark Horse.

"Don't give it a thought!" He beamed at me. "I found it sitting on the bar when Elijah took me down to breakfast. And now I must pick up my guitar before meeting up with him. We're heading down to the railway station—"

"You're leaving? Both of you?" I wasn't sure how I felt about Dad returning to Tottenham at this stage of Jonas's clever game.

Mr. Savage laughed merrily. "Don't worry; you're not losing us. We're going to stake out our busking pitch and take the village by storm. We even have our collaboration all worked out—I'm to do the strumming and the tra-la-las and Elijah will sing the verses."

Behind me one of the twins' breakfast spoons went clattering onto the booster chair tray and from there *ping-ping*ing to the floor. But I couldn't so much as turn my head. I was in shock! Dad had to be out of his mind, unless . . . oh, of course—stupid me! This was *his* way of forcing Mum's hand. She would have to beg him to come back when she found out he had been driven bonkers by their separation.

"I hope you won't feel I'm deserting you by moving out of my stable room." Mr. Savage wiped the mist off his spectacles with the back of his hand. "Elijah feels strongly that we should spend every waking and sleeping moment together if our careers are to advance. And helpful as Freddy has been, I have come to believe he might not be the best musical partner for me. You will make my apologies to him, Mrs. Haskell—Ellie—and please never forget that you are my inspiration." His voice broke. "There isn't a song I wouldn't sing for you, no plank I wouldn't walk . . ."

"That's very kind of you." My blushes were already turning into second-degree burns when he turned and stumbled down the steps in the manner of one whose eyes were blinded by rain or tears.

"He's round the bend, he is!" Jonas bent to pick up the dropped spoon and stood wagging it at me.

"Mr. Savage is a musician," I reproved, closing the door.

"By gum, you can say that again."

"Can I help it if I am a woman to die for?" Sashaying past him, I got busy rescuing Abbey, who had been kicking her heels against the chair long enough. And having put her on the floor with her building blocks, I turned my attention to her brother, who needed his face washed. "I fully appreciate, Jonas, that you prefer your women on the spicy side of seventy, but there are men who are prepared to settle for someone of my meagre years."

Having put him in his place, I asked if he would take Mum up some coffee.

"You think that's wise?"

"I know I can trust you, Jonas, to slip the cup and saucer under the door."

"If I have to go in, I'll keep me eyes closed."

Off he went at a speedy shuffle, having laid a single dahlia alongside the milk jug on his little tray. No doubt about it, I thought fondly, the old codger was playing his amorous role to the hilt. And he was doing it for me, so I would never have to run away from home again. Bless him! And bless Dad for taking poor Mr. Savage under his wing. I had meant well in agreeing to provide the man with a temporary roof over his head, but it might not have been the wisest of moves.

After helping Abbey stack her building blocks and watching Tam knock them down with his fire engine, it was time for me to remember that a woman's work has no beginning and no end. I was removing a pile of clothes from the dryer and reflecting sadly that it is a fact of life that socks do not mate for life when, blow me down, there was another knock at my door. And to think I had gone years without these many interruptions.

"Coming!" Throwing up my hands and sending the socks every which way, I went to open up, yet again.

"Why, Mrs. Pickle!" I couldn't for the life of me think what had brought her here, unless . . . my heart faltered . . . had something happened to Mrs. Malloy? Had my faithful daily in a fit of depression over being sacked decided to end it all?

"Do come in!" I backed up like mad.

"I don't want to be no bother." Her plump face was every bit as drab as her squashed felt hat and beige coat, but that didn't mean anything. Mrs. Pickle always looked as though she had just finished laying out her best friend.

"Please"—I scooped Abbey into my arms for moral support— "don't break it to me gently, I can take whatever you have to tell me."

"You're a lady, Mrs. Haskell, I've always said so." With these words she advanced into the kitchen with excruciating slowness. "But it isn't so much a matter of telling—as asking, if you get my meaning." This was worse than any form of torture practiced at the Tower of London other than being pressed to death. Happily, I was prevented from screaming by Abbey who, cheered on by her brother, got hold of my lips and twisted them into a knot. My bulging eyes must have spoken volumes, because Mrs. Pickle picked up the pace a fraction. "I've come along on the off chance—and you're free to tell me to go—so as to ask if you'd like me to do for you a couple of mornings a week."

"That's it?"

Mrs. Pickle looked blank, an expression she had plainly mastered years before.

"I'm sorry"—I set Abbey down with her brother on the rug—"it's been one of those mornings and I've been very worried about Mrs. Malloy."

"Yes, I suppose you have." Mrs. Pickle nodded slowly. "And from the sound of it, you've got your problems with Bill Watkins. I've never had much time for him, but he and me live two doors down from each other and he was telling me just this morning, when he come round to borrow some milk, about how come he got stuck on that balcony for hours on end."

"I hope he's feeling better."

"That depends on how you look at it," she said mournfully. "There's some I suppose as would say he's on the mend from how he was yesterday, and others as would say he's not as well as he was the day before that. You see what I'm getting at, Mrs. Haskell?"

"Absolutely. And next time you see him, please give Mr. Watkins my best and tell him I hope to see him back doing windows."

"I don't want to raise your hopes that'll be anytime soon." Mrs. Pickle stood with handbag in her hands and her Mother Hubbard shoes primly together. "But then again, I see as how Bill left his ladder up against the house here, so it could be he's planning on being back this year rather than next. Roxie didn't think he looked too bad when I was giving him the milk, along with a cup of sugar."

"That's right," I remembered, "Mrs. Malloy spent the night at your house. How is she?"

"That's hard to say, isn't it?" Mrs. Pickle bestowed a slow smile on the twins, who were fighting over possession of a rattle shaped like a lollipop. "Roxie's quite upset about the bust-up with your mother-in-law. Well, she would be, wouldn't she? She's fond of you and always has been. But she did brighten up enough to have a bit of a chin-wag with Bill Watkins. And afterwards she did say as how a change was as good as a rest, and if I would pitch in here until your mother-in-law leaves, she would be plenty grateful."

"That might work out very nicely." Removing the rattle from the twins' joint grasp, I placed it on a shelf out of jumping reach of Sweetie, who might mistake it for a bone as she had done St. Francis. Yes, I could see the method in Mrs. Malloy's magnanimity. After a week or two of trying to adjust to Mrs. Pickle's snail's pace, I would find myself remembering my former employee with tears in my eyes and counting the seconds, let alone the minutes, till her return.

Upon my urging, Mrs. Pickle removed her coat a slow button at a time; then she laboriously took off her hat which had done a nice job of covering her curlers, which—from the shiny-bright look of them—were her best ones. When I turned back from hanging the coat and hat in the alcove by the door, she was in the process of opening her handbag. In due course she produced what she called her "resoom."

"Oh, there's no need for that!" Swooping the socks off the table, I tossed them back in the dryer and pulled out a chair for her. "Why don't you sit down and I'll make us a cup of tea before showing you the house."

"I'd rather you looked at it, Mrs. Haskell, and I'll put the kettle on. It shouldn't take me above five minutes to find the cooker."

"This is very impressive." Taking my seat, résumé in hand, I read off the list of current clients. There was Lady Kitty Pomeroy, Mrs. Eudora Spike, and a couple of other names I recognized. "Are you sure you can take me on?"

"I can squeeze you in." Mrs. Pickle laboriously filled the kettle and in so doing splashed water to the four walls as if pumping it from a well. "Roxie said as you'd be happy with the odd morning and, when all's said and done, that works best for me, seeing as Lady Kitty asked me to go and give young Frizzy Taffer a bit of a hand for a week or two, but from the sound of it, she'll take me when she can get me."

"That's splendid," I said, wondering what Frizzy thought about being saddled with household help.

Mrs. Pickle brought my tea slopping over to the table. "What you should know in all fairness, Mrs. Haskell, is that different from Roxie, who's made a big-time career for herself out of being a char, for me it's just a job."

"There's no shame in that," I assured her.

"My life's work is wine-making, if you can see where I'm coming from." Mrs. Pickle was in fact coming towards me with the sugar bowl. "Every penny I can lay me hands on, one way or another, goes into modernizing my equipment. Some people might call me a woman with a mission—to see my labels on bottles all over the country. Then there's them as would put it different—that I'm trying to live down the shame of my great-great-gran being put in the stocks for being a witch and all, because she took her cat with her when she walked around the village with her clothes off."

"People can be very narrowminded," I said.

"You've never said a truer word." Mrs. Pickle staggered over to the table with the milk jug as if crossing the line after finishing a race from Land's End to John o'Groat's. "There's some as won't touch my rhubarb wine, and I'll admit straight off to you, Mrs. Haskell, that it is an acquired taste. Roxie said she'd sooner drink poison—you know how she is, but it's the iron that makes it just the tonic when you're run down or all to pieces with your nerves."

"The fact that your wines always win ribbons at the St. Anselm's Summer Fête speaks for itself." I was swallowing a sip of stone-cold tea when Jonas came stumping into the kitchen. His eyes met Mrs. Pickle's and I noticed that her face seemed to lose some of its cushioning and that her knees had buckled. Oh help, I thought. With Mum in the house, we had the makings of the eternal triangle. Was there no peace for the wicked Ellie Haskell?

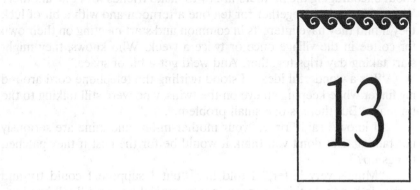

13

Had I done the right thing in not vetoing Mrs. Pickle's suggestion that Jonas show her around the house? While the twins sat on the floor talking to the suit of armour we call Rustus, I dithered about the hall with a fake duster in my hand and my legs at the ready to race upstairs if Jonas did no more than scream once. Luckily, the telephone on the trestle table rang and gave me something else to think about.

"Hello, Ellie!" The voice belonged to Frizzy Taffer, and I was delighted to hear her sound so bubbly. "I wanted to tell you my hair has grown back to an attractive stubble. Tom says he likes it this way and that I'll set a trend. Of course, in a place like Chitterton Fells it will take the women three years to catch on, and by then I will have gone back to my old mop."

"Tom's a prize and so are you," I told her. "Did you get home all right last night?"

"Eudora Spike gave me and Pamela a lift. By a mercy, everyone was in bed when I got in, because I wouldn't have fancied colliding with Tricks after spending the evening plotting to put her six foot under."

"We *were* wicked!" A soft padding sound caused me to look over my shoulder, but it was only Tobias Cat heading down the stairs.

"Weren't we?" Frizzy laughed merrily. "And I wanted to tell you it did me a world of good, so much so that I got up this morning determined to get on better with Tricks. I even came up with an idea that I think might help all of us—you, me, Pamela, and Eudora. What do you think about encouraging the mothers-in-law to make friends with one another? We could get them together for tea one afternoon and with a bit of luck they'll find they have interests in common and start meeting on their own for coffee in the village once or twice a week. Who knows, they might start taking day trips together. And we'd get a bit of space."

"It's a wonderful idea!" I stood twirling the telephone cord around my finger while keeping an eye on the twins, who were still talking to the tin man. "But there is one small problem. . . ."

"I know," said Frizzy, "your mother-in-law and mine are seriously not talking. But don't you think it would be for the best if they patched things up?"

"Mum's very bitter," I told her, "but I suppose I could try and persuade her to do this for me, as a very special favour. I'll tell her I am living in daily fear of bungling my job as chairwoman of the St. Anselm's Summer Fête, because the number of contestants planning to enter the homemaking events has dropped off since last year, and then I'll ask for her help in organizing a get-together for interested parties."

"That could work." I felt the warmth of Frizzy's smile all the way down the phone.

"Tricks mentioned when she came for dinner that she was entering the marrow-growing contest," I continued, "so with luck I can make Mum see it would be impossible not to include her ex-friend in the invitation."

"Ellie, this is wonderful. And wouldn't it be even better if one or more of the women came away from the fête next month with a ribbon or two? Something like that would boost their self-confidence and put them back in touch with their own lives."

"You're right." I watched Tam edge towards the grandfather clock and make a grab for Tobias, who was hiding around the corner. "Tricks has her marrows, my mother-in-law crochets a mile a minute, Bridget Spike makes the most marvelous marmalade, and Lady Kitty is famous for her apple pie. Mrs. Malloy says you just eat a slice and you die happy."

"The trouble with her ladyship," Frizzy said, "is that she is used to hosting the fête, not being a player."

"Then it will be up to Pamela to persuade her that she has been failing her subjects all these years by not setting the standard for a proper pastry crust to which the common woman should aspire. What do you think about my striking while the iron is hot and having the first tea party this afternoon?"

"Do I have to come and help?"

"Of course not, this is your afternoon off."

"What time do you want Tricks?"

"Three o'clock."

"Should I send along her pajamas in case it turns into a slumber party?"

"Good try, Frizzy!"

I could picture her crooked smile. "I'd better get off the phone before Mrs. Smith next door phones the police. Ever since Dawn got her new radio, you can't raise your voice above a whisper in this house without that woman banging on the wall."

"Heaven forbid I get you arrested," I said, and after hanging up I immediately telephoned Eudora, who, if not bubbly, was very agreeable to the plan for getting the mothers-in-law together. Reaching Pamela promised to be a bit more ticklish. I had my doubts that Lady Kitty would permit anyone but herself to undertake the responsibility of handling the telephone; but as it turned out, Pamela answered almost before I finished dialing.

"Allan"—her voice came in a breathless rush—"did you find a way to come up with the money?"

I felt my face flush for both of us. "Sorry, Pamela. It's me, Ellie Haskell."

"Oh, super!" She tried gallantly to sound pleased. "It seems *ages* since I saw you last night. Not that anything has changed here. Mumsie Kitty is being her usual beastly self, Bobsie Cat is talking about moving into the hollow tree down the lane, and I'm ready to do something desperate—like run off to Marks & Spencer and buy myself some new bras. That's why when I thought you were Allan I started babbling about money." Her voice trailed off, leaving an awkward pause which I filled with the image of her sad brown eyes and drooping ponytails.

"I rang to ask if Lady Kitty would come for tea this afternoon at three o'clock."

"By herself?"

"There's a reason," I said, and proceeded to explain all the well-conceived details of the mother-in-law campaign.

"Are you sure it wouldn't be easier to follow through with our original plans?"

"Pamela, last night was great therapy but . . ."

"I know." Her laugh was as hollow as the tree where her father-in-law was considering taking up residence. "It's just that you caught me in a really murderous mood."

"Don't worry," I soothed. "Things will work out, trust me, and in the meantime you get an afternoon's respite if you can talk Lady Kitty into coming to my house for tea. Tell her it won't be a *fête accompli* without her."

"If she does decide to enter the pie competition, she should win without question." Pamela seemed to be growing more depressed by the minute. "You'd never think hands had touched her pastry, which is why I was so scared when Allan told me about her decision to choose a wife for him by way of a bake-off . . ."

"But everything worked out," I reminded her.

"At a price."

I was searching for something to say, when Tam came across the hall at a racing toddle and slithered onto his bottom inches from my feet. Quickly making my excuses, I returned the telephone to its cradle and was about to pick up my son, when I saw Mrs. Pickle plodding down the stairs.

"Did Jonas give you a good tour?"

"We lost each other somewhere on the third floor." She was panting heavily as she sidestepped Abbey, who was lying on her back, pretending to be a throw rug. "This is a big house, and I can see I'll be using my broomstick more for getting around than cleaning. But that's what I'm here for, when all's said and done." She dropped down on a tapestry bench, stretched out her legs in their heavy lisle stockings, and closed her eyes. "You've got a lot of dust catchers, Mrs. Haskell, but all of them lovely."

"Thank you." I hoisted Tam higher in my arms and stroked his shiny copper hair.

"Anything particular wants doing?"

"Well"—I really hated to trouble her—"if it wouldn't be too much bother, you might give the drawing room a dusting. I'm having a few people over for tea."

"Anyone I know?" Mrs. Pickle opened one eye.

"Lady Kitty Pomeroy, Beatrix Taffer, and Reverend Spike's mother-in-law, Bridget." Feeling guilty in the face of her exhaustion, I added quickly, "It's not just a social occasion; we will be discussing their entries for the homemaking events at the summer fête."

"That goes for your mother-in-law too?" Mrs. P. now had both eyes open.

"She does the most wonderful crocheting." I waved my free hand at the hundred and one doilies gracing the hall.

"Sounds to me as how she's going to be here for some time."

"It's a strong possibility." I remained determined to face facts.

Poor Mrs. Pickle! Her face seemed to lose some of its cushioning as it turned a pale beige. That heartless Jonas! He must have told her that he had proposed to Mum and was anticipating a happy outcome. Men! I was tempted to wring his scrawny neck when I met him a few minutes later in the gallery upstairs, but he managed to get around me by offering to take the twins to his room for a game of peek-a-boo while I went and had a word with Mum.

She was dressed in a brown frock that wouldn't have done me for a sleeve, and it was clear to me our newfound relationship had taken a backwards turn, because she looked only moderately pleased at the interruption. Taking her cue, Sweetie poked her furry face out from under the bed to give me the evil eye. Mrs. Pickle could learn a thing or two from that dog.

"I decided to stay up here out of the way when I realized you had company." Mum kept right on rearranging her brush and comb on the dressing table.

"That's Mrs. Malloy's replacement." In my nervousness I almost committed the unforgivable error of straightening the reading-lamp shade. "She turned up uninvited and I simply wasn't up to turning her away when I am half out of my mind with worry."

"If that's a dig at me, Ellie"—Mum drew herself up so that she was almost as tall as the bedpost—"I can marry Jonas at once and get out of your hair. After all"—her eyes filmed with tears—"my dog does need a father."

Over Sweetie's woofs of agreement or denial, I stammered, "It's n-not y-you, Mum: *I'm* the problem. Why, oh, why did I ever agree to chair the summer fête when I am completely incapable of doing a decent job?" Sinking down on her bed, I buried my face in my hands. "Chitterton Fells isn't like London. Word will spread like wildfire that I've made a hopeless bungle of my responsibilities and Ben—your one and only son—will be put in the *horrible* position of trying to defend me. Business at Abigail's may even start to fall off, and then where will we be?"

I refrained from adding *Out on the streets, busking with Dad?* because I had decided to keep quiet for the time being on my father-in-law's current business venture. One hurdle at a time.

"Far be it from me to make light of your problems, Ellie." Mum's voice had perked up, just as I hoped it would. "And never let it be said I'm one to boast, but if you want to know what stress is, you should try doing the bingo books for your church the way I have for Holy Mother Mary's all these years. I don't suppose you believe me"—her sniff sounded somewhat perfunctory—"but if Father O'Grady were standing here now, he would tell you straight out that not once have I come up a penny short at the end of the year."

"I don't know how you coped, what with the Legion of Mary, the Altar Guild, and all your other commitments." I struggled valiantly off the bed. "Thanks for listening to my problems, Mum. Please say a prayer that I will muddle through and not make too big a botch of this afternoon's tea."

"This afternoon's what?"

"It's for women interested in entering the homemaking events at the fête—knitting, crocheting, gardening, baking—that sort of thing."

"Crocheting?" Mum's ears pricked up.

"It's one of our most prestigious categories." I stood, hesitating, with my hand on the doorknob. "This sounds awfully cheeky, but would you be willing to make some of your scones for this afternoon? Mine always turn out like rocks and—"

"We can't expect to be good at everything, Ellie."

"That's a kind way of putting it," I said humbly.

"You have to concentrate on your good points." Mum followed me out of the bedroom. "I've never liked to mention it before for fear you'd think I was trying to flatter you, but I have to say you do make a nice pot of tea."

To an Englishwoman there is no higher praise. Encouraged beyond my deserts, I said, "If you would help me make a success of this afternoon, I would be eternally grateful. But there is one problem I've been afraid to mention. . . ."

"You don't have any milk for the scones?"

"Worse than that." I took a deep breath. "Beatrix Taffer will probably show up and—"

"I understand, Ellie." Mum stopped dead in her tracks and assumed her martyr's expression. "This is an official function which Bea has every right to attend. And never let it be said I expected you to slam the door in her face. I'll make sure I keep out of the way when your guests arrive."

"But I want you at the tea. I *need* you there."

"Then"—her sparrow eyes shone and her hollow cheeks turned pink—"that's where I'll be."

She did not say *And may God have mercy on Beatrix Taffer's soul,* but the words vibrated in the air. And, unable to resist the urge, I gave her a hug and said, "Would you like me to curl your hair and try a little eye shadow on you? After all, it wouldn't hurt to put your best face forward and outshadow Tricks."

Catching sight of herself in the wall mirror, Mum stood shoulders back, chest out . . . as far as it would go. I could see the wheels turning. Would stuffing some cotton wool into her bra be an immoral act? Her eyes met mine, but all she said was "I'd better get started on those scones."

Just as well one of us had a sense of the imperative. The minutes always fly by when there aren't enough of them to go around. When Mum went off to the kitchen, I located Mrs. Pickle in the drawing room and was reassured to discover she was not driving the Hoover around the carpet at an unlawful rate of speed. Then it was back upstairs to collect the twins from Jonas, who, when he heard that women in twos and threes would be descending upon the house, promised to lock himself in with his chamber pot and a good book. And who was I to brand him a coward, with Mum and Mrs. Pickle already complicating his bachelor existence? All I needed was to have Tricks start making eyes the size of half crowns at Jonas and Mum might decide to elope to Gretna Green with him. After all, Mr. Watkins's ladder was standing ready and willing up against the house.

Abbey, bless her, ate her lunch like a perfect lady and made no attempt to distract Mum in her scone-making by throwing carrots and sausage chunks at her. Tam was another story. My son kicked and squirmed, dumped his food on his booster chair tray, and to show me he was well and truly prepared to do combat, put his tin hat, otherwise called a bowl, on his head. Great! I now had to wash his hair before putting him down for his nap. By which time Abbey, understandably, demanded some special attention upon being tucked into her own cot.

Bong went the grandfather clock when I made it back downstairs. Two-fifteen? So little time, so much to go wrong! Tobias Cat ate an insect that didn't want to be eaten, and got stung in the mouth. I dropped the vase containing Jonas's dahlias and spent five minutes picking up glass and getting most of it in my knees. And there was Mrs. Pickle. I had assumed she would depart by one at the latest, but when she made it clear she would stick around until the last chair leg was dusted—which, knowing her, could be the end of the century—I felt compelled to go and make her some lunch, a ham sandwich without any ham but with lots of mustard.

The only sustenance *I* got was an energizing whiff of Mum's rack of golden scones, but no doubt that was enough to make me gain two pounds. It took some persuasion to get her into the downstairs washroom for a fast makeover, but the results were well worth the effort. A few twirls with the curling iron, a couple of strokes of eye shadow, a dab of blush on both cheeks, and she looked pretty enough to take on Beatrix Taffer.

Speak of the other woman! I had barely unplugged the curling iron when *buzz* went the doorbell.

"Better early than never, that's what I say!" Brimming with mischief, Tricks bounded over the threshold, Indian draperies floating from her shoulders like a dozen or more print scarves, pudgy hands flapping. Today she had moussed down her hair so that it clung like a bathing cap. But otherwise it was the same Tricks. The moment the front door closed she remembered she had left the bag of vegetables she had brought for show-and-tell in the taxi. A desperate ringing of the bell produced the cabbie who had delivered my in-laws into my hands a few long days ago.

"Here!" He shoved a bag at me. It bulged with balloon-faced tomatoes that appeared to have been force-fed to bring them to maximum obesity in the shortest possible time.

Shutting the door on his indignant back, I discovered that Mum had also made good her escape. Who could blame her, in the face of her rival's apparent absence of remorse?

"What a cute pussycat!" Tricks had spied Tobias, sitting licking his chops, on the trestle table. "I'm nuts about all animals! That's why I can't eat them. Live and let live is what I say."

"That's a lovely attitude," I replied even as I thought about Goldilocks, who got poached by mistake.

As if reading my mind, Tricks did her best to look downcast when saying, "Young Dawn is still horribly cross with her old gran for that mixup with the saucepans yesterday. She told me I'd better sleep with one eye open in the future. Teenagers! I had to laugh at her! The child will learn fast enough that life is too short for fretting and fussing. And I only wish dear old Mags would finally get the good news." Tricks watched me trying not to drop the bag of tomatoes. "Talking of my best friend, wasn't she here a minute ago?"

"She'll be back."

"Goodness! I hope she hasn't gone off to pout. They say pouting is worse than smoking when it comes to causing wrinkles. A smile on your face keeps the doctor away has always been my thinking."

"I must remember that." I was about to suggest we head into the drawing room and see if Mum was playing lady-in-waiting, when—as if she had heard the magic mention of cigarettes—Bridget Spike appeared in the glass panel beside the door and thumbed the bell. In she came like a breath of Irish morning, her wrinkles unabashedly displayed, her parrot nose in full command of her face, and her shaggy hair making no apologies for scorning the comb.

"If it isn't grand to see you looking fresh as the daisy, Mrs. Haskell!" The fog rising up off the bogs was in her voice, and even more welcome than a pot of gold was the jar of marmalade she set down on the trestle table.

"How kind of you! And please, call me Ellie!"

"And who will this be"—she shifted her handbag up her arm as she turned to Tricks—"is it Lady Kitty Pomeroy or Beatrix Taffer I have the pleasure of meeting?"

After making the necessary introductions, I led the way to the drawing room. There we found Mum. The good news was that she wasn't hiding out behind the curtains, the bad news was that she had decked herself out with so many bead necklaces and bracelets, she resembled a refugee trying to escape with all her worldly goods. Another time after getting her ready for a social engagement I must remember to check her pockets.

"Don't get up, Mags my love." Scooting across the room, Tricks planted a kiss on the cheek of stone. "You stand there growing good and the rest of us will be our naughty selves."

Before Mum could start chewing on her beads and spitting them out, however, Bridget went up to her. "If it isn't a rare treat to meet you, Mrs. Haskell may never set foot again in Ireland. And is it you my daughter-in-law, Eudorie, tells me is such a marvel with the crochet hook?"

While Mum thawed visibly, I set down my burden of home-grown veggies on the table in front of the window, where they could soak up the sun and do some more growing. In refusing to leave me in the lurch, Mrs. Pickle had left the Hoover on the hearth rug and a dust rag draped over a lampshade, but what did that matter? Eudora and Frizzy had their afternoons to themselves and were hopefully making the most of every mad moment.

"Sure and away, Ellie," gushed Bridget, "it's a kind thing you did inviting me to your wee tea party."

"It won't be all that 'wee.' " Mum reacted immediately to the suggestion that there was anything cheese-paring about the company. "We are expecting more people."

"That's right; we have Lady Kitty coming and who knows who else will show up?" Given the uncertainties of this life, I did not feel I was telling a bald-faced lie.

"And isn't it exciting—all of us getting together to talk about our exhibits in the summer fête!" Tricks plopped down in a chair, her legs flying almost over her head, in a flurry of Indian muslin that revealed a tempting display of dimpled thigh. "I lie awake nights dreaming of one of my marrows being awarded the first-place ribbon. Me, Beatrix Taffer, famous in my old age."

"I'd say you've already made quite a name for yourself." Mum retreated to the chair farthest away from her friend while, seemingly unaware of any nasty undercurrents, Bridget placidly sat on one of the ivory sofas that faced each other in front of the fireplace.

"Would you be having an ashtray, Ellie, anywhere abouts?" Bridget was reaching into her handbag as she spoke. "We had a wee bit of a fire last night at the vicarage and Eudorie—who's a grand girl sure enough—is after me not to smoke in her house. It's to be banished I am to the outdoors, so it would be a splendid thing to light up here and suck all that good old muck into me lungs."

One hesitates to refuse a visitor lured into one's parlour, but Mum fortunately was not blessed with my social cowardice.

"My son, Bentley"—Magdalene exercised the force of his full name —"does not permit smoking in this house."

"Ah, it's a blessing—that it is, we don't all think alike." Bridget had barely finished making this equable reply, when the doorbell jarred me into action. In the hall I met Mrs. Pickle going as slow as her legs would carry her to open up. Sending her off to fetch the tea tray and scones, I did the honours.

"Lady Kitty!" I ushered her inside.

"You need to change your bell, dear." Her ladyship fixed me with a pained smile. "It doesn't go with the house at all. Has a very lower-class ring."

"I'll see to it," I stammered, having been promptly brought in line when confronted by her fierce fur coat and the voice that sounded as though she had a mouthful of plum pudding. On a brighter note, the cloth-covered dish she carried appeared to contain, if not a pud, a pie. When it came to anything with sugar and spice, I was always humbly grateful.

"You haven't done a bad job with the hall." Lady Kitty cast her eagle gaze over the swoop of banisters and the grandfather clock. "Of course, if it were me, I'd take up those flagstones and put down a nice, serviceable linoleum. And I'd get rid of those suits of armour; that sort of thing is considered nouveau riche these days." She prowled the area, making further inspection, then swivelled suddenly to face me. "I'm happy to give you these pointers, Ellie, because you're a girl who does her best."

"Thank you."

"My daughter Pamela is a different story. Would you believe she tried to talk me out of your suggestion that I exhibit some of my pies at this year's fête?" Lady Kitty tapped the cloth-covered dish with a forceful finger. "My life isn't easy, Ellie, but thanks to you I now see I was mistaken in not having set the standard years ago for the pie-baking community."

Before I could answer, she continued. "Don't think I'm not happy to stand here and listen to you chat, dear, but I'm afraid we'll have to save this for another time. If there's one thing I've learned, it's you can't run a village standing around twiddling your thumbs. Now, Ellie, why don't you take this delicious apple pie into the kitchen and cut it into nice neat slices, while I go in and get the meeting started?"

Duly dismissed, I retreated to the kitchen to find Mrs. Pickle stacking teacups and saucers in slow motion on a tray designed to hold at most one egg cup.

"Was that Lady Kitty?" Mrs. P. raised her head an inch at a time to look at me.

"Yes, and look what she brought!" I set the pie dish down on the table and raised the cloth to reveal a perfectly proportioned golden-brown crust. "If this tastes half as good as it looks and smells, she should be a shoo-in to win first-place honours in her category at the fête."

"As like as not, Mrs. Haskell."

"Oh, bother!" I exclaimed. "There goes the phone."

"That's the trouble with them things, make more work than they're worth, they do." Mrs. Pickle wiped her hands laboriously on her apron as she shuffled for the hall door. "That's why I've never had one put in my house for all Roxie Malloy keeps telling me I'm out of touch."

"You carry on here, I'll go and see who it is." My heart did not race along with my feet as I hurried to pick up the receiver, even though I had the feeling it would be Ben on the line. This would not be a case of his feeling an irresistible urge to whisper sweet nothings in my ear. He would be ringing to tell me about his talk with Dad.

"Hello," I said.

"Is this Mrs. Ellie Haskell?"

"Very funny, Ben," I said in response to the silly muffled voice, "but unfortunately I don't have time for fun and games."

"Then you'd better make time, hadn't you, Mrs. Haskell?"

"Who is this?" I was still thinking that someone, if not Ben, was tweaking my horn.

"Someone who wishes you well and would like to spare you any unpleasantness."

"Such as?" A chill was creeping down my spine.

"Oh, we do know how to play dumb, don't we?" The caller gave a hollow chuckle. "I'm talking about your chitchat at the Dark Horse and how you spent the evening plotting up ways to murder your mother-in-law."

"That was a joke!"

"Try telling that to the police, Mrs. Haskell."

"You're not scaring me." By now I was holding on to the phone with both hands to prevent it sliding out from my slippery palms.

"Aren't we brave? And I don't suppose you'd mind your hubby finding out what you have planned for his dear old mum. You could say I'm a pessimist by nature, Mrs. Haskell, but it strikes me he won't see the funny side. Could be he'd start to look at you different, out the corner of his eye, if you know what I mean."

"What exactly do you want?" I shrilled.

"Nothing a lady living in a swanky big house like yours can't afford. Why don't we say two hundred pounds? That's just a drop in the bucket." Again that nasty chuckle. "You're to leave it, sometime tomorrow, in the hollow tree at the end of the lane that leads up to Pomeroy Hall. Do I make myself clear?"

"Perfectly," I said numbly, and heard the phone go dead.

This couldn't be happening! I must be out of my mind to even consider the possibility of submitting to blackmail. The only sane—safe—thing to do was to make a clean breast of my sins and take the consequences. How bad could they be? Knees buckling, eyes squeezed shut against the sunlight breaking through the windows to point its accusing golden fingers at me, I saw Mum's wounded face rise up before me. All hope of establishing a better relationship with my mother-in-law would be doomed if she found out. She would think I hated her. And she was already in such a vulnerable state. Poor little sparrow.

Two hundred pounds wouldn't ruin me. But what about Frizzy, Eudora, or Pamela? Would they be hard-pressed to meet the blackmailer's demands if he played fair and put the squeeze on them too? Suddenly I found myself recalling that morning's telephone conversation with Pamela. What were her words when she thought she was talking to her husband Allan? *Did you come up with the money?* Her hasty explanation of wanting to go out on a shopping spree had not rung true.

And now a really ugly suspicion entered my head. What if Pamela— desperately short of cash, for whatever reason—were herself the blackmailer? The disguised voice of my caller could have been male or female. And was it pure coincidence that Pamela had mentioned the hollow tree in connection with her father-in-law, Bobsie Cat? No, I couldn't— *wouldn't*—believe it. There had to be someone else, some dark, tormented soul who had been made privy to that ill-advised conversation at the Dark Horse.

My heart stopped, then started up again with a hop, skip, and a jump. Heaven help me! I remembered fiddling with Peter Savage's tape recorder before placing it on the floor beside our table. That morning I had returned it to him—and perhaps when he turned it on he got an earful that suggested an easier way to make a living than busking for loose change. Oh, surely I was being ridiculous. The man was a slave to his art. Besides which, he had been vehement in professing his profound admiration for me. *Aha!* jeered a little voice inside my head. *Do you really need more evidence that he is a dangerous crackpot?*

"Mrs. Haskell!"

"Yes, Mrs. Pickle?" I came down to earth with a thud after jumping three feet in the air.

"I was wondering"—she was peering around the kitchen door—"if it would be an idea for Jonas to help me out with bringing in the tea, seeing as how there's more scones than I can carry in three loads."

"He's resting," I said, "so could you try and manage?" The wicked life I led was making me hard, I thought sadly as I went into the drawing room. Mum and Tricks were talking to each other under cover of a diatribe from Lady Kitty on the ready-made pies offered for purchase in the frozen section of supermarkets. Only Bridget paid any attention to my return.

"If it isn't herself come to join the company! Sure and away, I was picturing you like poor Martha in the Bible—slaving away at the cooker while her sister Mary sat buttering up to Jesus. . . ."

It was Mrs. Pickle who gasped. She had opened the door smack into my back and, with more speed than I had ever seen her exercise, dropped the tray of scones. Admittedly she would have made more of a statement if she had brought in the teapot and crockery, but she certainly caught the attention of one of those present. Lady Kitty did not descend from the raised hearth which comprised her podium. But she did stop talking—making it possible to hear what Tricks was saying to Mum.

"Now then, Mags love, you've no reason in the world to act upset. There's nothing between me and Elijah but a strong physical attraction. Believe me, it's you he needs for all the important things—like cooking his meals and washing his socks."

"Thank you very much" came the fuming reply.

"And, just between friends, I wouldn't go making a fuss about him giving up the greengrocery business."

Mum's answer was silence.

"Didn't you know?" Unabashed by the open scrutiny of Bridget and Lady Kitty, Tricks clasped her pudgy hands together and smiled broadly. "Elijah has taken up busking. I saw him this morning in the village square and—"

"The neighbours!" It was a cry to break a daughter-in-law's heart. "What will the neighbours say?"

"Don't worry, Mum." I spoke from the floor where I was picking up scones. "No one knows him hereabouts."

"If they don't, they soon will!" Tricks bounced in her chair with enthusiasm. "Take my word for it, Elijah and his busking partner are going to be famous. They were singing a song of their own composition—'The Fair Maid of Chitterton Fells.' And I don't suppose I need tell you that the woman who inspired it is sitting right here."

"Fancy that!" Mum drew upon some inner strength to come up with a thin congratulatory smile. "And here's me thinking you had already made a name for yourself as the kind of woman who would drop her knickers at the drop of a hat."

If ever a moment called for immediate interruption, this was it. Lady Kitty did look pointedly at her watch, and Bridget did fidget with the handbag holding her cigarettes, but it was the opening of one of the windows and the appearance of a leg extending itself over the sill that saved the day!

"Am I in time?" inquired my cousin Freddy as he sprang into the room with a grin as disreputable as his scraggy beard and unkempt ponytail. "A little bird told me that this meeting was for those wishing to audition for the job of reading tea leaves at the summer fête. And you know me, Ellie!" He scraped a bow, accompanied by a far-flung hand. "Have tent, will travel!"

"He's the limit," I informed all and sundry, including Mrs. Pickle, who was still picking up scones and no doubt thinking that as the rightful descendant of a full-blooded witch, she was the one with the third eye.

"Auditions?" Lady Kitty looked quite put out. "But surely you know, Ellie, that Frizzy Taffer's aunt Ethel always reads the tea leaves. "Hers is a true gift. She's been in constant communication with her husband, Herbert, since he passed over to the other side."

"I'm surprised," I responded, "that he takes her phone calls."

"What's that?" One of Lady Kitty's eyebrows went up and didn't come down.

"Just a joke," I said, not liking to repeat Frizzy's sad admission that Aunt Ethel was believed by her nearest and dearest to have pushed Uncle Herbert down the stairs to his death.

"The occult is no joking matter." Freddy smiled wanly in my direction as he moved about the room, hands extended, eyes half closed. He had us right where he wanted us. Lady Kitty on her podium. Bridget in her armchair. Mum and Tricks on their opposing sofas. Mrs. Pickle still on her knees. And yours truly not knowing whether she was coming or going.

"Those of us who see beyond the immediacy of the moment bear a heavy burden." So saying, he crossed swiftly over to the table in front of the window and plucked one of Tricks's bulbous red tomatoes from the brown paper bag. "But don't let me frighten you." He bit thoughtfully into the oozing red flesh. "I see fame and fortune, a handsome man of noble lineage, and a journey across the sea for someone in this room."

"Anything else?" Being a fool, I *had* to egg him on.

"Like sudden death?" Mum was looking at Tricks.

"As in murder?" Freddy's grin was made the more ghoulish by the bloodred juice dripping onto his chin. "That's certainly one way of taking destiny back into our own two hands."

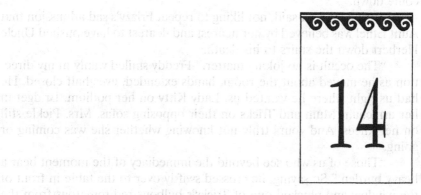

14

Morning can be extremely kind and sympathetic when it feels like it. On waking up the next day after a nightmare that was longer than *Gone With the Wind*, without even the hope of a sequel to provide a happy ending, I was really ashamed of myself for letting a trivial thing like blackmail ruin a night's sleep. As a woman on the go, I had to expect such occasional inconveniences and get on with my life.

Ben had the twins in their booster chairs and a cup of coffee ready for me when I entered the kitchen. What more could a woman ask, except perhaps the right to call her sins her own?

"You've got that look in your eyes," he said without glancing up from wiping the breakfast off Tam's face.

"What look?"

"The one that says you're hiding something."

"Such as?" I laughed glibly.

"Something really serious."

"Like what?"

"You forgot to buy toilet paper or scorched one of my shirts." He was now looking at me, more in sorrow than in anger. "These things happen, sweetheart, and you have to learn to forgive yourself. What bothers me is that you sometimes forget that marriage is about communication."

"Hark, who's talking!" If I had learned one thing from wedded bliss, it was how to turn the tables. "I could hardly get two words out of you last night about your meeting with your father."

"You're right." He stood, rinsing off the facecloth at the sink. "But there wasn't much to say. Dad was heading out of the Dark Horse when I went to see him on my way to work. And later, when I caught up with him in the village square, I could barely get near him for the crowd he and his partner had attracted."

"Did you at least find out if he is staying on at the pub, or whether he plans to camp out under his umbrella?" I removed Abbey from her chair and set her down on the floor.

"There was no talking to him. Each time I tried, I got elbowed out of the way by some person tossing coins into the collection box like it was some good-luck fountain. As it was, I could barely hear myself think above the strumming of the sidekick's guitar and Dad's booming baritone."

"What is to be done?" I put Tam on the floor, where he could squabble with his sister. "He and Mum are growing further apart daily."

"Parents are a worry." Ben shrugged into his tobacco-coloured tweed jacket, took a slug of coffee, and gave me a token peck on the cheek. "Two are enough, Ellie, I really don't think I want to have any more."

"Say, 'Bye-bye, Daddy,'" I urged the twins, and got ignored for my trouble. Who could reasonably blame them for wanting a little time to themselves? For a few moments I, too, relished the quiet, but before I had finished turning over the front page of the newspaper, I realized my ears were on the alert for a repeat of yesterday, when people never stopped knocking on the door.

I was pouring myself a second cup of coffee when there came the *rat-tat-tap* so urgent I felt compelled to answer it. But before I could raise a foot to go and open up, Freddy slouched into the kitchen. What a sight for sore eyes! He had shaved his beard down to a convict's stubble. His ponytail looked as if it had been used for sweeping up, and his shirt had a rip that exposed one nipple.

"You hate me, don't you, Ellie?" He stepped neatly over the twins to lounge soulfully against the Welsh dresser.

"Never!" I cried. "My little tea party would have been deadly dull if you hadn't come climbing in through the window to send chills through everyone present."

"Then what is your excuse," he asked pitifully, "for not welcoming me with a piping hot plate of bacon and eggs? Surely you haven't forgotten, Ellie, that this is my day off?" Having got that off his semi-exposed chest, Freddy dragged out a chair, spun it around, and sat straddling the seat. "If you'll cross my palm with silver, coz, I'll read your cup."

"Thanks, Gypsy Rose Lee. But I think you exhausted your talents yesterday."

"The ladies *loved* me."

"So you always say." I bent down to hand Abbey the building block she needed to complete her wobbly stack. "But if you don't mind, I have more important things on my mind than your escapades."

"Mother-in-law troubles?" Not being a complete cad, Freddy achieved an expression of familial concern.

"Yes, to put it in a nutshell."

"She's being difficult?"

"More accurately, she's having a difficult time." Opening a cupboard, I pulled out a frying pan. "But heaven forbid that should come between you and a good breakfast."

"You're too good to me." Freddy dabbed his eyes before giving the chair a spin that sent it skidding across the floor to stop with its legs tucked neatly under the table. "How would you like me to take you out for a cheap, greasy lunch?"

"Thanks"—I slapped rashers of bacon into the pan—"but I am having lunch at Pomeroy Manor with Lady Kitty."

"You're coming up in the world."

"We are meeting to talk about the fête."

"I thought you did that yesterday."

"Today we'll be discussing where to rent the little Bunsen burners for the jacket potatoes and how many gallons of lemonade we will need. Which reminds me"—I cracked an extra egg into the pan for luck—"when do you plan to go around collecting money for supplies?"

"Tomorrow, cross my heart and hope to die!" Freddy approached his nose to the stove and in the process almost lost what remained of his beard. "I would go today, but I think duty might be better served by my staying and chatting up the old girl while you're off gadding."

I brushed past him on my way to the table. "Promise me that when you show up at people's doors with your little tin can you will look respectable."

Before he could respond with more than a wounded look, the door opened and in came Mum, wearing a dressing gown that looked as if it had been passed down from an older sister and had yet to be grown into.

"I thought I smelled cooking, Ellie, but don't bother laying a place for me. I'll turn right around and go back to my room so you can have a nice, private chat with your cousin, as is your right."

"My! You do look fetching this morning!" Flopping down in a chair, Freddy cranked his legs up so the heels of his wretched sneakers rested on the table edge. "Don't ask me what it is, but there's something different about you. Something kind of nifty."

"Ellie did curl my hair yesterday. . . ."

"Gosh! That's more than she's ever done for me."

"I'm sure she's very good to you . . . in her way." Mum completed her compliment by sitting down at the table. And flushed, less from the heat of cooking than the realization that she and I had indeed made progress yesterday, I put a plate of bacon and eggs in front of her.

"This looks quite nice, even if the egg is a bit runny." She poked at it with her fork. "But a piece of toast would have been sufficient." Her words still hung in the air when the hall door nudged open and Sweetie made her grand entrance. For a harrowing moment I thought Mum was going to set her breakfast plate on the floor. Instead, she bowed her head and said grace, then gathered up her knife and fork. It would seem an example must be set if she wished to prevent her little dog from becoming a picky eater.

Sweetie was showing her annoyance by refusing to let the twins grab hold of her tail, when Jonas came *humph*ing and *grumph*ing into the room.

"Didn't you hear the breakfast gong?" Freddy tilted his chair on its hind legs and lowered a piece of bacon down his throat with the panache of a sword swallower.

"He can have some of mine," Mum said quickly. And there was something about the way she subsequently passed Jonas the salt and pepper that had me worried. There is a bit of the temptress in every woman, and I doubted not that Mum was still smarting from her latest go-round with Tricks. A complication for which we had no one to thank but yours truly.

"Don't mind me, I can always come back next Tuesday." Jonas planted his elbows on the table and stuck out his moustache. Unlike me, he was very much a morning person and usually saved his grumpiness as a sort of treat—to be savoured later in the day. Immediately, I worried that he wasn't feeling well. Could it be that his lumbago was acting up? Or was the problem something more serious? As I poured him a cup of coffee, my mind shied away from the thought that lovesickness, like mumps, might be the more severe for attacking later in life. Nonsense, I told myself, the man didn't have serious designs on Mum. His marriage proposal had been made merely to boost her spirits during a trying time.

Perhaps I needed to get out of the house for lunch. But first things first. Abbey and Tam were getting restless so, leaving my kitchen crew to do the washing-up, I took them for a toddle around the garden and afterwards to the nursery to read to them from one of our favourite picture books. Then there were beds to make, washing to be done and hung out on the line, and a half-dozen odd jobs, so that time got away from me, and I would have had to scurry to get the twins fed if Mum had not offered to do this for me.

"I don't know how I managed without you," I said in my new spirit of appreciation after getting dressed for my outing. She had the washing-up done, Abbey and Tam down for their naps, and was at the kitchen table crocheting at a speed that made me fear her fingers would fly off.

"You go and have a good time, Ellie!" Her eyes followed me to the door. "Don't think about me sitting here by myself."

"Jonas is in the garden," I offered.

"I know, but I'm trying to keep my distance until I decide about marrying him."

"What about patching things up with Dad?" I tried not to sound panicky.

"That's not going to happen." Mum's nose twitched right along with her crochet hook. "If Beatrix can make him happy, who am I to stand in his way? Let her have him. Marriage to a busker isn't for me, thank you very much. My parents would turn in their graves."

What stick-in-the-muds!

While backing the car out of the stable, I considered buzzing down to the village square to see Dad and give him a piece of my mind. My confidence in my ability to meddle was undaunted, but a glance at my watch suggested I might be wise to go straight to Pomeroy Manor. Once through the iron gates and heading down Coast Road, I fixed my mind in a straight line, refusing to let it veer left or right. The morning had been clear, if not exactly bright and breezy. Now a mist was creeping up from the ground in trailing wisps—as yet no bigger than puffs of smoke from a cigarette but promising bigger and better things to come. I was thinking, as I turned onto Market Street, that we hadn't had a good healthy fog in some time, when who should I see standing on the near corner but Frizzy Taffer, complete with headscarf. Her hands were laden with shopping bags so that it seemed unconscionable to pass by with a toot and a wave. What could Lady Kitty do to me if I arrived at Pomeroy Manor ten minutes late? Order that I be put in the stocks? Besides, it might not be a bad idea to ask Frizzy if she, too, had heard from the blackmailer. Which reminded me— Clutching the handbag at my side, I had to stop by the hollow tree on my way to the manor and make my deposit.

Pulling up alongside the curb, I rolled down the window and asked, "Want a lift?"

"Are you sure it's no trouble?" Was it only the shopping that made Frizzy look as if she had the weight of the world in her hands?

"Hop in!"

"This is nice of you, Ellie." Arms cradling her bags, she leaned back in her seat as the car took off. "Tricks says she had a wonderful time at your house yesterday. Nonstop laughs is the way she put it."

"There were some fun moments." I struggled to remember what they were.

"I hear your cousin Freddy is a scream." Frizzy swayed towards me as we rounded a curve, and I caught a good look at her face.

"What's wrong?" I asked. "And don't tell me nothing, because it's written all over you. Has Tricks poached any more goldfish, or . . . ?"

"Oh, Ellie, it's my aunt Ethel. She's really a lovely person and the children are ever so fond of her, really they are—even Dawn, for all she sometimes calls Ethel a nasty old cow. Auntie almost had a fit when Tricks went and blabbed about your cousin wanting to do the tea leaf readings at the fête."

"He was doing a leg pull." I turned on the windscreen wipers to get rid of the mist.

"That's what it sounded like to me, but Auntie was already in one of her tempers over what happened with my hair. Tom was really worried that she would knock Tricks out cold and"—Frizzy pressed a hand to her headscarf—"who needs that sort of thing in front of the children? It took me a good hour last night to get Auntie calmed down and afterwards . . . well, it couldn't be more awkward; she's decided to move in with us until Tricks moves out."

"If it doesn't rain, it pours," I said, looking up at the rapidly darkening sky.

"Really, Ellie, under normal circumstances I'd be glad to have her. Auntie practically brought me up, so I've learned to make allowances when she flies off the handle into one of her shouting fits, but what with children, and the neighbours being so difficult, and the upset with Mrs. Pickle . . ."

"What was that about?" I turned onto Robert Road.

"It was all Dawn's fault, the naughty girl. Would you believe she stamped and screamed—just the way Auntie does—and accused Mrs. Pickle of stealing her Barbie dolls. As if the woman would want them! Honestly, I didn't know where to look. My face must have gone as red as my hair . . . what there is of it."

"Was Mrs. Pickle upset?"

"She took her time—the way she does everything else, but when Dawn suggested we search her bag, she did flare up. And who could blame her? I didn't think I would ever stop apologizing. And I felt so sorry for the poor woman, knowing she had to go straight from our house to work at the vicarage."

"And you didn't look in the bag?"

"Of course not!"

"Mrs. Pickle didn't insist?"

"If she had, I would have died on the spot." We were now on Kitty Crescent. As we closed in on Frizzy's house, she exclaimed, "Look, there's Aunt Ethel at the gate, waiting for me. At least Tricks doesn't make me feel like a kid. In fact, most of the time I feel years older than her."

I pulled the car up against the curb. "I'm sorry you've been having such a difficult time."

"I deserve some sort of punishment for being a bad girl at the Dark Horse the other night."

Here was my cue to talk to her about the blackmailer. But surely if the money-grubber had put the squeeze on Frizzy, that would have topped her list of today's problems. And what was the point of scaring her on the off chance that he—or she—might phone? For all I knew, whoever it was might not even be aware of Frizzy's involvement in the mother-in-law plot. Or the villain could have decided it wasn't worth the cost of a phone call attempting to get money out of someone who didn't have it and who might in a state of desperation turn around and go to the police.

Whatever, it was too late to say anything. Aunt Ethel had the car door open and her arms halfway across the seat, scooping up shopping bags. "There you are, Frizzy!" Her voice was piercing. "I've been that worried, you wouldn't know. Up and down the streets I've been, asking everyone if they'd seen my little girl."

"You shouldn't have worried." Frizzy got out of the car. "My friend Ellie Haskell gave me a lift home from the shops."

"Now, isn't that kind!" Aunt Ethel had to bend almost double to loom in the car doorway. She had a face that looked as though it had gone sixteen rounds in the boxing ring. Her right eyelid didn't open properly and her nose looked as if it had been broken so many times, she had given up trying to fix it. She held those hefty shopping bags as if they were filled with candy floss.

"How do you do?" I stammered.

"Any friend of my little girl's is a friend of mine." Auntie gave me a smile that sported several missing teeth. "An awful time she's been having, as she's probably told you, and did I ever foam at the mouth when I found out about her lovely hair. But never you worry, if I don't get to black both Beatrix Taffer's eyes, I'll find another way to get even. And when I'm done with her, I'll lick young Dawn into shape, see if I don't! If there's one thing I won't stand for, it's anyone running roughshod over my little girl. She's never been what you could call strong, has our Frizzy."

"It's been lovely meeting you."

Aunt Ethel must have taken to me, because she did not ram my smile down my face, but when she closed the door with a slam that sent the car halfway across the road, I was relieved to be off. Frizzy and her aunt were still waving as I drove around the corner. I picked up speed despite the mist that was now billowing up like steam from a witch's cauldron. That reminded me. Poor Mrs. Pickle, I thought. The life of a daily help is not all it's cracked up to be.

Knowing that Lady Kitty would be very cross with me for being late, I still searched for the hollow tree as I turned off the road onto the wooded lane that looped its untidy way outside the walled grounds of Pomeroy Manor. Yes, there it was—a lofty oak, around which a cluster of scrub trees hovered, like courtiers waiting upon the orders of his majesty.

I had to hand it to the blackmailer, he or she could not have chosen a better place for the dropoff. In less time than it would have taken me to make a deposit at the bank, I knelt on the mossy ground and shoved the envelope containing four fifty-pound notes into the elf-size opening at the base of the trunk. What took up time was dusting off my skirt; I had to make a production of the business in order to rid myself of the feeling that I had been contaminated by an evil embedded in every stray blade of grass. Getting back into the car, I was glad I had left the motor running, because there was no way I could have grasped the ignition key, let alone turned it.

As I proceeded down the lane and turned through the brick pillars onto the drive that ran between an honour guard of trees for a good half mile up to the hall, I kept telling myself that I no longer had anything hanging over my head . . . until the next phone call. At which time I would talk tough to the blackmailer, explain that he had caught me on the hop the first time, but never again. Let him go to the police with his tittle-tattle and have them laugh in his face. Mum was alive and well and the bodies of the other mothers-in-law had certainly not started piling up.

Pomeroy Manor stood in the sort of leafy setting that might have welcomed Henry VIII on one of his trysts with Anne Boleyn. The house was a proud but friendly old-timer with a ruddy brick face and twinkling window eyes. But on closer inspection, the gardens were a disappointment. Every tree and shrub had been given an army haircut, and what flowers there were stood shivering in the grey mist as if afraid to put a petal wrong. Parking the car on a stretch of asphalt that would have put the average dinner table to shame, I went up the bleached white steps to ring the gleaming doorbell.

Before I could smooth a hand over my windblown hair, Lady Kitty opened the door. She ushered me into the wainscotted hall that must have seen many a baronial bash.

"Here you are, Ellie, at long last."

"So sorry I'm late," I babbled, "but on my way here I saw someone I knew and gave her a lift home."

"If you rode a bicycle, dear"—Lady Kitty closed the door with a thump—"you wouldn't get asked for rides. We have to think about the choices we make . . . and take the consequences."

"How true."

"Come along, then." She bustled me down the hall at a pace that allowed no time to gawk. "It's Hobson's choice, so I hope you like blood pudding. Pick up your feet, that's a good girl." Shoving open a door, she said, "This is the dining room, and as you see, Bobsie Cat and Pamela are sitting waiting to tuck in their bibs. Now, if you'll take your place, Ellie, I'll dish up."

"Hullo. It's nice to see you again." Pamela's smile gave no indication that we were anything other than mere acquaintances. Our tipsy evening at the Dark Horse and our phone conversation yesterday might never have happened. Today Pamela wore her hair loose with a headband. She looked disarmingly young as she turned to her father-in-law. "Bobsie Cat, this is Ellie Haskell from Merlin's Court."

"Is it, by Jove?"

"It's a pleasure to meet you, Sir Robert."

"Likewise, m'dear!"

He was a large, red-faced gentleman with a bald head and a tic to his left eye that gathered speed when Lady Kitty, armed with a huge spoon, *plonk*ed a chunk of pudding onto his plate, along with a goodly helping of vegetables. Hers were the ways of a woman who always served "Father" first, so he could hurry back to his plowing the moment he had wiped his mouth on the back of his sleeve. It mattered not that Sir Robert looked incapable of doing anything more strenuous than cleaning his duelling pistols.

A serving of pudding and vegetables landed with a thud on my plate. And after dolloping out portions for herself and Pamela, Lady Kitty took her seat at the head of the table.

"Tuck in, everyone," she ordered.

I opened my mouth to lie bravely and say I adored blood pudding, but all heads were down as the knives and forks sliced their way down to the bare bone of the china. Were mealtimes always this way at Pomeroy Manor? Sir Robert struck me as the quiet type who, at least in the presence of his wife, rarely risked saying anything more controversial than "What! What!" But Lady Kitty definitely had a voice of her own. And Pamela could be quite a chatterbox. Was I the reason for this constraint? Or had the family taken a vow of silence at table, to be broken only in direst need of asking for the salt and pepper?

Toying with my food, I took stock of the dining room. It must once have been very handsome with its cathedral windows and lofty timbered ceiling, but some nameless person had created the marvelous illusion of reducing it in size to a council-house boxiness, where all the furnishings had been bought with more thrift than taste, on the never-never.

"Anyone for seconds?" Lady Kitty raised her serving spoon on high, and when Sir Robert and Pamela shook their heads, I felt emboldened to do likewise.

"You can go ahead and speak now, Ellie." Her ladyship's smile could have been a frown—they would always be interchangeable. "I don't allow conversation during meals because it interferes with digestion, but when you've cleaned your plate you're free to chatter on as you like, isn't that right, Bobsie Cat?"

"Yes, m'dear."

"And I don't allow comic books at the table, do I?"

"No, m'dear."

"We'll save our talk about the fête, Ellie, until we've had our apple charlotte." Lady Kitty rose to her feet and began gathering up plates. "Who's ready for a nice big helping?"

"I'm full," said Pamela.

"That's not a proper excuse, is it, dear? You know you have to keep your strength in case the day ever comes when you find yourself in the family way with our little heir."

"Yes, Mumsie Kitty."

"That's better."

Lady Kitty took out the empties and brought in the apple charlotte and a jug of custard. Both were delicious, but we were not allowed to sit back and relish the memory. The moment we laid down our spoons, Lady Kitty was back on her feet, pouring out large tumblers of milk to be placed with no ifs, ands, or buts in front of each of us.

"I don't allow tea or coffee after meals, do I, Bobsie Cat?"

"No, m'dear!"

"Too strong for the tummy." Lady Kitty patted her own affectionately before sitting down and removing a sheet of paper from under her place mat and passing it over to me. "Here's the list of equipment we'll be needing for the fête and the estimated cost of purchase or rental. You'll see that the most expensive item is the hoop-la stall, but there's no getting around the fact we must have a new one this year. We don't want to be shown up in front of Bobsie Cat's cousin—the Honourable George Clydesdale—when he presents the Martha. Georgie is a remarkable man." Lady Kitty paused to draw breath. "Not only has he done a very nice job with his vineyards in France, he has also managed to hold on to all his hair."

"Marvelous!" I avoided looking at Sir Robert's naked dome.

Pamela raised her head. "I thought you said, Mumsie Kitty, that if he had an ounce of patriotism, Uncle George would move his vineyards to England?"

"That was before he and I had our little talk, and he promised to set up a bottling factory in this country." Her ladyship bestowed a quelling glance on her impudent daughter-in-law before handing me a pen. "So, Ellie, if you'll just initial the page, dear, we should be all set."

"There's nothing else we need to discuss?"

"Not a thing." She watched me trying to turn a blot into an extra-large full stop. "Like always, I have everything under control. And now if you, Bobsie Cat, and Pamela would like to go into the parlour and have a natter, I'll get back to the kitchen and start the washing-up."

"May I help?" I asked in hope of turning the visit to some account.

"I'm better on my own, dear, especially as I want to give the stove a cleaning. Every day has its set jobs and—" She broke off, possibly as a result of my look of surprise, but more probably because Sir Robert had seized the moment to slump forward on the table. His outstretched arms knocked over the salt cellars along with his brimming glass of milk.

Pamela let out a squeal. When that failed to bring him around, I rose from my chair, bent on rushing over to administer mouth-to-mouth resuscitation (according to Mum it *had* worked for Sweetie). Lady Kitty didn't bat an eye.

"Don't encourage him, Ellie." She was gathering up pudding plates with hands as steady as rocks. "This is the silly old duffer's way of trying to get attention. I'm the one with the high blood pressure, but that's life, isn't it? And it has to go on. So I'll get started with the washing-up while you girls make sure he doesn't do something silly like swallow his tongue."

To show she wasn't too cross, Lady Kitty patted her husband's bald head in passing and went out the door. Immediately after she left, Sir Robert cracked open a decidedly malevolent eye and croaked: "God save me from that woman. What! What!"

"Oh, Bobsie Cat, you were only teasing!" Pamela fell upon him with hugs as he straightened up.

"I thought, m'dear, it wouldn't hurt to show your friend Mrs. Haskell that your mother-in-law is a cold-blooded monster. Not often we have a witness. And, stap me, if I won't need a fresh-faced young filly to put in a good word for me when I'm standing in the dock at the Old Bailey, defending m'self for bludgeoning the old girl to death. What! What!"

"You really are naughty!" Pamela dimpled up at him; I stood by, speechless.

"You're right, m'dear, and now I'm going straight upstairs to hole up in my room." Somewhere out in the kitchen a pan clanged and, with his twitch back in full force, Sir Robert bade me a hasty adieu and exited the room.

"He tries to be brave, poor darling! But you can see he is a soul in torment." Pamela obviously shared Sir Robert's penchant for comic books. "If he dies—or I should say when, seeing it's never an option for any of us—I will be alone all day with Mumsie Kitty."

"Couldn't you find a place of your own?"

"We don't have the money. She takes Allan's paycheque and gives him only enough for expenses. And that's something I need to talk to you about, Ellie." Pamela crept up to the door and pressed her ear against it before returning to lead me by the hand back to the table.

"What is it?" I asked as we both sat down.

Her big brown eyes sparkled with tears. "I need to borrow some money. I'm in the most awful fix. I haven't known which way to turn."

"Are you being blackmailed?"

"Ellie! How ever did you guess?"

"Easy! I got a phone call yesterday, demanding a payment of two hundred pounds in return for him—or her—keeping quiet about what he overheard at the Dark Horse."

"When we talked about murdering our mothers-in-law?"

"What else?" I stared at her.

"But that's not why I'm being blackmailed. With me it's been going on since right after Allan and I were married. You know all about the matrimonial bake-off"—she brushed her hair back from her brow with a trembling hand—"but what only Allan and I and one other person know is that I *didn't* bake the pie that won me Prince Charming."

"You didn't?" My voice rose in a squeak; I immediately clapped a hand over my mouth.

"I'm a terrible cook. I was at my wit's end at the thought of losing Allan, until I remembered my aunt Gert. She's a professional baker in Norwich. She sells her frozen pies to a number of supermarkets, and when she knew what I was up against, she offered to make the all-important apple pie for me. On the day of the bake-off she arrived at my house with it nicely under wraps in her carryall. And while we were talking in the sitting room I . . . realized someone was outside by the open window. But I never thought about blackmail. And even when the phone calls started coming I didn't get too panicked. The demands weren't too bad at first—just a couple of pounds at a time. But they've been creeping up, and the little nest egg I had before my marriage is gone. I don't have any more jewellery to sell, and every time I mention getting a job, Mumsie Kitty has a fit. Her daughter-in-law's place is in the home, under her thumb."

"How much does our friend want this time?" I asked.

"Two hundred pounds."

"At least he or she doesn't play favourites."

"Ellie, can you lend me the money?"

"This blackmail is never going to end."

"Yes, it will!" Pamela's eyes narrowed and her dimples disappeared completely. "I *have* to find a way out, because I can't go on like this. Just help me this once, Ellie, please!"

Reaching into my handbag for my cheque book, I wrote out the required amount and handed it to her. "No mention has been made to you about the mother-in-law thing?"

"Not yet."

"Keep your fingers crossed." I capped my pen, put it away, and stood up. "We'll keep in touch," I said, crossing to the door.

"Do you have to go?" She followed me out into the hall, and I found myself hating to leave her in that house that should by rights have been cozy and wonderful even though the family portraits had been taken down and replaced by Woolworth prints.

"I really must." I gave her a hug before stepping out into the swirling mist. "Please explain to Lady Kitty that I had to get home and didn't like to interrupt her oven-cleaning. By the way"—I turned back on reaching the path that wove between the flower beds and the lawn—"how have you been able to keep up the pretense of being a great cook?"

"No problem," said Pamela. "Mumsie Kitty has never let me touch a mixing bowl since I married Allan."

"Typical!"

It also went without saying that I would wander around in circles, the way I always did in a parking lot, before stumbling upon my car. The trees lining the drive kept me on the straight and narrow, but when I got out onto the lane I was glad I had put my deposit in the hollow oak on my way to the hall. The fog was thickening with every turn of the wheels and I couldn't wait to be safely home. Making my way through the village didn't pose any particular problems. I just tagged along behind a friendly little car in front of me until we came to a parting of the ways at the foot of Cliff Road. Now I was on the home stretch and should by rights have been quite comfortable, seeing I had been known to boast that I could drive it blindfolded. We say these idiotic things and never expect to be punished for them.

Part of me wanted to hurry, the way you do when you think you're out of petrol, but caution dictated I take each wavering loop of road with caution. Every boulder that showed itself on the verge was as welcome as a beacon. The bus stop loomed up, looking lost and lonely. Visibility was down to two inches, and I suspected the car of squeezing its headlights shut as we approached the top of the hill. It was certainly making nervous noises. That is why, when I neared the vicarage, I thought the scream was mechanically induced.

But when it came again, high-pitched and wailing, I knew that someone was out there in the fog. Someone who was dealing with a bigger problem than a dropped picnic basket. Drawing the car to a lurching halt, I flung open the door. The ground not only looked soft and fuzzy, it felt that way as I stumbled blindly towards the voice which continued to scream with utmost helpfulness.

"Coming!" I shouted.

"Over here!"

"Don't move!" It was advice I would have done well to heed myself, for at that moment I almost went over the cliff, which would have been extremely hard on the shadowy figure who peered up at me from what seemed to be a narrow ledge some ten feet below me.

"If it isn't grand to see you, Mrs. Haskell," said Bridget Spike. "Would you be after having a cigarette on you to help steady me nerves?"

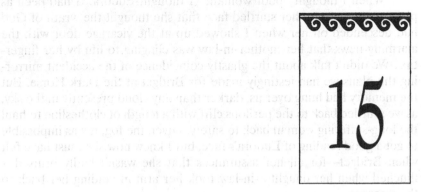

15

"**S**he could have been killed!" Ben was still stating the obvious the next morning. A concerned frown humanised his glamour-puss image as he reclined on the bed in his black silk dressing gown, hands under his head, looking for all the world as if he were posing for a fashion layout for some ultra-glossy gentleman's quarterly.

"Yes, dear."

"What a miracle you showed up when you did."

"Exactly."

"And you say she went out for a smoke, lost her bearings, and wandered right over the cliff?"

"Yes, dear."

"Thank God she landed on that ledge."

"Very true."

"One fatal slip and it would all have been over." Ben addressed his elegantly crossed ankles while I realized I had put my slacks on back to front and my blouse was inside out.

"Poor woman!" His sigh rattled me sufficiently that I couldn't get my zipper to go up or down. So much for all the hype about men learning to communicate with their wives. Here was one time when I didn't want to talk a subject to death, and there was no way to shut him up short of putting a pillow over his face. Perish the thought! I had once and for all put a rein on my murderous tendencies.

When I thought "poor woman!" I thought Eudora. It had been as plain as the nose on her startled face that she thought the wrath of God had descended on her when I showed up at the vicarage door with the alarming news that her mother-in-law was clinging to life by her fingertips. We didn't talk about the ghastly coincidence of the accident mirroring the plans we had jestingly made for Bridget at the Dark Horse. But the memory had hung over us, darker than any cloud presently in the sky, as we scuttled back to the perilous cliff with a length of clothesline to haul the long-suffering woman back to safety. Given the fog, it was impossible to get a good reading of Eudora's face, but I knew how she must have felt when Bridget—for all her assurances that she wasn't badly bruised—flinched when her daughter-in-law took her arm in guiding her back to the vicarage.

Eudora, being the pragmatic sort, would undoubtedly come to realize that she was in no measure responsible for the mishap. But I had been tempted several times the previous night to telephone in an attempt to comfort her with the reminder that I, with some help from Pamela, had come up with the imaginary scenario that had been coincidentally played out in real life. But on reflection, I had decided it was best to let the matter die a natural death. A fate to which Bridget Spike could once more happily aspire.

"Ellie"—Ben slid off the bed to wrap an affectionate arm around my shoulders—"I have a very special treat in store for you."

"Really?" Looking down at the blouse I had just finished buttoning, I wondered if I had wasted my time.

"I've decided to take the morning off. You need my manly support after your harrowing experience. And so, my darling, I will prepare you the breakfast of a lifetime—a golden crisp potato gateau layered with savoury cream and smoked salmon. And afterwards we will take a quiet walk in the garden." As he spoke, he led me over to the window, and we stood looking out upon a sunny scene of gently sloping lawns, colourful flower beds, and rustic benches taking their ease under the lush green shade of the trees.

"The garden is already taken." I pointed to where Mum and Jonas had come into view over by the copper beech, with Tam and Abbey toddling along on either side of them.

"This is beginning to look awfully cozy," said Ben.

"They make a nice couple," I agreed. "Anyone would take them for picture-perfect grandparents enjoying a special moment with the kiddies."

"And each other."

"But they don't belong together." I resisted stamping my foot.

"You think it's just a youthful infatuation?"

"I think we have to put a stop to it right now."

"Do you want me to put another flea in Dad's ear?" Ben's voice followed me across the room to the wardrobe, where I was rummaging around for a cardigan.

"Let me do it." I already had the bedroom door open and was halfway into the gallery. "We may get better results if I exert my feminine wiles. You'd feel self-conscious crying in the street. So why don't you stay here and keep the home fires burning?"

"I'll take the easy way out and go to work." He was untying his dressing gown on the run as I blew him a kiss and made good my escape. What I hadn't told him was that I felt a compelling need to put our house in order before my life got away from me. That my friends were in the same boat was no consolation. My heart went out to Frizzy, who now had to cope with hot-tempered Auntie Ethel in addition to Tricks, and to Eudora who—even as I was going out the front door—was probably taking down all her No Smoking signs. Pamela, admittedly, was a bit of a lame duck who could have done more to help her situation by standing up to Lady Kitty and getting a job. But having spent years bogged down by weight problems and a poor self-image, I knew too well what it was like to be caught in the trap of one's own powerlessness.

Mum, Jonas, and the twins must have gone back into the house, as I did not see them anywhere in the garden when I crossed the courtyard on my way to the car. It was completely irresponsible of me to leave without saying good-bye to my little darlings, but I was glad to avoid revealing my destination to Mum. She had to believe that when Dad returned to her, he was not responding to any outside pressure. Ben would explain I'd had to rush out and glibly avoid going into detail.

It was impossible not to feel optimistic on such a lovely morning. The sky was as blue as my children's eyes, and the scent of grass was worth fifty pounds an ounce as it came drifting on a soft, warm breeze through the open window of the car. Upon reaching the spot where

Bridget had plummetted over the cliff, I stirred uneasily in my seat. But that was nothing to my reaction when I saw her standing by the bus stop, a quarter of a mile down the hill from the vicarage. Even though the woman had claimed to be unhurt by her near-lethal experience, I had been picturing her tucked up in a bed with plump pillows, and sheets made up with hospital corners. Surely it was too soon for her to be out unaccompanied!

Stopping the car an inch from her feet, I stuck out my head to offer her a lift and got quite a turn, as Mrs. Malloy would say. That was a suitcase in Bridget's hand. I couldn't have been more shocked by the sight if she had been a known terrorist.

"Sure and away, it's kind of you to offer, but I'll not be putting you out," she said. "Is it not enough you've done for me already?"

"There won't be another bus for half an hour," I told her as I hopped out and stowed the case on the rear seat. "Get in and make yourself comfy."

"It's a grand girl you are"—she took her seat—"but I'll not be wanting to cause trouble between you and Eudorie. She was having a bit of a lie-down when I left, and Gladstone was off to the butcher's, so I didn't get to say me good-byes."

"Won't they be upset?" My hand hesitated on the gearshift.

"Indeed they will! Last night Eudorie was on at me to stay for good and all, but it's been pining I have for me own two rooms, where I can smoke without upsetting the apple cart."

"You're sure? I could run you back up to the house."

"That you won't!" Bridget made a grab for the door handle. "And you with troubles enough of your own. Sure enough, I left a note filled with songs of praise as would make the angels weep."

"I can't change your mind?"

"Not in a month of Sundays." Her smile was stretched thin and her sunken cheeks made her nose look beakier than ever. Only a fool could fail to understand her need to hole up in her own place within easy telephone reach of her own doctor. But from the way she kept glancing uneasily over her shoulder as we drove down the hill, I sensed Bridget had some reservations about bolting while Eudora's back was turned.

"Will it be taking you out of your way to drop me at the bus station?" she asked when we reached the village.

"Not at all," I assured her, and was shortly to discover I had never spoken more truly.

Parking the car outside the arena crowded with red and green double-deckers, I spotted the man I was looking for in the doorway of a flower shop on the corner across the way.

"Don't be coming in with me." Bridget reached into her handbag and brought out a jar of marmalade. "This here's a wee something for your kindness, and now it's off I am to me life of wickedness and sin."

Over her protests I carried her suitcase into the station, right up to the little kiosk where she would purchase her ticket, and with a hug and the feeling that all wasn't hunky-dory, I left her. Going was one thing, but taking her marmalade and heading home made me wonder if Bridget had sustained a head injury in her fall. The whole business was extremely awkward, and I was wondering, as I crossed the road, how I would explain my aiding and abetting to Eudora when next we met.

Luckily, I had other causes of concern. My father-in-law stood in front of the flower shop. He had a bunch of bananas under his arm and was calmly munching on the one in his hand. Of Mr. Savage there was no sign, but we would get to him later.

"Caught you!" I wagged an infuriated finger under Dad's nose. The breeze lifted his white hair from his bald spot and ruffled his beard. And *breezy* was the word for him all right. Really, it was too much.

"Don't let me block the doorway, Ellie," he roared for all the road to hear, and had the satisfaction of seeing a couple of pedestrians jump out of their skins or, rather, their raincoats. For wouldn't you know it had started to drizzle, but in a halfhearted fashion, like a child pretending to cry to get attention.

"I am not going into the shop," I informed him rigidly.

"What's that?" He affected a pout, most unbecoming in a man of his age. "Aren't you going to nip in and buy a bunch of flowers?"

"Whatever for?" I stared at the tubs of tea roses and sweet Williams set out on the pavement and wondered what Jonas would say if I paid good money for a nosegay wrapped in green tissue paper when our flower beds at Merlin's Court spilleth over.

"No need to jump down my throat." His brown eyes shone with the innocence of Sweetie at her most guileful. "Being a sentimental old fool, I thought Magdalene had sent you down to pick out a nice little bouquet to be delivered with her apologies for behaving like a . . ." He pursed his bristly lips.

"Like a woman?"

"That's the word." Dad stepped back to let a Darby and Joan couple totter past, their faces wreathed in wrinkles, their walking sticks tapping away in perfect harmony. "All alike, you women. Crying and carrying on for no good reason. But I'll say one thing for your mother-in-law, Ellie, she knows when it's time to come to her senses. So she doesn't say sorry with flowers. All the better. Would have come out of the house-keeping money and I'd be on bread and dripping for a week. What matters is she sent you down to tell me she's made a bloody fool of herself and wants me back."

"She did nothing of the kind."

If he heard me, Dad gave no heed. He was in full vigour, with the world at his feet and the bounty of nature under his arm. "It's not in my character, Ellie, to play the heavy husband. God knows you couldn't find a milder man than myself anywhere. And it's a sorry day when I'm turned out into the streets for taking a dip in the sea with a respectable female companion."

"At midnight! In the buff!"

I might as well have talked to the lamppost. The bananas were ripening while we stood and I experienced a gnawing fear that the twins would be teenagers and Ben have turned my side of the bed into a national shrine before this conversation was concluded.

"Mum didn't send me," I said, "but I'm here to beg you to come home and make an honest woman of her."

"She jilted me."

"That's neither here nor there."

"After nearly forty years!"

"Don't you care that Mum thinks you're up to tricks with Tricks?" Drops of rain, or possibly tears of frustration, dampened my face.

"Absurd!" Dad swelled up to twice his original size. A young woman caught in the glare of his scowl cut a wide swath around us with her thumb-sucking infant in its pushchair. "But I'll tell you something, Ellie, if I did end up in the arms of another woman, it would be because I was *pushed.*"

Here it was, the time for me to use the ace up my sleeve. What was good for the gander was even better for the goose.

"I don't want to frighten you, Dad," I lied. "The sad truth is Mum is feeling rejected and Jonas is on the spot—a rugged outdoor man in the prime of his golden years, ready and willing to put a ring on her finger."

"He doesn't know the woman!"

"These things happen. And I'm growing more afraid by the minute that she will accept his proposal."

"She must be in her second adolescence!" Dad's face had turned red as a traffic light. Cracks appeared in the pavement at his bellow, but I stood my ground.

"She's talking about dyeing her hair."

"Magdalene?"

"Yesterday she wore eye shadow."

"And you're letting this sort of thing go on?" he roared.

"There's not a lot I can do even if she decides to get engaged to Jonas. She's lonely and they are both single." I let the words sink in. "It may have slipped your memory, but Mum is a very attractive woman. And in the last few days she seems to have blossomed."

"Magdalene has her moments," Dad conceded gruffly. "Like when she dishes up her meat pud and two vege. Why don't you go back home, Ellie, and tell her I'm prepared to let bygones be bygones if she'll admit she was wrong and ask me to come back."

"I will do nothing of the sort," I told him angrily. "What's needed here is for you to pocket your pride and return to her, cap in hand. Fortunately for you, this does not appear to be one of your busier days as a busker. No screaming crowds, no little tin can, no Mr. Savage."

"Peter took the day off to stay in bed."

"Not feeling well?"

"Sore fingers, from plucking his guitar."

"It seems to me he might do well to rethink his chosen profession," I said coldly, "and you had better do some serious cogitating on the perils of life as a lonely old bachelor."

Leaving him to the dubious companionship of his bananas, I headed for my car without waiting for a policeman to see me safely across the road. I drove home in a state of blind fury. The man was as obstinate as a mule, and I had absolutely no business feeling sorry for him. It took some doing to stitch a smile on my face before entering the kitchen, but I made the effort in preparation for finding Mum crocheting away. But as it happened, the only sign of life was Mrs. Pickle. She was at the stove, standing over the kettle, which was puffing away like a steam engine.

"If it isn't you, Mrs. Haskell!" Were there beads of perspiration on her metal curlers as she smoothed her hands over her apron in an attempt to look hard at work? "I was just giving the inside of the kettle a cleaning."

"That's lovely," I said, not looking at the teacup set out with the ginger snap in its saucer. "I'd completely forgotten you were coming."

"I don't know as I said what days I'd be here." Mrs. Pickle reached for a rag and applied it a slow wipe at a time to the working surface. "But never you worry, your mother-in-law told me what to do and what not to do. She went upstairs a while back with the kiddies, bless their little hearts."

"Then I'll go up and have a word with them." I had just set my handbag down on the table, when Jonas poked his moustache around the hall door.

"There you be, girl!" he grumped. "You'd think the telephone would give itself heart failure the way it's been ringing all morning."

"I've been gone only an hour."

"And that Mrs. Spike do be phoning on the minute, every minute."

"You don't have to tell me what that's about!" With a quaking heart and dragging footsteps I squeezed past him and went to dial the vicarage's number. Was I about to hear that the doctor suspected a sneaky little blood clot lurking in Bridget's veins getting ready to race to her heart at any moment? And that by helping her do a bunk, I had signed her death certificate?

"Eudora?"

"Yes. Ellie, it's good of you to ring me back."

"I know you must be sick with worry."

"Then you've already heard?"

"I saw your mother-in-law at the bus stop, and gave her a lift to the station. She told me she had left you and Gladstone a note, but I can understand why you are upset."

"This isn't about Bridget, although we'll get back to her later. Ellie, what I'm about to tell you will come as a dreadful shock."

"Yes?" I kept my eyes on Jonas hovering a few feet away from me.

"Lady Kitty Pomeroy died early this morning."

"Oh, my goodness!" I had to hold on to the receiver for dear life.

"Sir Robert told me when he rang to make arrangements for the service that the cause of death would appear to be a massive stroke."

"She went in her sleep?"

"No, Ellie! She went on her *bike*. She was out cycling on her way to pick up some eggs from a nearby farm. Sir Robert happened to be at the window and saw her lose control going down the steep track that provides a shortcut to the road. He said Lady Kitty went over the handlebars into the pond, and by the time he and Pamela reached her and pulled her out, she was dead."

"I don't believe this!"

"We have to sit down and talk," Eudora told me. "How would it be if I came over to see you this afternoon?"

"Anytime," I said, and put down the receiver. Bridget had not made her way back into the conversation.

"What's wrong, girl? You look white as a sheet." Jonas's bushy eyebrows were way down over his nose, a sure sign that he was bothered.

"I'll be all right." I rested my head against his shoulder for a comforting moment. "And it's nothing for you to worry about. One of Eudora's parishioners passed away unexpectedly."

"Someone you knew?"

"Lady Kitty."

"Her what was over for tea the other day?"

"And I saw her yesterday at Pomeroy Manor. So, even though I didn't know her well, it's upsetting."

"You're too soft-hearted, that's your trouble, girl."

"Hark, who's talking," I retorted. "Why don't you go out to the garden and enjoy the company of your flowers while I sit here and have a little think."

"How about I get you a nice cup of Ovaltine?"

"Perhaps later."

I managed a smile to send him on his way out of the house, but the moment Jonas was gone I sank down on the tapestry bench to try to get my scattered thoughts together. What had happened to Bridget Spike had been one of life's horrid twists of fate. I would no more have suspected Eudora of pushing her mother-in-law over the cliff in fulfillment of the prophesy made at the Dark Horse than I would have believed myself capable of anything so spiteful. But Pamela was a different case.

She had hated Lady Kitty, as opposed to finding her a royal pain in the you-know-what. And she was in the clutches of a blackmailer whose revelations would have made her life more intolerable than it was already. Yesterday she had told me she was determined to find a way out of her troubles. Now it would seem she had done just that. But silly girl, surely it had occurred to her that if a blackmailer had put the screws on me in regard to that business at the Dark Horse, he might well get around to her. The delay could be due to something as simple as our man or woman being pathologically lazy.

What were Eudora and I to do? Was *murder* too strong a word for what Pamela had done in tampering with the brakes of the bike and trusting to a steep stretch of road and Lady Kitty's high blood pressure to produce a fatal outcome? A case of wishful thinking at its worst, no doubt, but did the girl with the big brown eyes and wistful ponytails deserve to be locked up for life for mother-in-law murder?

It was in a mood of deep gloom that I ascended the stairs. I looked for Mum and the twins in the nursery before finding the three of them in her tower bedroom. Abbey and Tam were happily engaged in lining up Grandma's shoes on the bed, an activity I would have expected her to veto on the grounds of hygiene. From the looks of her, however, Mum had something else on her mind. And the moment she spotted me, she let me know what was wrong.

"I can't find my mantilla."

"That black lace thing you wear to church?"

"I'm not blaming you, Ellie." She went right on lifting up candlesticks and peeking under doilies. "All I know is it was in my suitcase when I arrived and now it's gone."

"But who would touch it?" I asked as Tam staggered towards me with his arms outstretched and the biggest grin on his face. "The children wouldn't have been up here on their own."

"I expect that cat of yours made off with it." Admitting defeat, Mum put the powder bowl back in position on the dressing table. "Sweetie knows better than to pull a stunt like this."

Were we talking about the same dog who had fled into the great outdoors a few days earlier with poor St. Francis clenched between her thieving jaws? Never mind, I had no doubt the mantilla would turn up safe and sound in a drawer and Tobias's good name would be cleared. My cat had his weaknesses, but ladies' finery was not one of them.

"Did you have a nice time around the shops?" Mum asked with no more than a token sniff as she began reclaiming her shoes from Abbey, who had been trying one of them on her head.

"I had a couple of errands to run, nothing exciting. And now I'm ready for a cup of tea. Would you like one?"

"Not just now, if you don't mind." Magdalene squared her skimpy shoulders and lifted her chin. "I've a million things to do up here before I can enjoy a sit-down. But don't let me stop you from taking things easy."

"Then I'll get the twins out from under." I took hold of Tam's hand and reached towards Abbey. "We'll be just downstairs."

"That's nice to know." Mum put a real effort into her smile. "And don't think I'm criticizing, Ellie, when I say it's time you did something about that ladder the window cleaner left up against the house. It's not what you could call an ornament, and it's smack-bang next to my window."

"I'll telephone Mr. Watkins."

"One more thing, Ellie." She had the wardrobe door open and was stowing away her shoes. "Perhaps this afternoon, when those two are taking their naps, you and me could do something nice together?"

"Anything you like."

"I could show you how to make jam tarts"—she picked up another pair of shoes—"the proper way."

"That would be lovely."

If life could only be the way it sounds, I thought sadly as I returned with Tam and Abbey to the kitchen with its shining copper pans and the rocking chair drawn up in friendly fashion to the hearth. But anytime now Eudora would come knocking on the door and there would be no shutting out the grim reality that Pamela had done something that could not be dismissed as naughty. It would no longer seem monumentally important that Mum had brushed some rouge on her cheeks and done rather a good job with green eye shadow. It wouldn't count in the scheme of things that Tobias and Sweetie would seem to have signed a truce and were now lying in a comfortable heap over by the Welsh dresser.

There was no point in wishing that Pamela and Lady Kitty could have reached some sort of understanding. It was equally futile to wish that I had never gone to the Dark Horse and talked a lot of boozy twaddle with three other miserable, frustrated women. What's done was done, and all the tears and feelings of guilt wouldn't change a thing. I was telling myself off in no uncertain terms, to the great concern of the twins, when I realized that my sniffles and smarting eyes were being exacerbated by whatever Mrs. Pickle had left brewing in the dented old saucepan.

What could she be cooking that made me feel I had overdosed on smelling salts? Whatever it was had cooked down to a dried-out white paste with cracks all over its surface. I was gingerly removing the saucepan from the heat, when Mrs. Pickle came into the kitchen at what for her was a run.

"There I was, dusting around all them doilies in the front room, when I remembered I'd left that stuff bubbling away." She moved up close to me to peer down at the cake of plaster of Paris with what appeared to be a practiced eye.

"What is it?" I asked.

"Bicarbonate of soda and ammonia." Mrs. Pickle spoke with ill-disguised pride. "Works miracles, it does, for getting the burnt off the bottom of a saucepan."

"You're full of nifty ideas!" Some idiot I was to have thought for one moment that this twentieth-century daily, with her tightly wrapped curlers and faded floral apron, was practicing witchcraft in my kitchen. And all because she was descended from a woman accused of having the evil eye at a time when such bigotry was politically correct.

I was about to ask Mrs. Pickle if she would like to brew us up a cup of tea while I gave Abbey and Tam each a glass of milk, when from somewhere above us came a shuddering crash, followed by a piercing scream from Mum.

"You stay with the children," I told Mrs. Pickle as I fled the kitchen.

Terror clutched my heart and my legs seemed to be treading water, so that it took me what seemed like forever to gct up first one flight of stairs, then the next. With every agonizing breath I was more sure of what I would find on reaching Mum's bedroom. That monstrous ceiling-high dresser would be spread out across the floor, and she would be pinned underneath with only her fingertips showing. I should have had it moved out of the room, hacked into a thousand pieces, if that's what was needed to get it out the door. Instead, I had trusted my own assurances that it was safe and solid and no more likely to come tumbling down than Mount Everest.

My hands were so slippery, I couldn't turn the doorknob without using the front end of my blouse for traction, but at last I was inside the room. What I saw almost brought me to my knees. The killer dresser hadn't moved from the wall and Mum stood safe—if not completely sound—by an overturned chair and the smashed remains of the dressing table mirror.

"Are you all right?" I asked as I tiptoed towards her.

"I've had a terrible fright," she whimpered. Tears beaded at the corners of her eyes.

"I know! I know!" My arms went around her, and she nestled up close to me just as Abbey or Tam might have after a bad scare. "Come over to the bed and sit down."

"I don't think I can move!"

"Then we'll stay right here for a bit."

"Don't go thinking it's your fault, Ellie, but I could see a rim of dust on the top of the wardrobe. And when I pulled up a chair and climbed up to do a thorough cleaning all along the ledge, I found . . ." She started to tremble.

"What did you find?"

"That dreadful thing—over by the fireplace. I dropped it, along with the duster, when I fell off the chair and cracked into the dressing table, bringing the mirror down."

"Let me look," I said, moving over to the hearth.

"Don't touch it, Ellie!" Mum was wringing her hands. "I don't want you contaminated. At my age what do I matter? But you have to think about Ben and the children."

My mind reeled with the possibilities of what I would find. Top on my list of horrors was a dead mouse, but when I edged the cloth away and got a look at what was underneath, I couldn't have been more shocked if you'd paid me.

"It's a doll." I picked it up. "A Barbie doll."

"But look what it's wearing!"

"A dress made out of your black lace mantilla," I whispered.

"And a little beret just like the one I was wearing when I arrived."

"Awful!" I inched up a finger to touch the hair that had been hacked to wispy shreds and tinted a mouse grey; but what held me mesmerized was the metal meat skewer that had been plunged through the doll's plastic bosom.

"She's me!"

"The resemblance is only superficial." I was able to say this truthfully, seeing that Mum had the far more compact figure of the two. It was also on the tip of my tongue to console her with the reminder that voodoo is not an exact science, but she asked the question that had to be faced.

"Who would do this?"

"Mrs. Pickle." Even as I spoke, I hoped the accusation was as erroneous as my suspicions over the brew-up in the saucepan a few minutes ago; but the evidence was overwhelming. Young Dawn Taffer's Barbie dolls had disappeared yesterday and she had accused a certain person of taking them. I also remembered that Mrs. Pickle had appeared on the doorstep with her bottles of dandelion wine immediately after my in-laws arrived, when Mum had been wearing her beret.

"It makes no sense, Ellie!" Shock had given way to outrage. "The woman hardly knows me, and it's not like I've had a run-in with her like happened with that Mrs. Malloy."

"Maybe that's it," I said.

"Meaning what?"

"That Mrs. Pickle is seeking revenge on behalf of her friend. But rather than standing here guessing, let's go down and have it out with the witch."

"Before we go"—Mum made a brave attempt at sounding casual—"would you pull out that skewer? The power of evil is a frightening force, as you would know, Ellie, if you attended the Catholic Church. Don't get all worked up, but I've been getting these palpitations."

And so, I hoped, would Mrs. Pickle when confronted with the work of her hands. But when we met up with her in the kitchen, I was the one to panic. I didn't see the twins.

She read my face with surprising speed. "Don't you go worrying, Mrs. Haskell. Jonas come along and took the kiddies outside."

"That's one mystery cleared up; and now perhaps you will explain the meaning of this!" With Mum treading all over my heels, I held out the mutilated doll.

"You wasn't meant to find it." Mrs. Pickle sank down onto a chair and began twisting the front of her apron. "I put it in as high a place as I could reach."

"What made you do it?"

"It were because of Jonas." She kept her head bent. "I've had me hopes for ever so long that him and me would click. And when I found out he was thinking about setting up shop with a glamour girl from London, I was a mite put out, so to speak."

"You were jealous of *me*?" Mum sounded dazed, as well she might.

"Jonas never once noticed I was wearing me new curlers."

"That's a poor excuse for what you did. And what I would like to know"—I folded my arms—"is why you took more than one of Dawn Taffer's Barbie dolls."

"I never did nothing of the sort." Mrs. Pickle looked up at me with her first show of defiance. "That kiddie is a wicked little liar if ever I saw one. A real nasty piece of work. You should hear how she talks back to her gran."

Before I could respond, Mum touched my arm. In as gentle a voice as I had ever heard her use, she said, "Don't take this the wrong way, Ellie, but I think you're being too hard on Mrs. Pickle. Jealousy is a dreadful thing. It gets you by the throat and won't let go. It turns your whole world inside out. It makes you act like a crazy person."

Was it possible, I thought, looking down at the little voodoo doll, that the black magic had backfired, and what we had instead was a miracle?

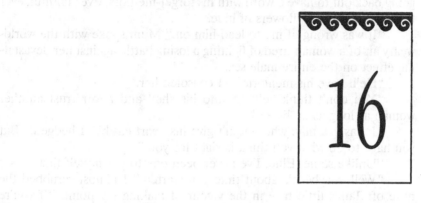

Happy is she who walks the path of righteousness to weekly Bible class—save for the occasional night off for good behaviour and the unmissable TV program. Believe me, I did not take my reward lightly. But I wasn't so far gone with excitement at the possibility of Mum reuniting with Dad that I now saw Pamela Pomeroy's role in the demise of Lady Kitty as a mere social gaffe. And I wasn't without feeling for the lovesick Mrs. Pickle when she left us in disgrace. That's the trouble with life. It's so rarely all of a piece. Sometimes all you can do is pick out the raisins—enjoy them, however few, and forget the bun is stale.

I was about to suggest to Mum that my new see-through nightie would be just the thing for a naughty weekend with Dad at the Dark Horse, when Jonas came in from the garden with the twins. From the looks of them, all three had been digging in the flower beds with their bare hands.

"We been looking for that statue of St. Francis"—Jonas completed the ruin of his toilet by touching his forelock—"but he b'ain't nowhere to be seen."

"God does not judge by results," Mum told him, and I wondered if he realized from the sad edge to her smile that she was lost to him and there would be no more morning walks through the dewy grass. To ease the moment, I made a big production out of lifting first Abbey, then Tam onto the working surface next to the sink. Over their squealing protests at the appearance of the dreaded face cloth, I heard Jonas say that he was going back out to have a word with his forget-me-nots. Ever faithful, ever true, are those little flowers of blue.

"It was wrong of me to lead him on." Mum spoke with the world-weary air of a woman tired of fighting a losing battle against her devastating effect on the entire male sex.

"He'll have his memories," I consoled her.

"You don't think he'll go into his shell and never trust another woman as long as he lives?"

"Jonas is a man who doesn't give his heart easily," I hedged. "But you have to do what you think is right for you."

"Unlike some, Ellie, I've never been one to put myself first."

"Well, maybe it's about time you started." I almost scrubbed the nose off Tam's little face in the vigour of making my point. "If you're miserable, we're all miserable. And that includes your grandchildren, who are too young to speak up for themselves."

"Me pretty!" My daughter would choose that moment to put two words together. Unlike her brother—the strong, silent type—who was scowling fiercely, Abbey was happy to have her face dried off and her barley-sugar curls fluffed up.

"Please God"—Mum crossed herself—"she won't end up breaking the heart of every man who crosses her path. But what can we expect with me for a grandmother?"

"When I get Abbey and her sidekick here out of nappies," I said, "I'll worry about what the future holds in store for our little adventuress. But one thing I do know is that children love the fairy tale with the happy ending. And even for grown-ups there is something infinitely appealing about a story of star-crossed lovers who against all odds end up in each other's arms."

Now was the moment, I thought, when Mum would tell me in plain words that she was planning to put the Tricks Taffer episode behind her and take Dad back. So much for wishful thinking. She picked up the kettle and said she would make us a cup of tea, leaving me to swallow my congratulations. A shame, but there you are! She would speak when the time was right. And I still had my dreams of having the wedding at Merlin's Court. Meanwhile the clock was looking down at me with a frown on its face. It was almost noon and the twins had to be fed.

After putting together a quickie lunch of fish fingers, leftover mashed potatoes, and peas, I got them into their booster chairs, tied on their bibs, and handed them their Peter Rabbit spoons and forks. Watching to make sure they ate more than they chucked on the floor, I drank my tea and left Mum to sit in the rocking chair, staring into space. Surely she wasn't having second thoughts already?

Squashing this pessimistic notion along with a couple of peas that landed in my path, I handed first Abbey, then Tam, a beaker of milk and was thinking in grandiose terms of setting the seal on their gourmet meal with some apple sauce and custard, when someone knocked on the garden door.

"That'll be Eudora Spike," I told Mum in a voice I had trouble hearing over the hammering of my heart. "She phoned earlier to say she would be popping in for a chat."

"Then don't keep her waiting on the doorstep on my account, Ellie. Never let it be said I get in the way of you and your friends." The wording was typical up to the point where she added, "You deserve some time for fun now and then."

Fun wasn't exactly what I had in mind when I opened the garden door; and when I saw Pamela standing on the step beside Eudora, I wondered just what was in store.

"Come in," I said to the accompaniment of Mum getting the twins out of their chairs and scooting them out of the room with maximum speed and tact.

"I hope we didn't push her out. . . ." Eudora stepped over the threshold with a heavy tread.

"Abbey and Tam were ready to go down for their naps," I jabbered while my mind veered off in all directions at once.

"Eudora and I met as she was leaving the vicarage." Pamela closed the door behind them, and for a sickening second I wondered if she would turn the key and slip it into the pocket of her frock. What an imagination! The girl did nothing more menacing than endeavour to steady her trembling lips as she looked at me imploringly.

"You'll have to excuse the muddle." I began rearranging the twins' booster chairs at more inviting angles and had waved at my guests to be seated before I could get a grip on myself. Blame it on my lackluster social calendar but, truth be told, I was more in the habit of sharing tips on child care with my friends than waiting for one of them to confess to activities that would mean the end of any hope of joining St. Anselm's Hearthside Guild.

"Ellie, I have to talk to you."

"Perhaps I should leave the two of you alone," offered Eudora. From her haggard appearance, the vicar was in dire need of a catnap similar to the one Tobias was currently taking under the rocking chair, with Sweetie for a pillow.

"No, don't go!" I said quickly. "I'm sure it's best for everyone concerned that you stay."

"Is that really what you want?" Pamela's soft brown eyes widened as she reached out her hands to me. "Oh, Ellie"—a sob caught in her throat —"the last thing I want is to make trouble for you."

"For *me*?"

"I know you were only trying to help. And I promise to visit you every month for as long as you languish in prison, but I do wish you could have kept me out of the picture."

"What on earth are you talking about?"

"Pamela has some bee in her bonnet that you had a hand in the death of Lady Kitty." Eudora's glasses took a distracted leap off her nose, and I watched in bemusement as my hand came out in slow motion to make the catch and hand them back.

"I don't believe this!"

"I wanted to believe Mumsie Kitty died from natural causes"— Pamela's ponytails drooped low—"but when we got her bike out of the pond it was obvious to me that someone had fiddled with the brakes."

"That doesn't surprise me."

"All of a sudden I thought about that woman who served our drinks at the Dark Horse."

"Mrs. Malloy?"

"That's her. I keep remembering, Ellie, how she mentioned that your mother-in-law took a spill down the stairs the night she arrived at your house."

"Elderly people are prone to accidents." Eudora spoke up for the defense.

"I know, but there was also that business of the potentially dangerous chocolate that found its way into the mousse." Pamela lifted her head to look at me more in pity than in condemnation. "And the day before yesterday you said to me on the phone that you would try to help me out. Honestly, I hate myself for thinking such awful things, when you had been so kind listening to my problems and pitching in with the blackmail money. . . ."

"The *what*?" Eudora sat down in the rocking chair with a thump that sent Sweetie and Tobias scurrying for more suitable cover.

"We'll get to that later," I said.

"Ellie, I understand you were trying to be a friend in the true sense of the word." Pamela kept trotting after me as I backed away. "I'd be lying if I said I was sorry Mumsie Kitty is dead, but—and this may sound awfully ungrateful—why couldn't you have done the job yourself instead of employing that Mr. Savage as your hit man and then sticking me with the bill?"

"You have finally lost me." I warded her off with an outstretched arm.

"Luckily my poor father-in-law wasn't anywhere near the front door when that ghastly man showed up within a couple of hours of this morning's main event!" Pamela was now shaking so violently, the twins' dishes rattled on their booster chair trays. "If Bobsie Cat had been there, he would have assumed I was involved up to my neck when Mr. Savage gave me his horribly gentle smile and said in a voice that went right through me, 'Madam, I am here to collect.' "

"Are you sure about all this?" Eudora spoke as if addressing a child not known for telling the truth.

"Did he say his name was Savage?" I demanded.

"He didn't have to!" Pamela blinked back the tears from her eyes. "He looked just like one—a savage, I mean—and what he did say—and I am absolutely clear on this—was 'Ellie Haskell sent me.' "

"Anything else?"

"I don't remember." A note of outrage had crept into her voice. "The walls started whirling around and the last thing I remember before everything went black was me screaming the place down."

"You look ready to pass out again," I said with a renewed sense of calm as I took her by the arm. "Why don't the three of us go and sit down somewhere comfortable, and when you feel better we'll try to make some sense out of all this."

"I told several people, including my solicitor, that I was coming here." Pamela darted an assessing glance over her shoulder at Eudora, who had followed us out into the hall and across to the drawing room. "The bus driver will remember that I asked to be set down at the stop nearest Merlin's Court and—" She broke off to let out a squeal that almost shattered the glass in the French windows that opened onto the moat-enclosed courtyard. "Oh, my gosh! That's *him*! Out there, peering in at us! Who could ever forget that murderous face or doubt for a minute that whatever his romantic feelings for you, Ellie, he will slit both our throats if we don't pay him what we owe!"

"But surely"—Eudora stepped farther into the drawing room—"that's none other than—"

Before she could complete her sentence, the glass door opened forcefully against the oak bookcase and, with the timing for which he was famous, in sauntered the villain of the piece.

"Pamela," I said as she dodged behind me, "I'd like you to meet my cousin Frederick Flatts."

"Who?" she squeaked.

"My God! It's her!" Freddy clapped a hand to his brow. "The woman who screamed bloody murder when I showed up at her country estate collecting for the St. Anselm's Fête."

"And don't think your efforts go unappreciated." Eudora conferred a smile on him that had all the trappings of a benediction.

"I'm so sorry!" Pamela whimpered. "I guess my imagination got the better of me."

"And no wonder," I told her. "You were in a state of shock when Freddy showed up at the door."

"You're not angry with me?"

"How can I be when I was just as guilty of jumping to conclusions? Before you got here I had you tried and convicted for Lady Kitty's murder. Now all I can say is you would need to be a better actress than I take you for in order to put on such a show."

"Oh, Ellie, that makes me feel so much better." Pamela sagged against me while Freddy stood looking the picture of unkempt bewilderment.

"Anyone want to fill me in on what I'm missing?" he asked the room at large. "Don't try to break it to me gently; I have my smelling salts in my back pocket should the details be unfit for a man's tender ears."

"Good for you," I said. "But this is a private matter."

"You're kicking me out?"

"That's right, Freddy dear."

"How can you be so heartless!" He dabbed at a mock tear with the end of his ponytail. "I wanted to tell you how much money I collected."

"Later."

"And I was going to offer to take your mother-in-law out for an afternoon jaunt."

"Well, in that case"—it was impossible not to backtrack when Eudora was looking at him through spectacles that had misted up—"why don't you go upstairs and have a word with Mum? But if you don't find her in the nursery, I would leave it, Freddy. You wouldn't want to interrupt her if she's taking a rest in her room."

"What a nice person," Pamela quavered when the hall door closed on him.

"The salt of the earth," I agreed.

"And what a pity"—Eudora crossed the Persian carpet to sit down in one of the easy chairs—"that Lady Kitty's death makes plain we have amongst us in Chitterton Fells a person without strong moral values."

"You don't think you could have been mistaken about those brakes?" I asked Pamela as we took our seats side by side on one of the twin sofas.

"Not a chance." She shook her head, causing the ponytails to slap against her cheeks. "Mumsie Kitty was riding the old bike that I had been using for ages. Trust me on this; I know how every strand of wire should be connected."

"And I have something to tell you." Eudora faced us squarely. "Last night, after you brought Mother back to the vicarage, Ellie, she told me and Gladstone that she had heard someone come up behind her as she blundered about, having lost her bearings. She *felt* whoever it was give her a push over that cliff."

"It was foggy." I was still clutching at straws. "People do stumble into each other under such conditions with unfortunate results."

"That being the case"—Eudora bit her lip—"why didn't the person respond to Mother's cries for help instead of running off down the road?"

"And you think that's why your mother-in-law left so abruptly this morning?" I asked. The elderly woman's frightened face loomed up sharp and clear in my memory.

"It's worse than that." Eudora looked from me to Pamela. "I could tell immediately as she spoke that Mother suspected me of the attack. And who can blame her? She knew I had been upset over the fire she started in my study. She definitely thought I had gone wacky when I insisted she smoke outside. Which at my age, in Mother's book, isn't all that unusual. Like many of her generation, she is steeped in horror stories about women who went off their rockers during the change."

"I don't believe this," Pamela said, meaning exactly the opposite. "We're in the midst of a full-scale mother-in-law massacre!" She let out a wail that shivered the timbers of the house. "And I didn't mean it, honestly I didn't, about being glad Mumsie Kitty is dead. I never liked the woman, but she was Allan's mother, and I'm not a completely unfeeling monster."

"Of course you're not!" I wrapped an arm around her.

"And you don't think that Frizzy Taffer is attempting to divert suspicion from herself as she prepares to get rid of the thorn in her side?"

"No, I don't." I spoke with more determination than certainty. "Frizzy strikes me as a thoroughly decent woman who wouldn't stoop to anything so low."

"I hope you're right, Ellie." Eudora rubbed her shoulder as if trying to ease a deep-seated ache. "But if what we have here is an enactment of our decidedly foolish conversation at the Dark Horse, then I am afraid we may be only halfway through this nightmare."

Pamela nodded. "Two down, two to go."

"Bridget isn't down, but she is out . . . of the picture," I said in a desperate bid to latch on to particulars and not let go. "I know for certain that word of our silly plotting did get out, by one means or another"—this was directed at Eudora—"because I got a phone call from someone who agreed to keep mum for the price of two hundred pounds."

"Ellie, how awful!"

"He or she didn't put the squeeze on you?"

Eudora shook her head, and Pamela confided that she was being blackmailed for an unrelated matter.

"It wouldn't seem to make good business sense for this person to be our murderer," I said. "But who knows what sort of a crackpot we are dealing with?"

"All I can suggest is that someone has a grudge against one or other of the mothers-in-law and wants to cover his tracks by bumping off all four of them according to our plan"—Eudora sat up straight in her chair—"so that the blame falls squarely on the scapegoats."

"The news media will dub us the Deadly Daughters-in-law. We set ourselves up pretty handily, didn't we?" Pamela sat twisting one of her ponytails around her finger. "Mumsie Kitty made more enemies than she did apple pies. But I can't think of anyone in particular, except Mr. Watkins, the window cleaner, who made quite a stink recently when she refused to pay him for a job badly done. . . ." Her voice faded.

"Mum had quite a run-in with him too," I said while gathering up my courage to bring up the name that I felt sure had Pamela worried. "What about Sir Robert? I know you're fond of him, Pamela, but you and I both heard him say yesterday, after his collapse at lunch, that he could be driven to murdering Lady Kitty."

"I confess!" She dropped her head in her hands. "I did tell Bobsie Cat about our talk at the Dark Horse. He had a good laugh, but the old codger is all bluster. He really wouldn't hurt a fly."

Eudora broke what became an awkward silence with the statement that, to her knowledge, Bridget had made no enemies in Chitterton Fells.

"Admittedly, she upset the bishop quite a lot with her comic-book commentary on the Bible, but that's hardly what we are talking about, is it?"

"In addition to Mr. Watkins"—I began ticking off on my fingers—"Mum has fallen foul of both Mrs. Malloy and Mrs. Pickle—the first for giving her the sack, the second for stealing Jonas's affections. It may not cut much ice with either of you, but I'm prepared to vouch for Mrs. M. not being the murderer. What I can believe, knowing her, is that she may well have spilled the beans about what she overheard at the pub to her friend Edna Pickle. Speaking of whom, we did have rather an unpleasant incident here earlier today."

While listening to my stark account of the voodoo dolls, Eudora looked appropriately shocked that such things were still going on in the twentieth century, to say nothing of in her parish. But when I was finished, she said, "Unpleasant as all this is, Mrs. Pickle may have found a way to vent her feelings of pent-up hostility that falls short of murder."

"Another thought has occurred to me." I brushed back a lock of hair that was falling over my eyes, thus obscuring my twenty-twenty vision. "Mrs. Pickle may have a motive for getting rid of all four mothers-in-law. According to Mrs. Malloy, the lady has a burning ambition to win the Martha."

"As does my husband." Eudora smiled in rueful amusement. "He's taken to sleeping in his apron and babbling recipes in his sleep."

Pamela leaned forward. "Are we talking about the trophy awarded at the fête for the best entry among the winners in the homemaking categories?"

"The very same."

"And you think Mrs. Pickle may have viewed the assorted talents of the mothers-in-law as a serious threat to her raging ambition?" Eudora looked at me in disbelief. "Ellie, that trophy is awarded every year. If she were to get pipped at the post this time, there would be other opportunities."

"You're right," I conceded. "It just sticks in my mind that Mrs. Malloy said she wouldn't be surprised if Mrs. Pickle had rid herself, by one foul means or another, of former high-quality contenders."

"But I thought those two women were the best of pals." Pamela appeared to be fast losing track of whose side anyone was on.

"So they are, which is why I didn't take Mrs. Malloy seriously. I thought it was just friendship talking, if you understand what I'm saying."

"We so often talk worse about our friends than we do about our foes," Eudora said sadly.

Deciding I had done a sufficient number on a woman who had her way to make in the world, I proceeded to close out my list of suspects on the home front.

"Mr. Peter Savage, being a stranger to these parts, is type-cast as an unknown quantity. He's in rebellion against his mother. And his current lifestyle does make him something of an oddity. Added to that, he did talk a lot of bosh that suggested he might have a crush on me. . . ." I attempted to look modest. "And if—as I fear may have happened—that unwise conversation at the Dark Horse got inadvertently immortalized on his tape recorder—which, thanks to me, was eavesdropping under the table—well, who knows?"

"And who do you suppose has sufficient reason to rid the world of Beatrix Taffer?" Eudora took a quick look at her watch.

One name unfortunately leaped to mind, but I wasn't about to toss it into the ring. And there was luckily another possibility.

"Frizzy may have talked to her aunt Ethel about what was discussed at the Dark Horse, and believe me the woman—who may or may not have given her late husband a fatal push down the stairs—looks eminently capable of murder. Especially where Tricks is concerned."

A heavy silence descended on the drawing room, of the sort that sometimes occurs before a particularly bad thunderstorm. The sky outside was a limpid blue and innocently devoid of cloud. But I didn't trust the day any more than I trusted myself and the other two women to discover the identity of the person menacing the mothers-in-law, before tragedy struck yet again.

"I think we should talk to the police," I said.

"Just what I was thinking," agreed Eudora.

"But what if the police station closes early on a Friday?" Pamela might have been talking about a bakery shop run by two elderly maiden ladies.

"We'll go down right away." I got off the sofa to stand at the ready.

Eudora gave another glance at her watch. "Ellie, I can't. Sir Robert is due at the vicarage in ten minutes to discuss the hymns for Lady Kitty's funeral."

"And I have to be there." Pamela jumped up and began smoothing down her ponytails. "Would you mind awfully going down on your own, Ellie, and explaining exactly what has us all worried to death?"

"I could wait for you both," I offered.

"Yes, but if the three of us went down without Frizzy, we might create the wrong impression about her. We don't want that, do we?" Eudora was almost back to her brisk self. "And if we wait to talk things over with her, we will waste precious time. We've already had one near-miss and a fatality in a very short space of time."

"We need to warn Frizzy," I said, "that Tricks could be in danger. She must confiscate her mother-in-law's bottle of health tonic immediately."

"I'll phone Frizzy as soon as I get home," Eudora promised me as she headed out into the hall. "You just worry about getting down to the police station." She and Pamela were on their way out the front door, when the younger woman tugged on my sleeve.

"One thing I don't have to worry about anymore is our black-mailer," Pamela said cheerfully. "I know it's beastly of me to be happy about anything right now, but it's wonderful to be free of that leech and to know that there is nothing to stop me . . ." The rest of what she was saying got blown away by the wind as she hurried after Eudora down the front steps of the house. Closing the door on their retreating backs, I experienced a fleeting moment of happiness for Pamela. She was right. Now there was nothing to stop her from telling Sir Robert that she had cheated, by submitting one of her aunt Gertrude's pies, in the marriage bake-off. Her father-in-law wouldn't care two hoots.

I was leaning against the front door, thinking that there was something . . . or someone . . . that I had failed to mention to my fellow investigators, something that might well have a bearing on the infamy at hand, when who should come out of the kitchen but Mum and Freddy.

"There you are, Ellie!" Magdalene's eyes were positively twinkling. "I made your cousin lunch and we've been having such a nice chat. He wants me to teach him how to crochet."

"But first I'm going to take her out for an afternoon spin, isn't that right, Auntie Mags?" Freddie gave the top of her head, which came somewhere above his waist, a fond pat.

"I've never been on a motorcycle in my life." Mum made this star-tling revelation in a voice that marvelled at so many, many golden moments lost.

"Are you sure this is wise?" I asked them both. "What if it starts to rain?"

"Life is a chancy business, Ellie," she said with a serene smile that did more for her than any amount of eye shadow, "and as I was explaining to Frederick, who is so understanding, a ride in the open air is just what I need to blow away the cobwebs in my head."

"Well, I do hope that if she gets blown off the bike in her entirety," I told Freddy severely, "you will at least stop to pick her up and dust her off."

"It's not like me to think of myself," Mum reminded me, "and if you think I'm being selfish, by all means say so. The last thing I want is to cause trouble between the two of us when we seem to be getting along better than I ever dared hope."

"Off you go and have a good time!" I cried. After all, any danger that awaited her on the open road was minimal compared to what might be lurking in the house in the guise of a wardrobe primed and ready to fall and crush her to death under its massive weight. "I may have to go out myself for a bit, but Jonas is here to look after the twins."

"If you're sure . . ." Mum hesitated as duty dictated.

"Ellie want us to be happy, isn't that right, coz?" Freddy gave me a scratchy kiss on the cheek that made me wish he would either shave off his stubbly beard or let it grow back to full bloom. But in the main I felt very pleased with him as he marshalled Mum out the front door, leaving me with nothing to do but get ready for the trip to the police station.

Well, maybe a bite to eat before setting out. It has been my experience that courage does not sit well on an empty stomach, so I hustled into the kitchen, where I found a plate of ham sandwiches covered with a dishtowel on the working surface, courtesy of Mum. There was no denying that our relationship had improved to the point where I would miss her when she returned to Tottenham—hopefully with Dad—but she had to go and that very evening, at the latest, if I were to ensure her safety.

I sat in the kitchen longer than I intended, letting my mind drift until it was suddenly roped in like a barge. It wasn't the distant *bong* of the grandfather clock that made me jump from my chair, but a far more ominous sound. Someone—a grown-up someone, from the heaviness of the footsteps—was walking around in the nursery. We had our Child Watch intercom to alert us when the twins woke up of a morning, or in the afternoon from their naps. And the intercom was letting me know now, in no uncertain terms, that I had an intruder.

Me and my overloaded imagination! I was telling myself that the culprit had to be Jonas, and I would have his head for clumping about in a manner liable to wake both Abbey and Tam, if not the dead, when I took a look out the window and saw Jonas innocently watering one of the flower beds.

The urgency of the situation forbade my taking a detour to the drawing room and equipping myself with the poker. I made do with the largest wooden spoon I could grab from the drawer. A carving knife would have made a lot more sense if I hadn't been afraid of doing myself bodily harm and scarring the twins emotionally for life in the process.

Taking the stairs ten at a time, I raced down the gallery. There I collided with Mr. Menace as he stepped out of the nursery.

I gasped. *"Dad!* What are you doing here?"

"I came over with a bunch of flowers for Magdalene!" He sensibly distanced himself from the wooden spoon.

"And how did you get in? Down the chimney?"

"No!" Sheepishly he looked down at his red cardigan. "I was going to knock on the door in the prescribed fashion, Ellie, but when I was coming up the drive I saw the ladder leaning up against the house, and it seemed to me"—he cleared his throat—"that if Jonas hadn't yet fixed the window latch and I could get into her bedroom without Magdalene seeing me, I could leave the flowers and a note on her bed as a means of paving the way, before . . ."

"Having to face her?" I supplied.

"Your mother-in-law is a pretty tough customer." He spoke with a note of pride. "I don't doubt it will take me another forty years to soften her up."

"If she lives that long." And I burst into tears.

17

"If you keep this up," Dad said in an unusually soft bellow, "we'll have to turn the windscreen wipers on *inside* the car."

"How can I help it?" I sobbed. "Going to the police was a complete waste of time. Sergeant Briggs was either rolling his eyes or staring out the window during most of our visit. The only time he perked up was when I told him about the blackmail."

"You've me to thank for him being that way, Ellie! It was too much to hope the man would take us seriously after catching me in the altogether the other night. He'd obviously written the entire Haskell family off as a bunch of lunatics."

"You've been wonderful," I told him, "hearing out my story without a word of condemnation for the part I played in this sorry saga." Tears continued to puddle the lap of my frock which happened to be dry clean only.

"Watch the road, there's a good girl."

"What road? I feel like I'm driving a submarine."

The rain was coming down faster than the wipers could keep up with it, and the sky was black as night and so low to the ground I was afraid I would run smack-bang into it. And, talking of waters that ran deep, we were at that moment passing the Chitterton Fells Leisure Centre, with its swimming pool capable of floating the *Titanic*. The pool had been opened the previous year by Lady Kitty, with all due pomp and circumstance, when she cut the ribbon between the shallow and the deep end. Now she had been cut down in her prime. The reminder was enough to make me start blubbering again.

"Ellie," Dad said for the fifth time, "you are not to blame because someone is making a dent in the local mother-in-law population. Good grief! If we had to worry about every single conversation we ever had among friends, we'd never know a moment's peace."

"Or say an unkind word about anyone."

"And a fine state of affairs that would be."

"I'm so relieved you believe my incredible story."

He patted my hand. "You meet a lot of ugly customers in the greengrocery business."

"What are we going to do?" I wailed.

"You're going to drop me off at the Dark Horse, Ellie, so I can pack my bags and settle the bill. Then I'll come over to Merlin's Court, tuck Magdalene under my arm, and off we'll go back to Tottenham."

"If she's fit to travel after being out on the motorbike with Freddy in this weather." I leaned forward to wipe a patch of window clear with my sleeve and saw the pub sign flapping to and fro like a hearth rug hung out on the line for a poorly timed airing. "Do you want me to wait outside for you?"

"No, you go home." Dad had the car door open before I had us properly parked. "After what you've been telling me, I don't feel comfortable leaving Magdalene unattended one minute longer than necessary. There is a time in the life of man when he doesn't count the cost of a taxi."

He waved me off. And I proceeded up Cliff Road with my eyes glued to the peephole that was fast fogging up again; my mind was spinning faster than the wheels of the car. If Mum was already back and had found Dad's bouquet, she might require no persuasion from me that Merlin's Court lacked sufficient privacy for the sort of reunion he had in mind. Determined to be optimistic, I drew up in front of the stable, wiped my eyes, turned off the ignition, and dashed across the drenched courtyard to the garden door.

The moment my hand touched the doorknob I was assailed by a panic every bit as blinding as the rain. What good were my plans for giving Mum the boot if the killer among us had finished her off in my absence? My knees were wobbling as I entered the kitchen. Damn! I let out a gasp when the wind snatched the door out of my hand and slammed it shut behind me.

Oh, the mercy of the mundane! Mum was seated at the table with both Sweetie and Tobias on her lap.

"What a picture you make!" I was tempted to take a flying leap and join them.

"A certain doggie is petrified of storms." Her lips twisted into a smile. "Tobias has been quite a comfort to her, so much so that I've been thinking about getting Sweetie a kitten for her birthday."

"What a lovely idea."

"And now, Ellie, for the bad news. . . ."

"What's wrong?" I stammered.

Her face grew grim. "It's going to come as a shock."

"Tell me?"

"Elijah has been here." Mum spoke in the strictly neutral voice of a television commentator announcing purported sightings of the great prophet. "From the muddy footprints leading from the window to the bed, he must have come up that ladder abandoned by your window cleaner. Anyway, he left some flowers and a letter for me and . . . all things considered, Ellie, I have decided to go back to him."

"That's wonderful!" I exclaimed.

"I expect you think me very weak."

"No," I assured her firmly, "I think you are doing the Christian thing."

"This has absolutely nothing to do"—Mum closed her eyes—"with sex."

"Of course not."

"Elijah has a shop to run and I will be way behind with my dusting when I get back, so if he should show up here in the next little while, I think we ought to make tracks for home tonight."

Things couldn't have worked out any better, or so I thought for all of ten seconds. Mum had just put the dog and the cat on the floor and was in the act of getting to her feet, when the door opened and Jonas came stomping into the kitchen.

"So you do be back, Ellie girl." His shaggy brows met in a frown over his nose. "I just got off the telephone from talking to that there

Beatrix Taffer's granddaughter. Seems the old lady's eaten or drunk som'mat that disagreed with her and she's in a bad way."

"No!" I cried while Mum opened and closed her mouth without making a sound.

"She's been asking for Magdalene," Jonas said.

"Where is she? At home or at the hospital?"

"At home as of now."

"Beatrix always had a dread of hospitals." Mum was turning in ever-narrowing circles until she was in danger of colliding with herself. "I'll have to take Sweetie with me; the poor little scrap is terrified of being abandoned during storms."

"Do you think that's a good idea?" I grabbed up a raincoat from the row of pegs in the alcove by the garden door and tossed it over her shoulders.

"Sweetie won't be any trouble. She never barks unless spoken to."

Jonas followed us down the steps into the courtyard. "There's som'mat else I need to tell you, Ellie. A policeman rung up just afore the kiddie did, and he left a message for you. Some rigmarole about him bringing a certain party down to the station for questioning."

Incredible! Sergeant Briggs must have taken my fears far more seriously than I realized. And to have acted so quickly! Much good it did Tricks, I thought bitterly.

"What's all that about the police?" Mum asked as she hurried after me through the rain to the car. "It doesn't have anything to do with Ben, does it? He hasn't been serving crème de menthe over the ice cream during nonlicencing hours?"

"No, nothing like that—" I reached for the car door at the moment Mum tripped over a rock . . . or whatever . . . on the ground and narrowly saved herself from pitching forward.

"It's St. Francis!" She picked him up with the hand that wasn't holding on to Sweetie, and held him aloft like a beacon to light our way, which given his phosphorescent nature, he did quite handily. "That he should turn up now, after being lost for days—don't tell me it's not a sign from above." Mum tucked the statue into her raincoat pocket. "It must mean Beatrix is going to be all right; even you must see that, Ellie."

"Absolutely!"

"You don't think"—Mum was having trouble getting the words out —"that Beatrix did something silly—like make an attempt on her life because of all the trouble there's been, between her and me over that swimming business and Elijah?"

"This was not a suicide attempt."

Neither of us spoke again throughout the ten-minute drive that seemed more like an hour to the Taffer house. Sweetie likewise appeared lost in thought, and did not so much as blink when lifted from the car. The rain had slackened, although the sky remained so black, it was impossible to see where it ended and the roofs began, and the Taffer house was forbiddingly dark. Not a crack of light showed as we scurried down the narrow garden path to the front door. But for the sounds of life in the form of rock-and-roll music coming from inside, I would have concluded no one was home.

"You did ring the bell?" Mum held Sweetie tightly in her arms.

"Yes," I said, and rang it again.

"Whatever's taking so long?"

"I've no idea." My voice came out in a croak. I pictured the entire Taffer family rallying round Tricks's deathbed for one last singsong. Moment by agonizing moment, the fear had grown inside me until it was the size and weight of a cannon ball. Realizing this was no time to "come over queer," as Mrs. Malloy would have put it, I was forcing myself to take slow, deep breaths when—at long last—we heard footsteps approaching the door.

Mum looked as surprised as I felt when it was opened in slow motion by Mrs. Pickle. She wore her coat and a woolly hat jammed down over her curlers.

"Why, it's you, Mrs. Haskell, and your mother-in-law too! Would you believe I was in the kitchen doing me last rounds, when I thought I heard the bell." Her currant-bun face was flushed—presumably from the exertion of her walk down the hall. "But what with all that racket from young Dawn's radio, I thought me ears must be deceiving me." She stepped aside an inch at a time, for us to enter, then closed the door. "And you brought the little doggie too, that's nice, isn't it?"

"We came to see my friend Beatrix," said Mum in quite a cordial voice.

"Oh, dear! Coming all this way for nothing!"

"You mean . . . ?" Mum dropped poor Sweetie on the floor without a word of apology.

"She went fifteen minutes ago," Mrs. Pickle informed us without taking the half-smile off her bland face. "And you do have to say as what it was for the best."

"Do we?" I whimpered.

"Hospital was the place for her is what the doctor said when he finally got here. He'd had a couple of other emergencies so no one's blaming him; well, it wouldn't be fair, would it?"

"Is she very bad?" I asked.

"It don't look hopeful is what Doctor told the family." Mrs. Pickle undid a couple of coat buttons to show we weren't keeping her. "Mrs. Taffer—Frizzy, that is—promised to give me a ring here, seeing as how I don't have a phone of me own, as soon as she knew something one way or the other. I only put on me coat because the house got downright nippy with the weather being so bad and all. So if you'd like to stay and wait for word, it shouldn't be very long, and I'll be glad of the company." She looked down at the floor. "Then again, could be you'd rather not, after that bit of bother this morning."

"At a time like this, nothing matters but Beatrix's full recovery." Mum's lips stiffened into a forgiving smile, for which she received a woof of approval from Sweetie, who apparently forgot doggies are meant to be seen and not heard.

"I'll take you into the back room." Mrs. Pickle went flip-flapping down across the hall in the down-at-the-heel plaid slippers that didn't do much for her coat. "It's not so cluttered with the kiddies' toys as is the front room." Her words were barely audible above a renewed burst of rock-and-roll music descending upon us from one of the upstairs rooms. "They left in that much of a hurry, young Dawn didn't bother to turn off that ruddy radio." Mrs. Pickle shook her head as she pushed open the door to the back room. "I've been meaning to go and see to it like, but it's a bit of a climb up those stairs."

"I'm surprised she wasn't made to turn it off earlier, with her grandmother so ill." Mum gave one of her signature sniffs.

"The family's so used to the racket, they don't even hear it. And if the doctor told the kid to lower the music, I doubt as how she would have listened to him. She's a willful one, that Dawn, and no mistake. Surprises me she even bothered going to the hospital; she wasn't much of a one for her gran. I kept out of the way when they was leaving so as not to intrude, and I can tell you I wasn't sorry to miss one of her tantrums."

Mrs. Pickle plowed a path across the box-size room that barely offered a place to stand despite the table being pushed flush against the French windows and stacked high with the dining chairs, a couple of ottomans, and a television set.

"I was thinking of giving this place a good top and tailing, when Mrs. Taffer took bad." She lifted a couple of light bulbs, one at a time, and a box of crayons from one of the two easy chairs, while Mum removed her damp raincoat and laid it cautiously over the empty clothes-horse in front of the fireplace. "One good thing about Frizzy Taffer, she don't never rush you. She says if she gets the place halfway shipshape by the time the kiddies is all grown, that's soon enough for her."

"Frizzy's a gem." Trembling, I sat and inadvertently put my hand on the little table between Mum's chair and mine. I watched it topple over, catching Sweetie on the tail before she could streak for safety.

"One of the legs is wobbly." Mrs. Pickle came forward at what for her was a rush. "Here, I know as how I can fix it." She reached into her coat pocket and brought out a piece of paper already folded in two, and proceeded to wad it up until it was a couple of inches square. "There!" She righted the table and stuck the paper under the peg leg. "That should help keep it steady. Now, how would it be if I poured both you ladies a glass of me rhubarb wine. I brought it over this afternoon as me way of showing I wasn't upset about Dawn accusing me of pinching her dolls."

This not seeming the time to point out that Mrs. Pickle was indeed guilty as charged, I smiled politely as she poured a couple of glasses from the bottle on the sideboard.

"I'm not much of a drinker." Mum watched Sweetie take a charge at the clotheshorse, sending it and her raincoat flying. "But if you think it will do my nerves good, I'll take a couple of sips. . . ."

"There's nothing better, and everyone that's tried it says they don't mind the iron taste none."

Upon this glowing recommendation, Mrs. Pickle handed us our glasses and said she would go out to the kitchen and make up a plate of sandwiches.

"Don't go to all that bother," Mum told her.

"It'll give me something to do to keep me mind off poor Mrs. Taffer. Now, just you sit tight and I'll be back in a tick."

"That means half an hour," I said when the door closed behind her.

"The woman means well, Ellie."

"That's true." I took a sniff of my wine and wasn't very keen on the bouquet, possibly because it smelled like very old rhubarb.

"You're on edge, and no wonder, with poor Beatrix in the hospital and that music blaring upstairs." Mum went to set her glass on the table, but before she even made contact, over it went again. "Obviously Mrs. Pickle didn't fold that piece of paper properly. Not that I'm criticizing." She gave me her wine to hold before bending down to remove the wad and smooth it out for geometrically correct restructuring. "I realize the woman's had a difficult day, first with us and that business of the dolls and—"

Mum broke off, to stand staring at me while Sweetie took a dive onto the sofa and began burrowing under the cushions, all without a word of reprimand.

"Take a look at this, Ellie." Her voice sounded unnaturally loud in the hush that indicated Mrs. Pickle had turned off Dawn's radio overhead. "It's a threatening letter. And it's not from the Gas Board either."

"Let me see." I took the piece of paper and read aloud: " 'Dear Mrs. Pickle, I'm sticking this through your letter box to let you know I saw you push that old girl off the cliff last night. In order for me to keep quiet about same, you must put two hundred pounds in the hollow tree at the top of the lane that leads to Pomeroy Manor. A sincere well-wisher.' "

Mum shook her head. "It has to be a joke. One of Mrs. Pickle's voodoo chums having a bit of fun with her; common sense tells you that if there was a word of truth to it, she'd never have used the letter to steady the table."

"She can't read," I said. "Lady Kitty told me so the other day. Bad luck for the blackmailer! And he had to communicate by letter, because Mrs. Pickle doesn't have a phone."

"I still say it's a prank."

"I don't think so," I said, trying to sound upbeat. "Bridget Spike did go over the cliff last night without suffering any serious injury, thank God; and she later told Eudora she was pushed. And this morning I learned that Lady Kitty has died in a bicycle accident."

"You never said a word to me!"

"I didn't want to alarm you."

"They were just at the house for tea! And now we have Beatrix, who's eaten or drunk something that's upset her!" Mum looked with horror at our wineglasses. "I hope I'm not one to get all worked up over nothing, Ellie, but it looks to me as if there's trouble in Chitterton Fells."

"We have to get out of here." I picked up Mum's raincoat from the floor and held it for her while she tried to put two arms into one sleeve. "This afternoon Dad went down with me to the police station to try to persuade Sergeant Briggs that we have reason to believe that someone hereabouts is targeting certain women."

"If you mean elderly women of your acquaintance, say so, Ellie." Mum finally freed one of her arms. "Now I understand that telephone message, the one Jonas gave you from the police. But they're certainly taking their time if Mrs. Pickle"—she lowered her voice—"is the person to be brought in for questioning."

"Let's not wait for them to get here." I looked towards the French windows blocked by the table with its tower of chairs and other odds and sods. Reluctantly I decided our best bet would be to try to slip out unnoticed by the front door.

"Now, hold on a minute, Ellie." Mum stopped fussing with her raincoat and looked at me steadily. "You're young—which no one is blaming you for—and one day you'll learn not to jump to uncharitable conclusions. We have only the blackmailer's word that Mrs. Pickle pushed Bridget Spike off that cliff and, to be completely fair to her, there was heavy fog, and—" Mum cut herself off as she bent to pick up Sweetie from the sofa. She gaped at what the little doggie had clenched in her jaws.

"Is it St. Francis?" I asked.

"No, he's still in here!" Mum pointed an agitated finger at her raincoat pocket. "This is"—prying it free from the canine jaws—"another of those voodoo dolls. Only this one isn't me! It's . . ."

"Tricks." I looked with revulsion at the spiky red hair and the frock made out of scraps of Indian muslin.

"Ellie, you suit yourself! Make all the allowances you like for Mrs. Pickle, I am getting out of this house while there is still time. And don't go telling me there's two of us to one of her, and there's really nothing to be worried about. . . ."

I had her by the elbow and was propelling her towards the door, when it opened smack in front of us. In came Mrs. Pickle, still in her coat and hat, and with a carving knife in her hand to complete her ensemble.

"Would you believe I was slicing up the bread for sandwiches, when I got to thinking as how you might be ready for some more rhubarb wine." Her face was as bland as rice pudding, and there wasn't a hint of ill nature in her voice when she looked at what Mum was holding, and said, "I see as how you've found another of them dolls. And to think I stuck it so far down the back of the sofa, I thought I'd never get me arm back out again."

"Dogs will be dogs." Mum looked down pridefully at Sweetie. "Thanks to this little bloodhound, we know that what the blackmailer wrote to you was true." Mum took a step backwards. "You are a murderer . . . not that I'm criticizing, you understand."

"She's referring to this letter!" Desperately hoping to reduce Mrs. Pickle to contrite tears, I brandished the sheet of paper in her face. "The writer claims to have seen you shove Bridget Spike off the cliff."

"Aren't some people nosy!" Whether she was referring to me or the blackmailer was unclear. "And to think I went to all the trouble of putting that letter in my pocket so as I could have Roxie Malloy read it to me the way she does all my correspondence. Do you know"—Mrs. Pickle gave a bemused laugh—"it's going to plague me all night long, wondering who could have wrote it? But there you are, if it's not one thing, it's another. All I do know is it was some skinflint who was too mean to pay for a stamp and came and stuck it through the letter box. What I have to keep telling meself is I'm not going to let nothing spoil the happy day when I win the Martha."

"So that's it!" I exclaimed.

"I was so sure this would be my year. Gladstone Spike gave me the willies till I got to realizing he'd never get to win. People would say it wasn't fair, him being the vicar's husband. But then the blow fell. I knew as how Mrs. Taffer's marrows were real marvels, I'd tasted Lady Kitty's pies and knew they was unbeatable, and that the same went for Bridget Spike's marmalade, and then there was *you*!" If looks could kill, the one Mrs. Pickle gave Mum would have worked on the spot. "In all me born days I've never seen no one crochet the like."

"We can't all be good at everything," Mum murmured kindly.

"But we *can* take our destiny in our own two hands, like what that fortune-telling cousin of Mrs. Ellie Haskell here said. I knew as how he had the gift when he said he saw a high-class gent and a journey across the sea for someone in the room that day."

"Freddy was talking out of the side of his head," I said.

"I suppose"—Mrs. Pickle looked down at her carving knife—"some people would say as how I've gone a bit overboard over a trophy given at the St. Anselm's Summer Fête, that there's always another year, and so on; but what they would be missing is that this time Sir Robert's cousin, the Honourable George Clydesdale, will be the one making the presentation—him who's such a bigwig in the wine-making business, with his own vineyards in France, no less! I couldn't pass up the opportunity of making him sit up and take notice of me dandelion wine. Not a man like that! For years I've had dreams of having me labels plastered on bottles all over the country. I'm not one of them women what sits back and waits for life to take her by the hand."

"So Mrs. Malloy told me." Lightning crashed. I edged closer to Mum. "She even suggested you might have done away with prior candidates in the annual race to take home the Martha."

"What a wicked fib!" Mrs. Pickle was completely outraged. "This is the one and only time I haven't played quite fair, so to speak. And none of this has been a piece of cake, let me tell you. I wasn't one bit sure as how any of the murders would come off according to plan, so I had to use the dolls to help me luck along. And after you found the one at Merlin's Court, I was at me wit's end." Her face strongly resembled a hot cross bun when she looked at Mum. "I'm not so daft I didn't know I'd never be welcome back in your house. There went me hopes of burying you under a wardrobe or such. But things seemed to take a turn around when I heard young Dawn ring up and leave word that her gran, for all she was delirious, kept saying her old friend's name. I'd put the herb killer in the rhubarb wine—when I couldn't lay me hands on Beatrix Taffer's bottle of youth tonic—and got her to drink some by telling her it would make her face soft and smooth as a baby's bottom. So all I had left to do was stay on here after the family left for the hospital and wait for you to show up like lambs to the slaughter."

"A pity for you we didn't drink the wine." Mum's sniff held a certain complacency.

"So I see." Mrs. Pickle looked at the full glasses. "A waste of perfectly good poison, if you ask me. And I had it all worked out a treat in my mind. I was going to tell the coppers I overheard Mrs. Ellie Haskell here accusing you—after she'd drunk the wine and realized too late it had tasted funny—of bumping off Mrs. Beatrix Taffer. All because you was jealous of her carryings-on with your husband. And I was going to say as how I rushed into the room to see you drinking down your glass. It would have looked like you took your own life in a fit of remorse. And that you'd tried your tricks on Bridget Spike and done away with Lady Kitty to confuse the issue, in a manner of speaking."

"But I was never in this house before today." Mum spoke up with the indignant courage of one who has truth for an ally. Thunder rattled deafeningly.

"And I'll say you was." Mrs. Pickle was fingering the carving knife in a manner that strongly suggested she could not be depended upon to exercise what little reason she had left. I was thinking that it wasn't a case of two against one—given Mum's size, but more like one and a half against one—when a miracle happened. The lights went out, plunging the room into impenetrable darkness, as will happen during a storm. Nothing inexplicable about that. The unearthly quality intruded when a misty white form, small in stature but giving off a wondrous glow, floated upwards to hover in limbo between floor and ceiling.

I might know that Mum had taken St. Francis from her raincoat pocket and was holding him heavenward in mute entreaty for spiritual sustenance, but Mrs. Pickle wasn't privy to this mundane fact. Understandably, she beheld an angelic vision sent to reclaim her from the forces of evil. Hadn't she been a Roman Catholic once upon a time, before she went to work at the vicarage? The knife fell with a thud, right on my foot, and I had just picked it up when the lights came back on and the doorbell rang.

"Excuse us." I grabbed Mum's hand, the one that wasn't holding St. Francis, and rushed past the cowering Mrs. Pickle on our way out the door and into the hall.

"I can't help feeling sorry for the woman." Mum tripped and righted herself. "All that talk of hers earlier today about her great-great-grandmother being a witch—meaning she was probably batty as they come—leads me to suspect there must be insanity in the family."

"We can't always blame heredity," I replied. "It's just as likely to be an environmental problem."

"In other words, Ellie, it's Mrs. Pickle's mother's fault for making her pick up her toys at night!" Mum was obviously well on the way to her own emotional recovery, when she opened the front door to reveal a policeman on the rainswept step.

"Evening, ladies!" Sergeant Briggs took no pains to hold back his sigh at having to deal yet again with nutty members of the nefarious Haskell family. "I've come round in response to a complaint from one of the neighbours about loud music. I'd have been here sooner, but it's been one of those nights. So"—he looked sternly from me to Mum—"who am I to take prisoner?"

"The mothers-in-law murderer," I told him as lightning crashed. "And here's a word of warning in your ear: If she should happen to offer you a glass of rhubarb wine, be sure and stick to your policeman's pledge of never drinking on duty."

Epilogue

Poor Mrs. Malloy! She took the news of her friend Edna's fall from grace extremely hard. And although she admitted that work was a great healer, she was still talking the subject out of her system a week later as she stood in the kitchen at Merlin's Court, pouring herself a cup of tea for the road.

"I knew she had her faults same as we all do, Mrs. H., but I never dreamed she had such a downright nasty streak. It don't do to look back, I know, but I can't get over thinking that if I'd only kept my trap shut and not told Edna about your bloodthirsty chat with the other ladies at the Dark Horse, Lady Kitty Pomeroy would be alive today."

"Now, stop that," I said for the fortieth time. "I've done my own share of blaming myself for what happened, but I have come to realize that Mrs. Pickle's obsession was such that she would have found a way to get rid of the mothers-in-law willy-nilly. What we have to focus on is that Bridget survived her fall off the cliff, that Tricks made a remarkable recovery after ingesting the weed killer, and that Mum came through physically unscathed."

"You're quite the pick-me-up!" Mrs. Malloy rinsed out her cup at the sink and stared out the window into the bright afternoon sunshine. "But before you get too cheerful, you'd better remember, Mrs. H., that you're stuck with having to find a replacement for Mr. Watkins now that he's all set to do time for blackmail."

"No problem," I said. "It turns out that Mr. Savage has decided he's not cut out to be a rock-and-roll singer, but that he does love the outdoor life. So he will be taking over Mr. Watkins's window-cleaning business. Did I ever explain to you"—I undid Mrs. Malloy's apron for her and hung it over the back of a chair—"that Pamela had guessed all along, on account of his having been doing the windows on the day her aunt brought her the pie for the wedding bake-off, that Mr. Watkins was the blackmailer?"

"You told me, Mrs. H., at least one hundred times."

"But did I mention that Pamela paid a visit to the police station immediately after Dad and I talked to Sergeant Briggs? She confirmed my murder story and conveyed her suspicions about Mr. Watkins. And did you know that the phone call Jonas received was intended to inform me that Mr. Watkins, not the murderer, was about to be picked up for questioning?"

"I believe you did." Mrs. Malloy refrained from rolling her eyes as she put on her fur coat and sequined cloche hat. "And if you don't mind, ducks, it's a sore subject, seeing as I was responsible for giving him the earful he used to put the clamps on you for money."

I followed her to the door. "It did puzzle me that I was the only one among the daughters-in-law that he contacted, but once you told me that you mentioned only my name in connection with the matter . . ."

"Well, I should hope you know me well enough by now to know that I don't gossip, except about people what I'm especially fond of!" Mrs. Malloy turned to look me up and down with a critical eye. "You look very nice in your party frock, Mrs. H."

"Thank you." I gave her a hug.

"And you're sure you don't need me for nothing else?"

"No, everything is all set for our little celebration." I held the door open for her and watched her teeter on her high heels down the steps. "Don't worry, I won't forget to save you a piece of wedding cake. And I'll be sure and explain to Mum and Dad that you had to leave to visit a friend in trouble."

"The way I see it"—Mrs. Malloy turned around to look up at me with eyes smeared with mascara—"I don't have to think well of Edna to feel sorry she's ended up in such a pickle."

"I'll see you on Monday," I said, and after closing the door picked up the silver tray of cheese straws to take into the drawing room, where our guests were already assembled, waiting for the bridal couple to descend the staircase for a reception prior to leaving for the registry office. We had arrived at this back-to-front approach because Mum and Dad, having elected to spend the preceding week with us, wished to leave immediately after the wedding for Tottenham. I gave Mum a lot of credit for agreeing to a civil ceremony as a sensible stopgap until a religious alternative could be reached. But I had to admit to a pang of regret that she wasn't going to have her big day with all the trappings of a white wedding. But as Ben had said to me the previous night, the time comes when we have to let our parents fly the nest and live their own lives.

Talking of my beloved, he came into the kitchen as I was going out into the hall.

"There you are, sweetheart." He took the tray of cheese straws from me with practiced ease. I thought he had never looked handsomer as he leaned with nonchalant elegance against the door—his dark hair crisp, his jewelled eyes alight to my every movement as I went to give him the restrained kiss that befitted the occasion of his parents' marriage. My hands did try to wander under his jacket to feel the warm smoothness of his shirt, but I snapped them back to my sides when he said, "I wish I could break this to you gently, Ellie."

"What is it?" Instinctively, I reached for a cheese straw.

"I just went up to Mum and Dad's room. . . ."

"Yes?"

"It was empty."

"So?"

"The window was wide open, and when I looked out I saw a white bow tied to the top rung of Mr. Watkins's ladder. It would seem, my darling"—Ben helped himself to a cheese straw—"that my parents have eloped."

"Oh, I do hope they are headed for Gretna Green!" For the first time in a week I remembered that life could be wonderful. Love was the great healer. I longed to sing and dance and toss the tray of cheese straws in the air. "Come on, darling"—I grabbed hold of Ben's hand—"let's go and tell our guests that great romance *is* wasted on the young!"

The people Mum and Dad had wanted included in the festivities were all there in the drawing room. Jonas, bless him, was not looking heartbroken. Tricks was looking the picture of health, and had high hopes that she would be the woman to win the Martha now that the other mothers-in-law were out of the running. Frizzy was looking lovingly at her husband, Tom, and baby Laura was crawling across the floor towards Tam and Abbey, who were both looking unabashedly adorable in wedding finery. It was a scene to warm the cockles of your heart until that heart-stopping moment when my one and only son took a couple of purposeful steps forward, and with a look in his periwinkle-blue eyes that I had never seen before, pointed his finger at baby Laura and said in a voice that brought a hush to the room: "Her *pretty*."

"That's my boy!" Ben looked down at the budding Casanova with intense pride, while everyone else smiled admiringly at the little he-man. Everyone, that is, except his mother. For at that moment I took a long, hard look down the years and saw my fate etched in cold, hard stone.

"Excuse me a moment, darling!" I gave Ben a nudge into the room. "I've just realized I have to make a *very* important phone call."

"You want to invite Eudora and Gladstone to join us?" His tender smile was an exact replica of the one my son was wearing as he looked deep into the eyes of that nice but quite ordinary nine-month-old girl.

"No." I managed to keep my voice light. "I need to phone the priory over at Pebbleworth."

"Is that the prep school you mentioned?"

"No." I laid my head against his shoulder. "It's a monastery, and you know how those places are—they probably have a huge waiting list. So, as a mother who wants *only* the best for her son, I think it would be wise to get Tam enrolled as early as possible. . . ."

ABOUT THE AUTHOR

DOROTHY CANNELL is the author of *The Thin Woman,* which won the Best Paperback Novel of the Year Award from the Romance Writers of America; *Down the Garden Path; The Widows Club,* which was nominated for an Agatha Award as Best Novel of the Year; *Mum's the Word;* and *How to Murder Your Mother-in-Law.* She was born in Nottingham, England, and currently resides in Peoria, Illinois, where she is at work on her next Ellie Haskell novel, *How to Murder the Man of Your Dreams.*